ically set up in the mind that exist in the world.[3] When a man
has an idea about something—even about an idea itself—

THE BROTHERS
KENNEY

BOOKS BY ADAM MITZNER

STANDALONE NOVELS
The Brothers Kenney
Love Betrayal Murder
The Perfect Marriage
A Matter of Will
The Girl from Home
Losing Faith
A Case of Redemption
A Conflict of Interest

THE BRODEN LEGAL SERIES
Dead Certain
Never Goodbye
The Best Friend

THE BROTHERS KENNEY

ADAM MITZNER

BLACK STONE PUBLISHING

Copyright © 2024 by Adam Mitzner
Published in 2024 by Blackstone Publishing
Cover and book design by Sarah Riedlinger

All rights reserved. This book or any portion
thereof may not be reproduced or used in any manner
whatsoever without the express written permission
of the publisher except for the use of brief quotations
in a book review.

The characters and events in this book are fictitious.
Any similarity to real persons, living or dead, is coincidental
and not intended by the author.

Printed in the United States of America
Originally published in hardcover by Blackstone Publishing in 2024

First paperback edition: 2024
ISBN 979-8-212-63133-4
Fiction / Thrillers / Psychological

Version 1

Blackstone Publishing
31 Mistletoe Rd.
Ashland, OR 97520

www.BlackstonePublishing.com

To the brothers Plevin, Michael and Benjamin.

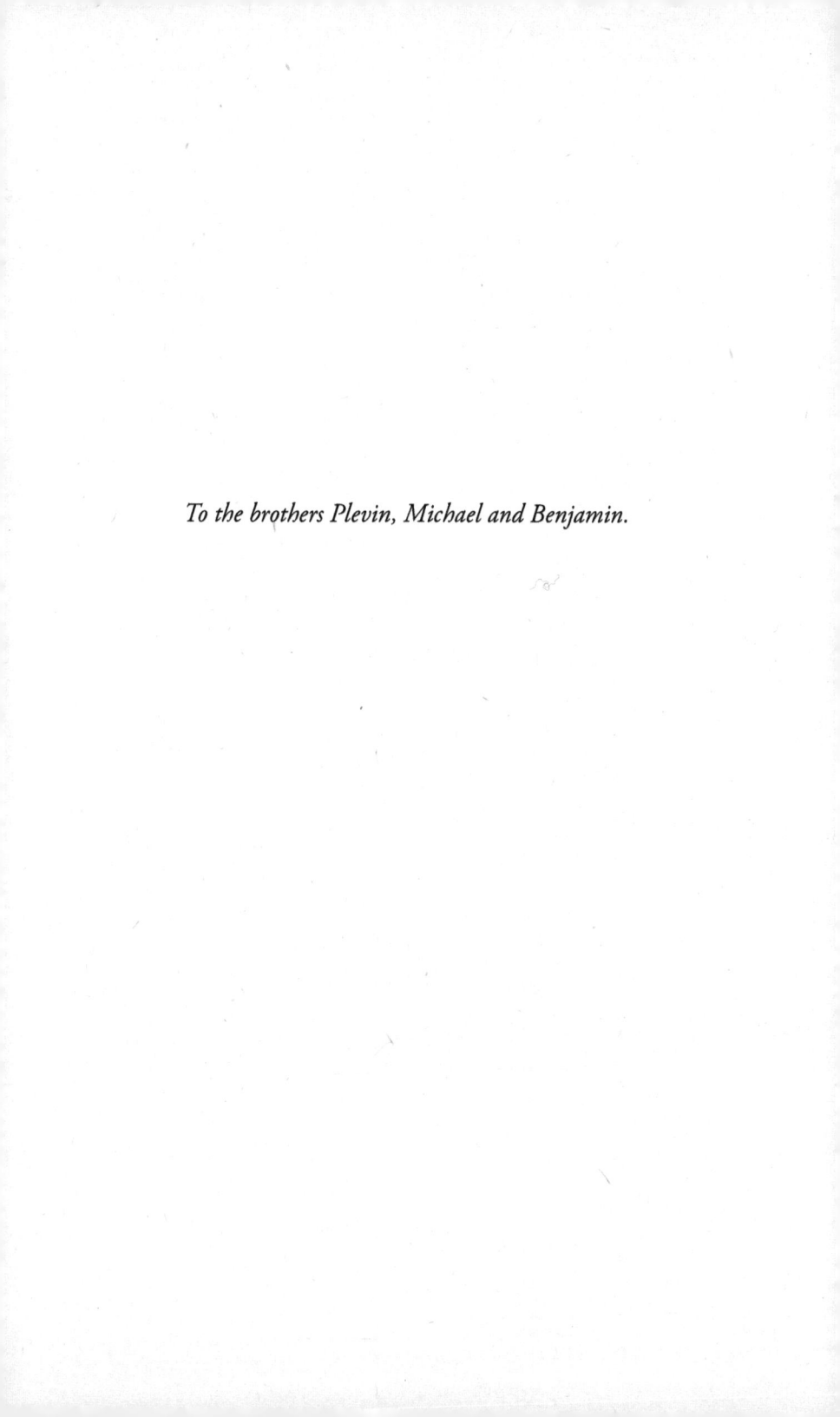

1.

For a split second, I thought I'd seen a ghost.

My mother's disappointed face was staring right at me. The way she crinkled her nose and pursed her lips, as if I'd missed curfew.

I actually had to remind myself that it was impossible for her to have returned from the grave. Not to mention that I was thirty-seven. Which meant I was on the receiving end of someone else's disapproval.

My sister inherited our mother's hazel eyes, ski-slope nose, and narrow mouth, but in her adulthood, Katie took on our mother's physical bearing as well. That hand-on-hip thing that a sculptor might have captured to unlock Mom's true essence.

To her credit, Katie immediately discarded that expression for one more appropriate for the reconciliation of estranged siblings. Even so, she could scarcely hide that the transition had been performed with some difficulty.

"Sean," she said, and then threw her arms around me, her head pressed against my chest.

Even in the best times, the Kenneys were not a physically

demonstrative clan. I couldn't recall our father ever touching us unless it was in anger, and our mother was not prone to affection, in word or deed.

We kids learned by example. Occasionally, I'd been on the receiving end of a high five from my older brother, or my younger sister would greet me with a peck on the cheek, but a full-on embrace wasn't part of our sibling dynamic.

The circumstances at hand more than warranted the display of affection, however. I hadn't seen Katie in nearly two years, and we'd only spoken or texted a handful of times in that span. She'd initiated all of those communications, and more often than not, I ignored her efforts to reach out.

But I suspected that the actual reason Katie held me so tightly was because there had been a death in the family. My conclusion on that score was not due to any particular sense of morbidity on my part, but only a tragedy of that magnitude would have prompted her to fly to New Orleans unannounced.

"You here because of Dad?" I said when we separated.

"Yeah. Two days ago. His heart. It just gave out."

The last I'd heard, our father wasn't doing well, although my family always spoke about declining mental acuity rather than anything physically wrong. He'd been diagnosed with early-onset Alzheimer's right before my mother died, about two years earlier. He'd shown symptoms prior to that, but our mother had done a yeoman's job of masking the worst of them so none of us would worry.

We all knew he wouldn't be able to last long without her. Still, I thought he had a few more years in him. Or at least I'd assuaged my guilt for being away by convincing myself there'd be time to come back and make amends.

Yet, like so many other things in my life, I'd been proven wrong. It was the irony at the core of my existence that, once upon a time, my greatest strength was to make the most of every second, and yet for more than a decade I seemed always to be misjudging time.

Katie eyed me up and down. "Not too worse for wear, I'd say."

My hair was all present and accounted for, and I wore it on my shoulders, longer than most men closer to forty than thirty would dare. I also still maintained my runner's physique, weighing less now than when I was in my prime. That had nothing to do with being in shape, however. I hadn't run a step in . . . well, in a very long time. Nowadays, I kept my weight down largely by drinking most of my calories. Nevertheless, the entire package gave me what many a woman had said was a boyish look.

But it was only on the outside that I was no worse for wear. Inside I was worn out to the core.

The thing I'd once upon a time appeared destined to succeed at, running four times around a track faster than anyone else, had not been the saving grace I'd dreamed it would. And while for years, I'd been trying to convince myself that my failure at the one thing I was best at didn't presage defeat elsewhere, the joke was on me because that turned out to be precisely what it meant.

After complimenting my physical well-being, Katie returned to her Mom-like demeanor, surveying my surroundings with a *Look what's become of you* expression. I didn't need to follow her line of sight to know she was right. She'd found me living in an efficiency apartment over my boss's garage. It had a bathroom, but the toilet was in the shower and the sink in the outer room, which was also the only other room.

My landlord-boss was this drunk named Clarence Boudreaux. He spoke English with a thick Cajun accent and was prone to turns of phrase that made no sense, like telling me *You wanna git down wit me*, when he wanted me to follow him.

Boudreaux had a small construction business. I worked

sixteen-hour days in that hot and humid muck they call weather in the Big Easy. On the last day of the month, Boudreaux paid me just enough so that I'd remain in his employ rather than choose homelessness. Never a penny more.

I found myself there as a result of being beset by a parade of horribles in my last few years in East Carlisle, a commuter town in central Jersey where I'd grown up and returned to after my running career ended. First, there was Meghan divorcing me. We'd been high school sweethearts, and married for seven years, with two beautiful children, Phoebe and Harper, when she told me that she no longer wanted to be my wife. I muddled through that for a while, until I got sacked from my job in the insurance industry, which was hardly a passion, but at least it paid my bills. Covid body-checked me further into the hole, giving me little hope of finding gainful employment. After we all locked down, Mom died of a recurrence of her cancer, and with her gone, the realization of just how sick Dad was became undeniable.

As soon as we were allowed to resume our lives, my ex-wife remarried. I would have added that to the list of my misfortunes except for the fact that her husband took over Meghan's mortgage payments, and as kind of a reverse wedding gift, Meghan relieved me of my obligation to pay child support, given my unemployment and the fact that Steve did very well.

The last of my misfortunes, the double-shot that threw me over the edge for good, occurred in rapid-fire succession. First, I got dumped by the woman I loved. Within hours, my brother and I had a massive blowout fight, following which I left town, ultimately landing in the hovel where Katie had found me.

"No offense, but I expected Kick would be the one to come fetch me," I said, referring to our brother, Michael, by his high school nickname, as everyone once had, but now only I did.

"Well, you haven't spoken to him in two years, so I'm afraid you're stuck with me."

Before I could reply, Katie said, "That's enough catch-up for now. Get yourself packed. We're on the four o'clock back to Newark."

It took me all of five minutes. I threw every article of clothing I owned into a beat-up canvas duffel bag. No matter what my future held, I knew I'd never be coming back here again.

"Home sweet home," Katie said, pulling the SUV into her driveway.

Her mouth was in a sad smile. "Everything okay?" I asked.

"Yeah," she said, rather unconvincingly.

I felt like an idiot. Of course everything wasn't okay. Our father was dead.

Katie's husband must have heard the car pull up. He opened the front door before Katie reached the stoop, while I was still pulling my bag out of the car's hatch. After she embraced Ben, Katie shook her head in response to a question I hadn't heard him ask.

"You need any help?" Ben called out.

"Thanks, but I got it," I replied.

Since I'd last seen him, Ben had lost the rest of what had once been a very curly head of hair and put on some weight. He now looked even more like the poster boy for suburban dads than he had before, which I hadn't thought possible the last time I'd seen him.

"I'm sorry, Sean," he said, when I made it to the porch.

"Let's get you inside," Katie said even before I could thank her husband for his condolences. "There's something I need to talk to you about."

I had expected to have some time before Katie took me to task for the way I'd been living my life. Besides which, I assumed it would fall to my older brother to read me the riot act, not my baby sister.

"Okay," I said. "But would you mind if I got something to drink before we talk about whatever it is that you want to talk about?"

Katie gave me the look members of my family often did whenever I asked for alcohol. Not that it wasn't warranted. My lack of control in that area was one of the many factors contributing to my current sorry state. But no one ever stopped drinking because their little sister cast a disapproving eye, which was a lesson Katie must have taken to heart because she said, "Ben, could you get Sean something?"

"What'll it be?" Ben asked.

"Depends on what we're going to be discussing," I said, smiling at Katie.

With a stern expression, she replied, "Get him a scotch."

"Jesus," I said.

"Yeah," she replied.

Katie and her brood now lived in our childhood home, a 1970s split-level colonial. They'd moved in after Mom's passing to better care for Dad in a place he found familiar and also so that they'd have a bit more space for their family. They hadn't changed any of the downstairs furniture, so I took a seat against one arm of the same sofa I'd braced myself against so many times when I was a child. Katie joined me on the other end. Neither of us said anything as we waited for Ben to return from the kitchen. When he did, I saw that he'd poured some liquid courage for himself too.

It might have been appropriate to drink a toast to my old man. But I said something different. "So what's on your mind, Katie?"

Whatever news she had to impart was apparently sadder

than our old man's death. Katie had kept a stiff upper lip about that during our trip back from New Orleans, but now she looked at me with tears in her eyes.

"I . . . I don't know how to tell you this, Sean."

She might have said something after that. Probably did, in fact. But I had completely tuned her out.

My father had entered the room.

For a dead man, he looked pretty good—clean-shaven, his hair parted neatly, wearing pants with a fly and a shirt with a collar. The only disconcerting thing about him, aside from reports of his death being greatly exaggerated, was that my old man didn't seem to register that his middle child, whom he hadn't seen in two years, was front and center.

For a moment I thought I must be hallucinating, and Dad wasn't really there. But when I turned to Katie, she brushed away a tear with her finger, and said, "I'm sorry I lied to you."

I wish my immediate emotion had been joy that my father was still alive, but it wasn't. I was furious regarding what I presumed was the actual reason I'd been summoned home.

It could only be one thing: an intervention.

"You need to tell me what's going on right now," I said, rising to my feet. "Or I swear to God, Katie, I'm out of here, and I'll buy my own plane ticket back to New Orleans."

It was a hollow threat. I didn't have the wherewithal to buy my own plane ticket. I could barely buy my own lunch.

"Please sit down," Katie said with more sadness than I could have imagined her giving voice to anything. It was as if she lacked the strength to utter the words.

There was a momentary standoff, during which I was uncertain whether to accede to her request or make a break for it. I looked over to Ben, who nodded slightly that I should do as his wife had asked.

After retaking my seat, in a more measured, but I hoped equally serious tone, I said, "I really need for you to tell me what's going on. Now please."

Despite the urgency in my voice, Katie didn't offer a reply. I couldn't imagine that she was at a loss for words. She'd obviously planned for this discussion at least long enough to concoct a cover story about our father's passing. Yet for whatever reason, she still hadn't yet come out with the truth about why she'd brought me home.

At last, Katie said, "I told you it was about Dad because I was afraid you wouldn't come if I told you the truth."

I'd intuited that much already and my patience was running even less than thin. "Well, you got me here. So why don't you tell me what was so goddam important to justify making me think Dad was dead for the last five hours?"

I said it like I meant business, but immediately realized that something greater than my anger was afoot. Katie was shaking, seemingly unable to get the words out.

"Michael," she finally said, her voice breaking. "He . . ."

She stopped talking, although her mouth continued to quiver.

Ben finished her sentence. "Michael's dead."

Just as I thought that nothing could be more shocking or terrible than that, Ben added, "Your brother shot himself. On his birthday for Chrissakes."

I had the sensation of falling. Not down, but through.

Even though Kick and I hadn't seen each other in two years, I had never doubted that our estrangement would someday end and we'd again be the brothers we'd once been. Now the specter that I would never again see him seared through me. It seemed outside the realm of possibility that I could exist in a world in which Kick did not.

I hadn't cried for a very long time. Not tears of joy when my daughters were born. Or in sadness when Meghan told me our marriage was over. Not even when my mother died.

I wanted to cry now, more than I'd wanted anything in a very long time.

But I'd been numb for so long that I'd apparently lost the muscle memory to conjure any emotion. Or even to find the words to ask about the how and why of Kick's death.

In the silence, Katie reached over to commandeer her husband's scotch. The few swallows of alcohol that followed must have centered her because without my asking, she began to explain the circumstances that led to our brother's life ending on his thirty-ninth birthday.

"Jenny told me that when Michael hadn't come home at the usual time, she'd begun calling, but he didn't answer. At first, she wasn't too worried because she assumed he'd been strong-armed by coworkers to get a birthday drink and then lost track of time. But by ten she knew something was wrong. There was no way Michael would be unresponsive for that many hours, especially on his birthday."

Katie spoke impassively, like a news anchor reading off a teleprompter. As if she was describing someone else's horror rather than her own.

"The next morning, the police came to the house. They said they'd found Michael's body at this fancy hotel about ten minutes away. He'd killed himself the day before."

"He didn't," I said. "He couldn't have."

Katie closed her eyes tightly, as if trying to ward off the pain. Ben leaned over to place his hand on her shoulder, but she shook it away.

Opening her eyes, Katie said, "I know. It doesn't make any sense. Michael was living the life. Beautiful wife, beautiful kids.

More money than God. Everybody healthy. That's the one thing I asked Jenny. Was he sick or something? You know, like Robin Williams when he took his own life. Jenny said he was in perfect shape. In fact, he had started running again about eight months earlier and had lost ten pounds."

"Did he leave a note?"

"No," she said, shaking her head.

"Then how do they know it was a suicide?"

She looked at me sternly, as if I'd entirely missed the point. My sister had apparently concluded that while there might be a host of unfathomables surrounding our brother's death, the fact that he'd taken his own life was not one of them.

"They just know," she said. "They just know."

I was no stranger to losing battles with your demons, but I couldn't comprehend that Kick had fallen prey to his. Not because he was rich or had a perfect family. I understood all too well that what seems ideal on the surface can often be anything but. Nor was my skepticism about my brother's cause of death on account of some outdated notion that only weak people take their own lives. Strength or character or what have you has nothing to do with falling ill, no matter the malady, and that includes mental illness.

I didn't believe that my brother had taken his own life for one reason, and one reason alone: Kick had never lied to me. Not once. And the last thing he ever said to me was that we'd see each other again.

2.

The 2008 Olympic track and field trials were televised on ESPN. During the pre-race commentary, Parker Swanson, who had placed fifth in the 1992 Olympics, told his viewers, "The 1500-meter champion will be Sean Kenney and I predict he's going to win gold at the Olympic Games."

Kick later told me that everyone sitting around the television back in East Carlisle erupted in cheers. But after a pregnant pause, Swanson added, ". . . in four years," which immediately quieted my family.

"For today's race," Swanson continued, "it's a pretty safe bet that Duane Washington and Paul Cochrane are going to run one and two, although which one wins gold and who has to settle for silver is far less certain. But either way, they're both punching a ticket to the Olympic Games. The question for the other ten men on this track, including young Mr. Kenney, is who's going to finish third and join them. And given the very strong headwind they'll all be pushing against, I think that a 3:43 will be enough to make you an Olympian."

I hadn't expected to secure an invite to the 2008 Olympic

trials. My sights had always been set on the games four years later. But two months earlier, I'd posted a personal best—3:39:07—and that was fast enough to earn a spot at the starting line in Sacramento for a shot at making the Olympic team.

When the starting gun fired, I stuck to my pre-race plan and settled into position about ten meters behind the front pack. The entire field ran in the same sequence for the next four hundred meters. I couldn't tell who was in the lead, but I knew it wasn't Washington or Cochrane because they were both slightly ahead of me, leading the middle pack.

The pace quickened a bit in the straightaway of the second lap, at which point Washington and Cochrane went out in front. I stayed with them and we ran as a troika until the race's halfway mark.

At the beginning of the third loop, I revved it up a notch, running by Washington and then Cochrane to take the lead. Even with the wind in my face, for the next four hundred meters everyone chased me until shortly after the bell signifying the last lap sounded, when Washington overtook me on the outside. Even before I could register that I needed a higher gear to catch him, Cochrane went by me and then shot past Washington.

Despite the fact that there were still four hundred meters to go, I answered back by going the sprinter's pace I usually reserved for the last hundred meters, which was enough for me to retake the lead. I expected Washington or Cochrane to challenge again, but neither did. Rather, they fell back a step.

I was in the lead at the Olympic trials with less than one lap to go. Even with the wind pushing against me, I was running at top speed and had no intention of slowing down.

Legs fast; mind faster; heart unstoppable, I said to myself, believing every word.

I held my pace through the first turn and even found the strength to accelerate in the back straightaway. The wind was whipping through my hair and the crowd was deafening to the point where I couldn't hear my own footsteps, let alone Washington or Cochrane, even though I knew they were right on my heels.

As if I was in a trance, I kept churning, pushing myself ever harder, my legs kicking ever faster. Coming out of the third turn, the finish line came without view, pulling me toward it as strongly as the fiercest ocean current.

And then it all turned.

Out of nowhere, Washington burst past me like he was on wheels. A blink of an eye later, Cochrane followed.

I tried my best to stay with them, but Washington and Cochrane distanced themselves from me with each step. The moment I realized there was no catching them, I heard footsteps to my rear.

Hornet Field had two enormous scoreboards situated where the end zone would have been if it had been laid out as a football field. After I crossed the finish line, I could see the winning times flashing.

Washington had captured gold with a 3:40:52. Cochrane was right behind him at 3:41:21.

I posted a 3:42:37.

Swanson turned out to be wrong, though. You needed a time of 3:41:53 to make the Olympic team.

I'd finished fourth.

Mom, Dad, Kick, and Katie had called en masse after the race ended. Each shouting into my voicemail words of encouragement—that they were proud of me and I should hold my head high.

Kick called by himself right after. In that message he said that he knew I'd be hurting, and he was there for me if I wanted to go over the race or just talk.

Meghan called too. She didn't reference the race, however. Instead, she said only that she loved me.

I didn't return any of the calls. I just didn't know what to say.

The irony was that I hadn't expected to win or even to make the team. Going into the race, I would have been pleased with a top half performance, and capturing fourth would have seemed like a godsend.

I had long known about myself that winning never felt as good as losing did bad. It wasn't even a fair fight. I'd won races and couldn't remember a thing about them the next day. But when I lost, that failure lingered for months, years even, and in some measure, never truly left. Sitting in that hotel room in Sacramento, I had little doubt that I'd carry this pain with me forever.

I turned the TV on to a superhero movie that I'd seen a dozen times before and ordered a dinner that I didn't expect to eat. About a half hour into the movie, the hotel room phone rang. If I hadn't thought it was room service, I wouldn't have answered.

"Is this Sean Kenney?" asked a familiar voice.

"Coach . . . I'm such an idiot."

"I don't want to hear that," Coach Pal said sharply. "You came in fourth among the best 1500-meter runners in the nation. And let's not forget, you were the youngest guy in the field. Now, I know it hurts. Going to the Olympics, that's obviously been the dream you've been working toward for years, and nobody ever complains about their prayers being answered earlier than expected. So, you're allowed to feel bad. Don't let anybody, not even your old high school coach, tell you different. But I want you to listen to me now because I'm going to give it to you straight." He paused. "You ready for it?"

"Yeah," I said, not at all certain I was prepared for Coach Pal's version of straight talk.

"Those guys who are going to the Olympics, yeah, they get to walk in a parade, but none of them is the runner you'll be in four years. Mark my words, no American will come close to the podium this time around. But you, Sean, in four years you're going to win gold."

"Thanks, Coach."

"No. Don't *Thanks, Coach* me. That's loser talk. I didn't train you to be a loser. And as God as my witness, I'm going to be beating this into your goddam skull until my last breath. There's a huge difference between losing—which is a part of life, and in some ways, the most important part of life—and *being* a loser. You lost today. Maybe it's good that you did. You've gone too long without that feeling, and sometimes you need a little reminder of how much it hurts. But you're not a loser, Sean. That's what matters. It's the only thing that does."

"Okay," I said, with the same cadence that I'd used to thank him a moment ago. The type that said I was acknowledging his words but not agreeing with them.

"You remember the guy who walked that tightrope across the Twin Towers?"

Coach Pal was never the most linear of thinkers, but this segue seemed disjointed even for him. "No," I said.

"You do remember the Twin Towers, though, right? You weren't too young for 9/11, were you?"

"Yeah, I remember the Twin Towers and 9/11."

"Okay, well, back in the '80s, it might have even been in

the '70s, this French guy, I don't remember his name, but he set up a tightrope between the two towers. He did it without anyone knowing about it. Then one morning, he just started walking across it. A hundred stories up, no net."

"Okay," I said, still not sure how Coach's story was relevant to my situation. Or anyone's situation, for that matter.

"Every step was life or death for that guy," Coach Pal said. "But all that French guy could really do was not fall. I mean, if he made the step, he had to take the next one. But if he slipped, then it was game over."

"So is this your way of saying that at least I didn't die out there?"

"Maybe that too, but no," Coach said with a chuckle. "It's my way of saying that you're never, ever going to have a competitor as tough as yourself. If you can beat that guy, you win. Every single time. When you get right down to it, nobody else ever matters. That's not only on the track. It's everywhere in your life." He paused a beat. "And it's also my way of saying that track, even at your level, is not life or death."

He was wrong about that, though. For me, each step of a race was life or death.

"Say it, Sean."

I knew what he meant, but I pretended otherwise. "Say what?"

"You know."

I sighed loudly enough that I'm sure he heard it through the phone. Then I did what Coach wanted.

"Legs fast; mind faster; heart unstoppable."

"They're not just words," Coach Pal said. "Today you ran with your legs. From here on out, you're going to run with your heart. And when you do, I promise, you're going to be goddam unstoppable."

Legs fast; mind faster; heart unstoppable.

For a very long time, I took those words to heart. They allowed me to believe that by sheer force of will, I could make my dreams come true. It was a conviction I held before and after that phone call with Coach Pal.

I've long since abandoned that belief, however. Now, whenever I recall Coach Pal's words, I consider them not merely a lie, but a curse.

3.

My brother was a runner too. Whenever I phrased it like that, Kick was always quick to correct me.

"I was a runner first," he'd say, emphasizing the last word to make the point that he paved the way for me, and as a reminder he'd bested me the one time we'd gone head-to-head.

There's this joke that goes, *There is magic in misery. Just ask any runner.*

And like many a joke, there's more than a little truth to it. Running can be a cruel mistress. Even when you're good to it—eating right, stretching—it causes you pain. Your chest aches and your lungs burn, to say nothing of the toll on your feet and back.

Nonetheless, Kick loved running. The wind in his hair. The thrill of his body delivering more than he thought possible.

My own feelings were less pure. I loved myself when I was running, but not the act itself, which is a critical distinction. One that I tragically realized only after my competitive days had ended. So whereas Kick could take what running had meant for him and build upon that base, I failed to adapt to adult life after my career on the track.

Worse than that, when I lost my ability to outpace anyone else at 1500 meters, my self-worth vanished as well. From the moment I ran my last race, I could feel a pressure building inside of me and knew it was only a matter of time before I imploded. The only real surprise was that I'd held it at bay for as long as I had.

———

Kick was christened Michael Patrick Kenney, Jr., but at East Carlisle High School, he went by the nickname given to him during his sophomore year, when he'd been last place in a race with about two hundred meters to go and won going away. I called him Kick at home, although my father bristled every time, which, looking back, was probably part of the reason I did it. For Dad, he was Junior, which, needless to say, Kick hated as every junior in history has and every junior in the future will.

Kick had initially gone out for the football team. Our father had been a football hero, a member of East Carlisle High's storied state championship team of 1979. That my old man's firstborn would follow in his footsteps was never much in doubt, as he'd been preparing Kick for gridiron success since practically the time my brother could walk.

The high school football coach thought Kick wasn't fast enough to be a wide receiver or a cornerback, and that he was too slight to play fullback or anything on either side of the line, so he relegated my brother to special teams. Dad said that was a pretty common role for underclassmen and not to be discouraged, but Kick saw it as a suicide mission, running as fast as he could down the field while other guys ran full steam the other way until they collided.

Mr. Palomino, who helmed the track team—and whom

everyone called Coach Pal—talked Kick out of being a two-sport athlete. "You've got real talent as a 1600-meter man," Coach Pal said, "and football is just going to be a way for you to get hurt."

Upon hearing that Coach Pal was denying him a football hero for a son, Dad marched right down to the school to rip Kick's track coach a new one. Dad's recounting of this meeting featured him telling Coach Pal never to contradict a word he said to his son or the next thing he'd experience was a size thirteen boot being so far up his ass that he'd taste shoelaces.

Coach Pal's rendition was different. "He's your father, so you got to respect him," he told my brother the next day at school, "but it remains my very well-considered opinion that you shouldn't risk injury playing football, and I told your father that I will continue to advise you to concentrate your full attention on track, where I believe you stand a pretty good chance of getting a spot on a college roster someday. But, of course, the choice is yours. It's your life, Michael. You get to decide how to live it. Not me. Not your father."

That night at dinner, Kick announced he was never going to play football again. Dad told him that he was making a big mistake, and seemed as angry as I could recall him being, to the point I worried he might actually strike my brother, which was something he might have done had he been a few more beers in.

Instead he said, "Suit yourself, but you're not going to get me to come to one of your meets, that's for damn sure."

I, on the other hand, never missed one of Kick's home meets. East Carlisle High School was a three-year stretch back then, so my ninth-grade year was spent in middle school. The minute the bell rang at the end of my school day, I hightailed it across the street to the high school, always arriving at Theodore C. Quinn Field before the starting gun fired for the 1600 meters.

I used my father's stopwatch to clock my brother, recording

his times in the back of the composition notebook I used for English class, which quickly had more writing from back to front than the other way. When we got back home, Kick and I would go straight to our room, and while both of us sat on his bed, I'd provide my analysis of the race with the aid of my notebook.

I joined the track team in March of my sophomore year. By then, Kick was a senior and the owner of the school's six fastest times in the 1600 meters. I would have wagered my allowance that for the entirety of that season nobody on the team knew my name.

At first, everyone referred to me simply as *Kick's Brother*, which I rather liked. Then somebody suggested *Kick Junior*, but Kick shot that down, which was undoubtedly more about his relationship with Dad than anything having to do with me. Finally, someone had the clever idea to call me *New Kick*, which was even better than *Kick's Brother* because the implication was that I would take over my brother's place on the squad someday.

An irony about the brothers Kenney: from high school and even into our early adulthoods, I was the more goal-oriented and the more successful, whereas Kick was directionless, without a plan for the future. Then it all turned on a dime. Just as my dreams came to a shattering conclusion, Kick found his path in the world of finance, quickly becoming more successful than we could have imagined possible outside the world of sports or entertainment.

Up until last week, the safe bet was that he would continue his ascent and I might never get off the ground. And now, only one of us had a future.

———

On the day that turned out to be my brother's last, I awoke remembering it was his birthday. I gave serious consideration to ending our two year silence by reaching out to him. Then again, the previous year I'd had that same thought and never called.

The reason I didn't call Kick that day, however, was not because I decided against it. It was because there was no need.

He called me.

From the timeline Katie presented, Kick had left work at around three, took the ferry from Wall Street like he always did, and arrived on the shore of Atlantic Highlands at four. I've checked my phone's call log at least a half dozen times since Katie told me all of this, looking at its digits the way I might a photograph of my brother, a way of holding on to that moment in time.

4.

When we were kids, our basement wasn't insulated. The hot water heater and furnace were exposed, and the floor was uncovered cement.

After the house became theirs, Katie and Ben finished the basement, decking it out with a big-screen television, black leather reclining sofa, complete with cup holders in the arms, and wall-to-wall carpeting. More importantly for my purposes, the sofa converted into a bed, the kind that didn't have the bar dissecting the mattress, and there was a full bath, so I didn't have to traipse through the house to shower.

"You can stay for as little or as long as you want," Katie said as she put clean linens on the mattress.

"Thank you," I said. "I promise, I won't overstay my welcome."

"Don't be silly. Family is always welcome." Then she added, "Hand to God," which was a turn of phrase my mother often used.

After Katie wished me a good night, and I was alone in my new home, I took the opportunity to call my ex-wife.

Six years ago, while Meghan and I were in bed, watching *Mamma Mia!*, after I'd said something about not knowing James Bond could sing, rather than comment on Pierce Brosnan's vocal range, Meghan said, "I need to say something. Something I've been holding inside for a long time, but I just . . . I just can't keep it bottled up anymore."

I knew what was coming. I'd been expecting it for some time, which lined up with Meghan's preamble of how long she'd resisted saying it.

"I know you're very unhappy," she said. "No mystery there, right? I honestly thought I could get you through it. But recently, or not all that recently, if I'm being totally honest, it occurred to me that I can't give you what you want. I've been killing myself for God knows how long trying to convince you that everything is going to be alright. Better than that. About how fortunate we are. And then, I had this light bulb moment. The reason why it's not enough for you—why nothing will ever be enough to make you happy—is because you don't want to be happy. I truly believe that you want to suffer because that's the only way for everything you need to believe about yourself to make sense. If your life is good, if you have a wife who loves you, children who are happy and healthy, then you can't be the failure you imagine yourself to be. And for reasons that I'll never understand, you can't conceive of yourself as anything but a failure. I'm sorry, but I can't be part of that self-pity anymore."

"Is there someone else?" I asked, ignoring what she'd just said about the reason she wanted to end our marriage.

"Just you," she said.

So we divorced, amicably, as those things go. Meghan got

our house, and I moved into the apartment complex across town. I saw my daughters on Wednesday night and every other weekend.

Meghan and I co-parented well. We spoke no less than once a week, usually about our daughters, but sometimes just to catch up. If we had a disagreement, again usually about the girls, we were respectful to one another and always reached common ground in the end. I'm not saying it was perfect, but as relationships between former spouses went, we were above average.

Even after she started dating the man who later became her husband, things between us remained good. But not so after I left. While I was in New Orleans, Meghan was often short with me. Never outright hostile, but also no longer willing to bring me up-to-date with the girls if there was something she thought I'd missed. I assumed that it was her way of ensuring I paid a price for my absence.

I was reasonably certain that she hadn't heard about Kick's death through whatever grapevine operated in the age of social media, however. Meghan knew what my brother meant to me and wouldn't have stood on ceremony if she'd heard news of Kick's passing.

Sure enough, when she answered the phone, she sounded like she always did. That said, her tone was also not too dissimilar to the one she likely used when responding to telemarketers.

"I'm afraid I have some bad news," I said. "Kick died."

"Oh my God," Meghan said. In an instant, whatever hostility she had toward me about the last two years gave way to compassion. "I'm so sorry, Sean. What happened?"

I was about to reveal that I wasn't entirely sure, but decided it was better to keep my suspicions about Kick's cause of death to myself, at least for now. So I said, "He shot himself."

"Oh my God," she said again, this time sounding even

more alarmed. "I . . . can't believe it. I really don't know what else to say."

For the first time since I learned of Kick's passing, I could feel emotion overtaking me. Meghan often had that effect, bringing out feelings I'd previously suppressed.

At first, it trickled in my throat, and then tears pushed forward from behind my eyes, until, without warning, I was overwhelmed, crying for the first time in more than a decade. I tried to hide it from Meghan, but pressed the mute button a second too late.

"Sean, are you okay?"

"Yeah," I lied, and then put myself on mute again so I could sniffle back my tears. After a deep breath, and while still a bit unsteady, I unmuted and said, "I'm at Katie's now. I got back today and I'm going to be staying with her for a little while. Through the funeral, at least. But probably longer than that too. Please don't tell the girls about Kick. I think I should be the one to break it to them. We're going to Jenny's tomorrow morning, but I can come over after if that's okay."

"Yeah, of course," Meghan said. "Jenny and the kids, they must be . . . I can't even."

"Katie says they're doing the best they can, but yeah, I can't imagine what it's like for them."

A part of me wondered if Meghan was thinking that I should be able to imagine a father leaving his children after what I'd done. My ex-wife didn't make that point, however. Instead, she said, "How are you doing?"

"Okay," I replied, even though a moment before I'd been inconsolable.

Meghan exhaled loud enough for me to hear. "It's me, Sean. You can tell me how you really are."

Early in our marriage, Meghan claimed she had the

preternatural ability to detect whenever I was being less than honest and that was the reason we'd always be together. In the end, it turned out she was right about her gift, but her skill proved not to be the fail-safe she'd imagined. As she told me more than once, it didn't help at all when I was lying to myself.

"Like I said, I'm doing fine. All things considered, I mean."

"Okay, but if you want to talk, know that I'm here for you."

Meghan's tone made clear that her superpower to detect my lies was still as strong as ever. But I also heard something else too: that tending to my well-being was no longer her responsibility or concern.

After hanging up with Meghan, I set out to memorialize my last phone call with my brother. I didn't write down the first part, when he told me about wanting to end our feud. It was what he said next that had been weighing so heavily on my mind, to the point that I needed to get the words out of my head and down on paper.

I've gotten myself in a bit of trouble. It's my own damn fault, and I know that the grown-up thing to do is be a man about it. And I will. But when I do . . . well, things may get very real, very fast. Everything is still in motion, but when all the smoke clears, I just want to know that you'll be there for me.

I didn't commit my response to writing because I remembered it verbatim. I'd said, "Absolutely. I'm here for you. Always."

I was about to inquire about his problem, to ask Kick how I could help, when he said, "Thank you, little brother. It means everything to me to hear you say that." Rather than saying goodbye, Kick's final words to me were: "I have to go now, but we'll see each other soon. I promise."

5.

Kick lived in Rumson, a New Jersey shore town that was a haven for financiers because they could commute to Wall Street via a high-speed ferry. It was hardly surprising therefore that Rumson consistently placed among the nicest places to live or best public high schools or whatever other metrics are synonymous with rich people.

I never really understood what Kick did to earn his millions. I didn't even know which Wall Street behemoth he worked for at any given time because he seemed to be always switching jobs.

"So, if I've got, let's just say for round numbers' sake, $500 million under management, then I'm spinning off $5 million in annual commissions," Kick explained to me once. "Now, that gets split up among my team, but let's say yours truly keeps $2 million. To incentivize me to bring my book over to them, some other firm will offer me $20 million up front in a zero-interest loan. The deal is that I'll pay it back in ten annual installments of $2 million each. I don't actually pay them anything, though. They mark the loan against my commissions, so that after ten years, we'll be all square. But my commissions go up every year because my book is growing, which means that even after I'm making the principal payment, which, as I said, I'm not really paying, at least not out of my own pocket, the firm is still paying me commissions on anything north of that. So, if three, four years into my deal, I'm earning $2.5 mil a year, I'm banking the $500,000 difference. But now some other firm is going to offer me $25 million over ten years to join them. By this time, maybe now I only owe fifteen or sixteen of the original $20 million loan, and I just got paid twenty-five from the new place, so I'm up $9 mil overall. And remember, the twenty I originally got, I'm not paying taxes on because it's a loan, not income, but I am putting all of it in the market, so that's another ten million in profit right there."

I can't say that the math ever made much sense to me, but it was undeniable that Kick made a boatload of money. Exhibit A in that regard was that his home looked like a small airport terminal, all sharp angles and glass, situated on two acres of waterfront real estate.

Staring up at Kick's mansion, I recalled the last time I'd been here. Two years earlier, I'd shown up unannounced and uninvited, at two in the morning. And I was drunk.

My brother had greeted me looking appropriately bleary-eyed. "What are you doing here?" he'd said.

"I need to talk to you."

I wasn't sure if it was my breath or my slurred words, but Kick immediately registered that I was intoxicated. Which obviously meant that I'd been too drunk to drive to his home. And, of course, that also meant I was too drunk to drive away from his home.

He shook his head in disgust. In that moment, I saw myself the way he did. Pathetic. An utter embarrassment. A loser.

Brothers can be like mirrors in that way. I'd always been able to see the strong family resemblance when staring into

Kick's face, and more importantly, the man I wanted to be. That night, however, all I could discern was Kick's contempt for the man I was.

In a soft voice he said, "I just don't understand what you're doing with your life. I really don't. You had a gift that most people would kill for, and somehow you've been able to convince yourself that it was a curse. And, yeah, I'm not saying you didn't have your fair share of disappointments. I know for a fact you did. But I am saying that a lot of good things have found their way to you too. Really good things. Phoebe and Harper being atop that list. And yet for reasons that I can't begin to fathom, you are determined to push everything that's good in your life off a cliff."

Rather than provide a considered rejoinder, I opted for brevity: "Fuck you."

"That's always your answer, isn't it? Look, I get it. We all get it already. You're mad as hell that things didn't work out the way you had once dreamed. Join the club, little brother. It's not a very exclusive one. Every single person on earth is a member."

"Easy for you to say about how life sucks in your mansion on the ocean."

"I'm not going to apologize to you for working hard and doing well. Nothing ever gets handed to you. You want something, you need to work for it. But it looks like you have no idea that's the way life is."

I remember the feeling even now. Like I'd just cocked a firearm. I let Kick have it with both barrels.

"You know what I do have an idea about?" I goaded.

"What?"

"Fucking Rachel Fischer."

The way Kick's eyes twitched made clear my blow had landed. "Is that right?" he said.

"That's absolutely right. Been doing it for the last six months. She says she's never had it better."

I should have added that she'd just dumped me and the reason I'd gone on my bender and was now at this house in the middle of the night was because I was suffering and needed his support. But as was my nature, I'd opted instead to inflict pain on him, as if that would lessen my own.

"Good for you," he said. "Why on earth do you think I would give a single fuck about you screwing my high school girlfriend who I haven't spoken to in forever?"

I tried to wipe that smug expression off his face with my fist, but he saw my haymaker coming and moved out of the way, causing me to fly over him, rushing headlong into the floor. He pounced on top of me, his knees pinning my elbows down, a position he'd taken many a time when we were kids.

"Get the fuck off me," I snarled.

There was a momentary standoff, as if Kick didn't quite know what to do. Then he rolled away from me.

After I came to my feet, Kick said, "Give me your keys. Sleep it off. We can talk like grown-ups in the morning."

I was operating on lizard instinct at this point. If Kick wanted me to stay, I was going to leave.

"I never want to see your goddam face again," I spat.

That was the last thing I said to my brother until the day he died.

Standing in front of his home, however, I was more focused on the last thing he'd said to me. *We'll see each other soon. I promise.*

That turned out to be untrue. What was less clear to me was whether it had been a lie.

"You ready?" Katie said, right before knocking on the door.

Her words brought me back to the present. "As I'll ever be, I suppose."

My sister-in-law opened the door. Jenny had always been breathtakingly beautiful. Tall and lanky, she had a swanlike neck, fiery red hair, and deep green eyes. Today those eyes were rimmed red. She was without make-up, her hair was pulled back in a ponytail, and she was clad in dark sweatpants and a hoodie.

Jenny hugged Katie first. After a moment it was my turn.

During our embrace, she whispered in my ear, "He loved you, Sean. Even though you weren't speaking, he still loved you."

Jenny was apparently ignorant about our rapprochement. That stood to reason, as Kick likely never spoke to her after I had.

"We brought you some muffins," Katie said.

"You didn't have to," Jenny replied. Then, in the direction of the winding marble staircase, she shouted, "Kids, come say hello to Uncle Sean and Aunt Katie. They brought muffins."

Their kitchen was blindingly white, with a center island the size of a queen bed, surrounded by six stools, even though there was a table that sat twice that many less than ten feet away. A dining room that could host a banquet was situated on the other side of the wall.

Jack was the first downstairs. He wasn't yet ten but already had the same long hair his father sported in high school. I wasn't certain whether he was too old to hug, so I didn't make any physical contact. Katie had no such reservations, embracing him at once.

Molly joined us a minute later. She was two years younger than her brother, and whereas Jack evoked the Kick with whom I shared a bedroom once upon a time, Molly was a mini-me of her mother.

Jack grabbed a chocolate chip muffin, but his sister wasn't interested in any food. After a minute, she asked to be excused.

Jack followed as soon as he finished his last bite of muffin. Not even, getting up from his stool while he was still chewing.

When it was just the adults, Jenny started talking about the arrangements she'd made. She spoke in a halting manner, as if she was struggling to hold it together.

"Tomorrow is going to be the wake. From six to eight. I still need to hear back from the mortician on whether we can have an open casket."

Katie recoiled. I also felt the pain of imagining our brother's face, which had always been flawless, now misshapen and bloody as a result of a bullet's trajectory.

"I know that your family has an attachment to the church in East Carlisle," Jenny continued, "but I thought it would be better if the funeral was held in Rumson, so more of the people in Michael's life could attend. I hope that's okay."

"Of course it is," Katie said. "We know we're Michael's family too, but you and Jack and Molly, you need to honor him in the way you think best. You won't hear any judgment from us."

A false-looking smile came to Jenny's lips. "Thank you for saying that. I feel like everyone is judging me now. I swear, I had no idea that Michael was so desperate."

I was about to ask Jenny about my brother's last days, but Katie spoke first. "We haven't for a single second thought that any of this was your fault, Jenny. Hand to God."

I hadn't yet shared my suspicions about Kick's cause of death, or even that the last phone call my brother made had likely been to me. The reasons for my playing this close to the vest were twofold: first, my sister made clear that she'd accepted the police's conclusions that Kick had taken his own life; and second, she'd for some time considered me to be a highly unreliable narrator about matters large and small, which meant that Katie wouldn't take my murder theory seriously unless I had some hard proof to back it up. All of which meant that my cross-examining Jenny would not have been well received.

As a result, Katie's absolution of our sister-in-law would be the official Kenney family position on the matter. At least for now.

Kick's bedroom, like every other room of the house, was right out of a magazine. Views to die for from picture windows, a magnificent four-poster king bed, artwork that I assumed had been purchased at auction.

Jenny opened a door to a walk-in closet that was organized like a men's clothing boutique. Suits lined along one wall, sweaters neatly folded on shelving against the other, and a shoe rack that held at least a hundred pairs.

"I assumed that you didn't have appropriate clothing for..." She stopped, as if she couldn't even say the word *funeral*.

"No, I don't."

"Pick something. Whatever you want."

"Are you sure?"

"Well, they don't fit me," Jenny said with another off-kilter smile. "But, yes, I'm sure. I think Michael would have wanted that. I've already pulled aside his favorite suit for . . . for him. But you can have your pick of the litter. Also select a shirt, shoes, and a tie."

Growing up, we wore dress clothes to church, but I didn't own a proper suit. After I won the New Jersey state championship, there was an awards banquet, and Kick took me down to the Carlisle Square Mall to purchase my first one.

He'd been beside me when I purchased my second suit too. The one I'd worn to marry Meghan. By then he'd already begun working on Wall Street and knew the jargon, telling the tailor that I wanted a single break and two-inch pant cuffs.

I ran my hand along the shoulders of about twenty garments before pulling out a thick navy wool suit, which I brandished for Jenny's approval. She opened the jacket, apparently so she could read the label.

"Good choice. Try on the jacket, make sure it fits," she said.

I slid the jacket over my T-shirt. It felt as if it had been made to my measurements. Jenny brushed her hand along the back.

"Perfect," she said.

———

"Do you really believe what you said?" I asked Katie when we were in the car on the way back to her house. "About not blaming Jenny."

"I do. There's only one person to blame, I'm afraid. And that's Michael."

I didn't respond, which must have caused Katie to assume I agreed. But I didn't.

Someone else was to blame for my brother's death. At that moment, I thought that someone else was Jenny. Not simply because the spouse is always guilty on *Dateline*, although that had something to do with it. I found troubling Jenny's claim that she had no inkling that Kick was in extremis. He'd told me straightaway that he was in some serious trouble. If Jenny was to be believed, then Kick hadn't shared the difficulties with his wife that had prompted him to reach out to me, which suggested that those problems had something to do with her. The only other possibility was that she knew all too well about my brother's troubles and was lying when she claimed otherwise.

Either way, it was more than enough for Jenny to be guilty in my eyes.

6.

After returning to Katie's home, I borrowed her car and drove to Meghan's, which was on the other side of town. I was downright terrified at the greeting I'd receive once I arrived, even though I was certain my children's judgment could not be as harsh as the one I'd self-imposed.

Meghan answered the door wearing jeans and a T-shirt. Her hair was blow-dried straight, but she wasn't wearing any make-up, which told me that nothing about her appearance was for my benefit.

"It's good to see you," I said. "You look good."

"Thank you," she said, but didn't return the compliment. That was either because she was adhering to boundaries, or a believer in the old adage not to say anything if you had nothing good to say. Probably both.

My mental image of my eldest daughter still involved a princess costume, but seeing Phoebe in the flesh brought home that she was much closer to the woman she'd soon be than the child I conjured in my mind. My youngest still had the skin and bone structure she'd possessed since losing her baby fat, but Harper's

T-shirt, which proudly proclaimed *Smash the Patriarchy*, suggested she wasn't a little girl anymore either.

It had been eight months since I'd seen them. At the end of the past summer, when they'd come to New Orleans for a week and slept in my bed while I slept in a sleeping bag on the bathroom floor. We'd spoken on the phone since then, of course. But not with scheduled regularity, and when we did make contact, very little of consequence was shared.

"Come in and hug your old man," I said.

My daughters moved in sync, like conjoined twins. I wrapped my arms around them and breathed in their scent. Back when we were married, Meghan and I would joke that they should bottle the smell that came off our daughters' scalps and call it *Pure Joy*.

"You both . . . God, you're both so beautiful."

My compliment made Harper smile, but Phoebe held her emotions in check. I got the sense that my eldest would be reluctant to let me back into her good graces. She took after me in many regards and her ability to hold a grudge was one of them. Harper, on the other hand, had always been more forgiving, like her mother.

"Your father has something to talk to you about," Meghan said. "I'll be in the kitchen if anyone needs me."

We all silently watched Meghan disappear behind the swinging door. Once she had, I could feel the adrenaline rise in me, like at the start of a race, when I was able to block out everything except the mission at hand.

"I'm sorry that the first thing I have to say upon seeing you both is that I have some very bad news. Your uncle Michael has died."

I stopped there, waiting for my daughters' reaction. Before I'd left, we'd been a close-knit family and so I imagined they'd feel the loss beyond their empathy for me. Then again, perhaps they'd heard that Kick was part of the reason I'd left and held him at least partly responsible for my absence. Whatever the cause, rather than display any emotion, they looked back as if they didn't quite understand what I'd just said.

"How?" Phoebe finally asked.

I didn't want to lie, but at the same time, my teenagers were not the first people with whom I intended to share my theories about my brother's death. So I said, "He took his own life." Then, to cut off further inquiry, I added, "I don't know why. I suspect we'll never know that."

"Didn't he leave a note?" Harper asked.

"No. Or at least none that anyone has found yet."

Jenny said she'd scoured the house and even opened their safety-deposit box looking for some final goodbye. A wife whose husband had committed suicide would do that, after all, so she would have done so too, even if she'd killed him. Kick's employer also reported that they hadn't found a suicide note at his office.

"The wake is tomorrow and then the funeral the day after that," I continued. "I'm going to be staying at Aunt Katie's for a little while. Maybe a silver lining out of Uncle Michael's death is that it's made me realize I've been away for way too long."

My girls closed ranks. Harper pulled herself tighter to her sister's side and Phoebe grasped her younger sister by the elbow.

Phoebe said rather matter-of-factly, "Uncle Michael didn't have to die for you to see us, Dad."

Her words hurt more than if she'd plunged a knife into my skull.

Sitting around our old family dining room set made that evening's dinner a bit of a time capsule of my childhood. Katie was in Mom's seat, the resemblance downright spooky, and I occupied the same chair as I had as a child. A meatloaf in the middle of the table, surrounded by a plate of roasted potatoes, filled the air with the scent of our long-ago family dinners. The major difference—aside from the fact we were all much older—was that my father was beside me, in the place Kick had sat all those years before. Across from us were Katie and Ben's daughters.

"How was seeing the girls?" Katie asked.

"Good." I caught myself. "All things considered, I mean. They'll be at the wake tomorrow."

My father, who'd been looking off into the middle distance, said, "Wake?"

"I told you, Dad," Katie said. "Tomorrow is Michael's wake."

"Oh," he replied. She might have been telling him the time for all the difference it seemed to make.

My father had once been an imposing figure. He was nothing like that now. He was sixty-three years old but might have been a hundred, completely at sea while sitting at his own dining table surrounded by two generations of his offspring.

Even at his best, he'd never been like some television dad who always has the right words to motivate you to be your best or soothe your pain when things didn't go your way. Like most parents, he fell between the extremes, providing his family a much more comfortable life than had marked his own childhood by working hard, without complaint. Although he never said it, I believed that, in his own way, he loved us and wanted us to be happy. On the other hand, he was aloof, drank too much, and had a temper that sometimes got the better of him, which were traits I'd inherited, unfortunately.

Of his three children, Katie was probably our old man's favorite, a status she cemented by her role as his caregiver after our mother died. Growing up, though, I always had the sense that my father didn't understand my sister, and it often seemed as if they were communicating in different languages. What was undeniable, however, was that he appreciated her presence in our family as a reminder that children did not have to be so difficult all the time. Kick and he seemed perennially at loggerheads, as oldest sons and fathers are wont to do. When I was younger, I hated the conflict that seemed ever-present in our home because of them, but when I got older I realized that Kick had actually cleared the way for me and Dad to have a more harmonious relationship. By the time I followed in my brother's footsteps, our old man had lost the will to fight those same battles again.

I put my hand on his shoulder. "You doing okay, Dad?"

He didn't answer at first, as if he was considering how he was, in fact, doing. Then he said, "Good," although it was so weak-sounding to belie the claim.

Later that evening, Katie and I were alone in the living room. Some Netflix movie was on, but neither of us was paying it any attention. Katie was focused on a needlepoint, which had been a hobby of our mother's once upon a time. She was at the beginning stages of a pattern that looked like the house. Only one of the trees in front had been finished, and not even, as half the leaves remained to be stitched.

I, on the other hand, had no interest in the movie because my mind was consumed entirely on who might have murdered my brother. So far, my list only had one name on it: Jenny.

Having failed in my own marriage, it wasn't much of a stretch to imagine that either Jenny or Kick wanted a divorce. Rather than half their assets and every other week of seeing their children, Jenny might well have decided to claim all of it for herself.

"Can I ask you a question?"

Katie's voice punctured what had been a half hour, maybe more, of silence, aside from the television. Lifting her head from the stitching, she seemed to be waiting for my permission to proceed.

"Okay," I said with some hesitation.

"Why haven't I seen you in the last two years?"

I'd asked myself that same question countless times, never coming up with a satisfactory answer. I had no expectation that any response I managed to provide would adequately explain the reason I'd exiled myself from those I loved.

So I didn't even try. Instead, I said, "I'm sorry."

"I don't know if that's true or not, but either way, it isn't an answer to my question. *Why*, Sean? What happened that made you hate your family?"

The starkness of the question pierced through me. When I left, I'd been angry at Kick, although jealous might be the more accurate emotion. And at Meghan too, although once again, my feelings about her were also complicated, but certainly not fueled by hate. If anything, I thought they'd been right about every word they shared with me and every unspoken thought they hadn't.

"I didn't hate my family. I hated . . . I hated me."

She shook her head in apparent disbelief. "My question remains. Why?"

Had I answered honestly, I would have said it was because my entire existence was a failure that I could never rectify. That everyone knew it and they lied to my face when they claimed otherwise. But that would have only begged other questions, and that was a path I had no interest going down.

"I don't know."

"Maybe you should know. Maybe you should give therapy a try or something."

"Okay, maybe."

She was looking at me with daggers. "Yeah, that's very convincing. So, if you're not going to go to therapy, and you won't—or can't—tell me why you have this deeply entrenched self-loathing, can you at least assure me that it's going to end?"

"I feel like I'm just starting to get good at it, you know?"

I was smiling when I said it. Katie was most definitely not smiling when she heard it.

"Sometimes I think you convinced yourself that when you disappeared our memories of you were wiped clean," she said. "But that's not the way it works. Even though we weren't part of your family anymore, you still remained a part of ours. Do you have any idea how many phone calls Michael and I had where one of us asked the other, *Have you heard from him?* and the answer was always, *No, have you?*"

She was right. I had convinced myself that I'd vanished from my family as if I'd never been born, like George Bailey in *It's a Wonderful Life*. And I thought everyone was better off for my absence, and, at least so far, no angel had appeared to prove otherwise.

My only response to the accusation was to hang my head. If Katie understood that I did so as an act of surrender, she didn't care because she still had one more blow to land.

"I know you like to believe that the first thing that comes to mind whenever anyone thinks about you is that you were this great runner. But that was a very long time ago. The truth of the matter is, when I think about you, when I consider the place you have in my life, and the place you held with our brother, and if I'm being honest, for Meghan and your daughters too, you're the guy who breaks the hearts of those who love him."

7.

The first wake I ever attended was for my uncle John, my father's oldest brother. I was nine and scared out of my mind about seeing a dead body.

When it came my time to view Uncle John in repose, I was surprised to find him with a huge grin on his face. Later, I overheard some chatter that he'd fallen on hard times, which caused me to conclude that maybe Uncle John wasn't all that upset about how things had turned out for him.

Peering at my dead brother, I came to the opposite conclusion. The mortician had done a masterful job, but no amount of make-up could alter the fact that Kick seemed angry to be lying in that box.

"He looks like he wants to beat the crap out of whoever put him there," I said to Katie.

"I think he already did that," she replied.

Out of my peripheral vision, I caught sight of Jenny. She was dressed in black and engaging with a well-dressed couple. They were all smiling.

"Jenny seems to be doing okay," I said.

"Don't," Katie said.

"Don't what?"

She gave me an eye roll that said I knew exactly what she meant. Then she told me anyway.

"Judge her. Everyone grieves in their own way. We have no idea what Jenny's going through. The life she thought she'd have forever ended three days ago. Now she's alone with two children to raise by herself."

"With all of Kick's money, I'm sure she'll be fine."

"Do you even hear yourself sometimes?"

After uttering her exit line, my sister walked away, leaving only disgust in her wake.

"You're Michael's brother, right?"

The woman who'd posed the question looked like an old photograph of Jenny—that same fiery red hair and sparkly emerald-green eyes.

"Yes. I'm Sean Kenney."

"My name is Arielle Taylor." She stopped there, as if to gauge whether I recognized her place in Kick's life. When my silence conveyed that I did not, rather than provide their connection, she said, "I'm very sorry for your loss."

"Thank you. I take it that you worked with my brother?"

It was an assumption I'd made solely based on her business suit and what appeared to my untrained eye to be expensive jewelry. That and the fact that she seemed exactly the type of woman my brother was drawn to, which probably made it an easy decision for him to hire her, regardless of her credentials.

"Yeah. Not at Buchanan Partners, but at the place he worked before that, Richmond Capital. I was the most junior person on the team, right out of college, although in my case, I was right out of a few years kicking around in Paris after college. I didn't know anything about finance. Michael taught me the business. I was heartbroken when he left the firm. But even after he did, whenever I had a question, he was always my first call."

"How'd you know we were brothers?"

"That was pretty easy," she said with an inviting smile. "You could be his twin."

"It's the suit," I said. "It's his."

"No, it's not that. You both have the same look in your eyes. Like you're watching everything, a little removed from what's going on, trying to make sense of it all."

I was about to remark that Kick had figured it out far more than I had, but that was obviously untrue, as evidenced by the fact he was lying in a coffin thirty feet away. That said, I was hardly faring any better. I wasn't even sure where to start in my effort to ascertain why he was in that coffin.

———

By eight, when my daughters had not yet appeared, I reset my expectations, assuming that something had come up and Meghan decided their attendance at the funeral tomorrow would suffice. But not long after, Meghan and Steve entered the room. Phoebe and Harper were right behind them.

It was Steve, rather than Meghan, who made the first overture. Stretching out his arm, he said, "I'm so sorry for your loss."

I shook his hand and thanked him for coming, which prompted Meghan to say, "We're going to go express our condolences to Jenny. Why don't you and the girls spend some time together."

After my ex-wife and her current husband crossed the room,

and I was alone with my daughters, I found myself at a loss for words. I wanted to say something meaningful about the preciousness of life. About regrets. About learning from your mistakes. But the words stuck in my throat, as if to prove that I was unworthy to impart any life lessons that I'd so clearly failed to observe.

"You figure out the mystery of time travel?" Coach Pal would say whenever I obsessed over a mistake I'd made in a race. "If not, then you better accept that there's no going back. All you can do is be better the next time."

Now was the next time. With my daughters. With everyone.

"I'm sorry, girls," I said.

I hadn't expected them to say anything in response, and they didn't. Instead, they looked at me with uncertain eyes, perhaps wondering for which of my many failings I was apologizing, and as they had the previous day, pulled closer to one another, as if to symbolize that they were a united front.

"I need to say goodbye to my brother as my first order of business, but as soon as Uncle Michael is laid to rest, I want to do everything I can to come back into your lives. I know that it'll take time, but the good news is that time is all I have right now. I thought maybe we'd start by having breakfast on Sunday. We can talk through what's been going on with me and what's been going on with you and maybe think about a plan forward for all of us."

Phoebe looked as if she was facing down a rival gunfighter, her face tight and unemotional. Harper, by contrast, was trying to fight back tears.

I put my hand on each of their shoulders, trying to forge a connection through contact if nothing else. "How does that sound?"

It took longer to get a response than I had hoped, but finally

Phoebe said, "Okay." Once her older sister accepted my olive branch, Harper nodded that she, too, was on board.

The air was cold and the night was particularly dark. I was clad only in Kick's suit, and while it kept me warmer than I would have imagined, it was no substitute for an overcoat as I walked with my former family, plus Steve, through the funeral home's parking lot.

At the car, I thanked them for coming, as if it had been a party.

"Michael is my—and the girls'—family too," Meghan said. And then she added, "Just like you are, Sean."

I nodded to acknowledge the sentiment and she offered a sincere smile in return. There had been a time when Meghan's smile was all it took to buoy me, but that was a very long time ago. Seeing it now no longer reminded me of how lucky I was, but of all that I'd lost.

As I headed back inside, my attention was captured by two silhouettes standing just outside the front door. After I'd moved a few steps closer, I realized that the darkened figures were Jenny and Ben.

Even though I was shivering, I remained in the cold to watch the scene unfold. I couldn't hear what they were saying, but their body language told me that they were discussing something serious. I considered that Ben might merely be offering his condolences, but I couldn't imagine why he would need to do that outside the funeral home, especially because, like the rest of us, he'd already extended such sentiments to Jenny when we arrived.

After Ben's monologue, Jenny said a few words. He said

something in response, which caused Jenny to take his hand into hers. They didn't talk after that. Instead, Jenny leaned into him and they engaged in a full-on embrace.

By the time I reentered the wake, Jenny was among a group of banker-looking types. Whatever she and Ben had been discussing so earnestly moments before had apparently been forgotten or hadn't been disquieting in the first place because Jenny seemed at ease, acting every bit the hostess of a party, rather than a grieving widow.

A few minutes later she extricated herself and headed toward me. A younger man was in tow.

"Sean, this is Brandon," Jenny said. "He works—*worked*—with Michael. Jesus, I'm never going to get used to referring to him in the past tense. Anyway, Brandon wanted to meet you."

Brandon was in his early twenties and dressed like he was going trick-or-treating as Kick. His gray suit, white shirt, and red power tie weren't all that different from the ones my brother was wearing that evening. Then again, I was hardly one to criticize. I, too, felt like I was in costume in Kick's finely-tailored suit, his shirt, tie, and shoes.

Jenny's mission complete, she bid us farewell. I watched her leave, but was quickly brought back to my new acquaintance by the sound of his voice.

"It's a real honor to meet you," Brandon said, a bit too enthusiastically for the circumstances. "I ran 1500 at Pomona, which I think is the only reason Michael hired me. He talked about you a lot, so I just wanted to say hello." And then, as if he had suddenly realized where he was, Brandon added, "I'm very sorry for your loss."

"Thank you," I said, but wanting to move on from the condolences, I added, "It's always a pleasure to meet a fellow 1500-meter man."

"I was never in your class, not even close. My PB was a shade over 3:54."

He was right. That wasn't in my class.

"Very respectable," I said nonetheless.

"Michael and I would go running sometimes at lunch. Just jogging, really. Three miles or so. But this one time I was feeling a little cocky, so I said to him, you know, *Race you to the finish*. I'll tell you, Michael was fast. I was two years from running competitively, not to mention that he was a good fifteen years older, but your brother, he still pushed me. Swear to God."

I smiled at the thought of Kick trying to outrun someone almost half his age. "Sounds like my brother."

Brandon's smile suddenly vanished. His eyes darted around the room. Then he took a step closer to me.

"I want you to know that I don't believe the stuff they're saying about him," he said in a whisper.

My first thought was that the *stuff* in question was that Kick had committed suicide. Rather than telling Brandon that I didn't believe it either, I recited the party line.

"You never really know what's going on with someone. I know it's hard to believe because on the surface it looked like he had the perfect life, right?"

What I said didn't seem to register, though. Brandon kept looking over my shoulder. I turned slightly to see that his focus was on the bankers with whom Jenny was still holding court.

I assumed they were Buchanan men. In other words, Brandon's bosses.

"I probably shouldn't be telling you this," Brandon said, still sotto voce. "The lawyers told us not to talk to anyone about it, and when people hear Russian names and crypto they immediately think money laundering, or worse. But I don't believe Michael would have put himself or the firm in that kind of legal jeopardy. I really don't."

Russians? Crypto? Money laundering?

Before I could ask Brandon to start over, this time from the beginning, and much more slowly, one of the men who only a moment earlier had been in Brandon's peripheral vision entered our discussion circle. His white hair told me he was in his sixties, which meant he was almost certainly a muckety-muck at Buchanan. He offered the obligatory condolences before providing his name. It went in one ear and out the other.

I looked hard at Brandon, trying to will him to explain why lawyers had become involved in my brother's workplace. The moment had passed, however. Brandon looked scared now. He wasn't going to say another word. Not with this guy bearing witness. In fact, it seemed very clear to me that Brandon sincerely regretted what he'd already told me.

―――

The nurse who looked after my father had taken him home when he'd started to grow agitated. Before he left, I spent some time with him. Not very long, but enough for me to realize he understood someone had died, but that it didn't register it was someone he knew particularly well. Nor did my father grasp that my mother wasn't present because she'd died two years ago, as more than once he asked me to tell her not to leave without first saying goodbye.

By 10:15, everyone had left except Jenny and her kids, Katie, Ben and theirs, and me. And, of course, Kick in the open casket in the corner.

Ben was holding a bottle of Irish whisky and a tower of

paper cups. "I thought that we should drink a toast to Michael," he said. He poured two fingers' worth into the paper cups, handing one to each of the adults.

There had never been much love lost between Kick and Ben. There were a myriad of reasons my brother cited over the years for why he found our brother-in-law unworthy of Katie, some of which I thought had validity too. But in that moment, I was reminded that what rankled Kick most was the way our brother-in-law sometimes leered at Jenny.

"Jenny, would you like to say something, or would you like one of us to do the honors?" Katie asked.

"I'll try," Jenny said. Then she shut her eyes, as if to suggest she needed a moment to reign in her emotions. "To my beloved husband and Jack and Molly's cherished father . . . brother, uncle, and son . . ."

That was as far as she got. Then tears overwhelmed her.

Ben, who was closest to her, put a supportive arm over Jenny's shoulder. She melted into his embrace, as if she'd been there before. So much so that I instinctively looked at Katie to see if she was bearing witness. But rather than focus on her husband soothing her sister-in-law, Katie's attention was on the rest of us as she finished Jenny's toast.

"To Michael," she said, and then we all drank.

———

A few minutes later, I pulled Jenny aside. Although I still wanted to know about her tête–à–tête with Ben, I now had bigger fish to fry.

"Did you know that Kick was having some trouble at work?" I asked.

Her response was not the immediate denial I'd been

expecting. Instead, she seemed to be considering how to answer, which suggested that despite what she'd told Katie and I the other day, she'd indeed been aware that her husband was in dire straits at the time of his death.

For a split second I thought she might even come clean. Say that she didn't want Katie to know, which was why she'd denied it the other day, but the truth was that Kick had run afoul of some Russian mob types. But just as I was considering how I'd respond to that, she said something completely different.

"Why would you ask me that? Today of all days?"

I couldn't discern if the question was meant at face value or a rebuke. Probably the former, but I pretended it was the latter.

"Because I thought that maybe it would explain some things."

Her nose crinkled, as if she smelled something foul, confirming that my initial assumption about the meaning of her question had been correct. It had been rhetorical.

"Sean, listen to me about this. Don't go looking for answers to questions that make no sense. There won't be any. Trust me, I've been thinking about nothing else since Michael died, and it's forced me to come to terms with two very hard truths. Number one, I'm sure that Michael had his reasons for doing what he did. And number two, which is more important, at least to me, I'm never going to understand what caused him to believe number one. I think that's why Michael didn't leave a note. He knew all too well how I'd feel about what he did, and he saw no need to try to justify it because he knew he couldn't. At least not to me."

I nodded that I understood, but my own truth was different. I believed that there were answers to be found. I just had to keep asking questions.

8.

The Rumson cathedral was twice the size and had three times the marble as our family's church in East Carlisle. It must have had two hundred seats, and every one of them was occupied, with people standing two and three rows deep across the back wall. People who cared for and admired my brother.

A moment of self-pity made me mentally count who would attend my funeral. Meghan and the girls. Steve too, probably. Jenny and her kids. Dad, if he was still alive when I cashed in. Katie and Ben and their children. That was it. Twelve.

"This is some building, isn't it?" my father said, looking up at the church's dome.

It was better this way, I told myself. No need for him to have to come to terms that he was attending his son's funeral. I envied my old man for his obliviousness.

I, on the other hand, was all too aware of the enormity of the loss I'd suffered, as well as the fact that my pain would only increase in the coming days. Kick had always been the person to whom I was closest, even when we were miles apart and not speaking. I'd miss everything about him, but perhaps nothing more than the fact that, beyond anyone else in my life, my brother believed in the version of me that I'd never achieved. At my lowest, I clung to the hope that if he could see it, I might someday too. Without my brother's faith, I worried that better version of me might be lost forever.

The priest might have come straight from central casting, the map of Ireland on an eighty-year-old face. He began his eulogy by reducing Kick's life to the headlines.

"A graduate of East Carlisle High School and Rutgers University, where he excelled on the track team, a prominent member of Buchanan Partners in New York City, a proud resident of Rumson, a valued member of our community, a friend to many, the son of Michael Kenney Senior and Margaret Kenney, who predeceased him, brother to Sean Kenney and Kathleen Whitting, and most importantly, husband to Jennifer and father to two beautiful children, Jackson, aged ten, and Molly, aged eight."

When I was in Sunday school, the nuns told us that suicide was a sin of the worst kind. Whereas other infractions were against your fellow man, self-harm was an attack on God because your life was the property of the Almighty and to end it was to assert your dominion above the Creator's. About a decade before those lessons were imparted, the Catholic Church amended its centuries-long position and allowed those who died at their own hand to be buried in a Catholic cemetery, but I suspected that the old priest, like my Sunday school nuns, still held to the prior belief.

"Whenever someone young leaves this realm to be with God, we question how it could be," the priest continued. "But the answer to such questions are beyond are comprehension and must wait until we are in Heaven ourselves, at which time God's plan is finally revealed in all its glory."

In the pew in front of me, Jenny sobbed quietly, her children clinging to her as if she was mooring that kept them from being cast away. Beside me were Katie and Ben, their daughters between them, each holding the hand of a parent. My own daughters were several rows back, so I took my father's hand.

Although it had not been my intention when I'd originally decided to engage him, I leaned over to whisper into his ear. "I love you, Dad." When that didn't elicit any response, I added, "And I'm sorry."

He looked at me through a bewildered smile, but then he said, "I know you are. It's okay. It's all okay."

My old man patted my hand, which was holding his, and then he turned his attention back to the priest. It made me wonder if my father had any true understanding of what had just transpired between us. The irony was not lost on me that perhaps I didn't either.

The priest said, "The gospel tells us that while Jesus prepared for his journey to Jerusalem, his disciples feared the worst. Jesus understood that they were worried he'd meet his death at the end of the journey—and he knew that their fears would ultimately be realized—but he told the chosen twelve that they would see each other again, which, of course, was also true. It was Jesus's love and faith in God that gave him the strength to move forward in his life toward death, and then, after he was crucified, his disciples were fortified by Jesus's faith to love him all the more. We must each find that strength within ourselves now that Michael has left us to take his place in the Kingdom of Heaven. Psalm 23 tells us that God is there for us even when we have turned away from him. It is a love that can never end. We have that same love for Michael."

Someone didn't love my brother at the end.

Everyone in that church thought that person was him. I was convinced it was someone else.

Brandon's words echoed in my head. *Russians. Crypto. Money laundering.*

The cemetery was a twenty-minute drive from the church. The mercury was slightly above freezing, but the sun's warmth was strong when it hit you directly, a reminder that spring was only a few weeks away.

Katie was tasked with delivering the graveside eulogy because Jenny claimed to be too grief-stricken to do it. No one asked me, which stood to reason, given that my family believed Kick and I were not on speaking terms when he died.

"Here's what I want to say about my brother," Katie began. "He was a very good man. But more important than that was that Michael was always trying to be an even better one. And I mean that in every facet of his life. He was an extremely successful financial professional, but where he strived to be his absolute best self was with his beautiful wife, Jenny, and his wonderful children, Jack and Molly."

My sister bit her lower lip, and then wiped her eyes with the tips of her fingers. In our childhood, Kick and I viewed Katie as a sidekick more than an equal, but in adulthood she had become the glue that kept our family intact. More than once over the past two years, she'd tried to broker a truce between my brother and I, but her efforts were lost on two such stubborn people.

"My heart breaks today, and I'm sure each and every one of you feel that same pain," Katie continued. "But I know that my pain is nothing compared to that of the three people closest to my brother. I'm so, so sorry, Jack and Molly, that you are not going to get to know just how wonderful a man your father was, but I will do my best, as will everyone else who loved your dad, to keep his memory alive for you. And I think, no, I know, that you both will do that for the rest of us too. Because in each of you, your father will always live on. Always."

After Kick's coffin was lowered into the ground, and the dirt shoveling ritual was completed, the priest told the assembled that we should all go with God. I walked alone, however, in the direction of the parking lot.

I must have been lost in my thoughts because I collided into an older man with a large belly. I didn't recognize him, and began to offer my apologies, when from behind his girth crept a smaller figure who was unmistakable to me, even though it had been years since I'd laid eyes on him.

When I was in high school, Coach Pal had a bit of an Abe Lincoln face, without the beard. He'd retained that haggard appearance through the years, and still looked as if he would fall over in a stiff wind. Since I'd last seen him, Coach Pal had shaved his scalp clean. He also now sported a neatly trimmed white beard, which oddly enough made him look less like the sixteenth president.

"I can't believe you came," I said as I embraced him.

"I'm so sorry about Michael," Coach Pal said. "It's . . . unfathomable."

"Thank you. It truly is. How are you?"

"I'm as good as I have any right to be, I suppose. Oh, this is my husband, George."

"It's good to meet you, Sean, although I'm sorry it's under such sad circumstances," George said. "Bill talks all the time about you and your brother—the brothers Kenney as he affectionately calls you. The two finest runners he ever had the pleasure of coaching, that's a direct quote from the man himself."

I nodded to accept the compliment, but wondered what it meant all these years later. The divide between being a fine runner and having a full and happy life was an ocean, it seemed. The ballad of Kick and Sean proving that point rather emphatically.

"How have you been, Sean?" Coach Pal's voice was frailer than I'd recalled, but I could still hear the faintest trace of the bellow that had encouraged me so many times as I rounded the final turn. "I haven't seen you since . . . I can't remember the last time, I'm afraid."

"I've been living in Louisiana the last couple of years."

"I asked how you were, not what state you voted in," he said, his voice rising to signify his displeasure with my response.

"I'm doing okay."

I could tell just by the look on his face that Coach Pal knew otherwise. "Let me ask you something. When was the last time you did any running?"

To anyone else it would have seemed a non sequitur. Not to me, though.

"A very long time ago, I'm afraid."

I could have told him the exact date. But that would have been too sad for both of us.

"Well, get your ass out there and run. It'll do you good. Clear your head. Get your heart pumping. Cleanse your soul."

I nodded. "Okay."

"Nope. Not good enough. Show me that you mean it. And by that, I mean, let me hear you say it."

Back when I ran in high school, Coach Pal would make me recite this corny mantra, which I likened to a prayer, so much so that I called it *Coach Pal's Prayer*. Once I asked him where it came from and he said it was his own creation, which made sense because it was hardly the height of eloquence. Nevertheless, it served as a beacon throughout my running career.

Coach was telling me that I should find strength in it even now. Unfortunately, I'd long ago stopped believing that anything, let alone mere words, could save me.

I did as he asked, however. "Legs fast; mind faster; heart unstoppable."

"Not just words, Sean. Remember that."

"I will. Promise." A lie.

Like before, he looked at me with skepticism, but his nod told me that there would be no further cross-examination. "I hope I'm not being presumptuous here, but perhaps you could do something for your old coach."

I expected his request to be in the order of a motivational quip. To keep my head high or not to give up. Which was why I said, "Of course. Whatever you need."

"It's actually not for me. It's for a former student. Do you know Andy Leeman?"

"The name doesn't ring a bell."

"He was ECHS class of . . . I'm going to say 2010. Maybe even after that. Fine runner in his day, although not like the brothers Kenney, of course. Anyway, he's got the best job in the entire world now." Coach Pal broke into a huge smile, as discordant with a funeral as imaginable. "He's the coach of the East Carlisle High School track and field team. And wouldn't you know it, he could use an assistant."

Once upon a time, coaching was the natural next step in my life. But I rejected the offers that came my way because I simply couldn't see myself dealing with people who had it all ahead of them, which would have been a constant reminder that my best days were behind me.

After more than a decade, I should have been over that feeling, but I wasn't. It was with me every single day.

"Thank you, Coach. I'd love to help out, but I don't know how long I'll be in East Carlisle. I do appreciate you thinking of me, though."

9.

Everyone was invited back to Kick's house after the funeral.

A photograph of my brother in a silver frame was on a table beside the front door. On the opposite side of the foyer was a whiteboard with a broader array of pictures. In those from his childhood, Kick almost invariably wore athletic garb—Little League double knits, Pop Warner shoulder pads, the green and white of his East Carlisle track uniform, all the way up to the scarlet red he wore when he competed for Rutgers.

The timeline continued when Jenny entered my brother's life. The first image of the two of them was captured at my wedding to Meghan. That was also the day I met my future sister-in-law. Before then, I didn't know Jenny existed.

We'd sent the invitation to Kick with Rachel Fischer designated as my brother's plus-one. He'd been dating Rachel since his junior year in high school and we had no idea they'd broken up. To the contrary, we were so certain that they'd be next to walk down the aisle that Meghan had planned to throw Rachel the bridal bouquet.

My first thought upon meeting Jenny—aside from wondering

why she was at my wedding with my brother—was whether she was more beautiful than Rachel. Until that moment, I hadn't thought such a thing was possible, my own bride included. But Jenny's beauty was as undeniable as Rachel's, while also being utterly different. Like comparing a glorious sunset and a moonlit sky.

When I managed to get Kick alone, I didn't mince words. "What the hell?"

He laughed, knowing exactly what I meant, even though I hadn't prefaced my question. "Don't you like Jenny?"

"I don't know Jenny."

"You will. And trust me, she's amazing."

In the ensuing years, I'd never quite come to consider my sister-in-law to be amazing. She was certainly nice enough, never uttering a harsh word, but she always gave me the impression that she preferred the idea of our family to actually being a part of it.

Katie was harsher in her assessment. "Jenny thinks she's better than we are, which is ironic, because her elevated opinion of herself comes from good genes and our brother's money, rather than anything she brings to the table."

I'd hitched a ride to Kick's house with Meghan and Steve, sandwiched between my daughters in the back seat of their car, like I was one of their children myself. Upon our arrival, Phoebe and Harper sought out their cousins and Steve left to fetch Meghan a glass of wine, leaving me momentarily alone with my ex-wife.

Meghan lightly put her hand on my elbow. "You holding up okay?" she asked.

I remained unprepared to tell Meghan—or anyone else—the truth about how I was really doing in the aftermath of my brother's death, or what I was really thinking about its cause.

So as I had when she'd asked a similar question the prior evening, I dissembled.

"As well as can be expected," I said.

Like before, I could tell instantly that Meghan saw through my act. She moved a half step, until she was standing nearer to me than I could recall her being in a very long time.

"I know that maybe this isn't the time or the place, but I'm going to give you a little tough love. You ready for it?"

I nodded that I was, even though I was fairly certain that I wasn't.

"We're all here today because your brother somehow got it into his head that the people who loved him, the people who would today give up everything for just a little more time with him, were somehow better off without him. The only thing I can say about the difference between what you did and what Michael did is that you can come back into your daughters' lives. But I swear to God, Sean, if you don't, then you're making the same choice he did, except that, in your case, it's maybe even worse. At least Michael made it final. Everyone knows where they stand with him. And that, if nothing else, gives them the freedom to move on with their own lives. To hate him if that's what it takes. But you're not even giving the girls that. They've got no choice but to keep loving you because if they stop, then you really are dead to them."

I held her gaze for a second so she knew I heard her loud and clear. But then I said, "Where was the love in that?"

She smiled. "Okay. So maybe it was just tough."

———

Katie caught up to me almost as soon as Meghan made her exit. "That seemed . . . intense," she said.

"Only your ex-wife can make you feel even worse than you already do on the day your brother is buried," I said.

"Yeah, well, Meghan was always gifted in that area."

"She wasn't wrong in what she said, though."

"That's what makes her so good at it, Sean."

I knew that was the reason too. What Meghan said cut deep because it was true.

I found Arielle Taylor talking to an older woman. Like the way Kick's colleagues all looked alike, I surmised this woman was Arielle's boss based on her clothing and blunt-cut hair. After introducing myself and accepting her colleague's condolences, I requested a moment alone with Arielle.

"To what do I owe the honor of a private audience?" Arielle asked as soon as we were on the other side of the room.

"I had this weird discussion with one of Michael's coworkers at the wake and I was hoping that maybe you could help me make some sense of it."

"Weird . . . how?"

"He said that my brother may have been in some legal trouble at work, but before I could get him to tell me what was going on, one of his more senior colleagues joined us, and he shut down. I guess I was hoping that because you don't work at Buchanan, but still know about Michael's business from when he was at Richmond, that you could fill in some stuff for me."

"If I can, sure. So what did this guy say was the legal trouble?"

"That the clients were Russian and it involved cryptocurrency and money laundering."

"That doesn't make sense," she said.

"What doesn't?"

"Well, any of it. But the first part, that the clients were Russians. That can't be."

"Why not?"

"Because ever since the war in Ukraine, we're not allowed to do business with Russian nationals or entities operating out of Russia."

"Maybe that's the legal issue."

"Can't be. Buchanan must have a million people in compliance and all they do is make sure the firm doesn't run afoul of the Know Your Customer rules. There's no way a Russian becomes a client of the firm. That just doesn't happen."

Had I misunderstood? I was fairly certain that's what Brandon had said. *Russians*.

"What about the other things? Crypto and money laundering?"

"No law against trading in crypto, so I'm not sure what he was even saying about that. And it's true that some of Michael's clients invested in that space. Or at least they did when he was at Richmond. But that isn't a problem. Lots of people really believe in that stuff."

That was strike two. I still had one more swing to take, though.

"And the money laundering part?"

"No idea what he could possibly have meant on that front. But I can say with some confidence that there is no way that Michael would be involved in money laundering. Not in a million years."

"That's what the guy at Buchanan said too. That he didn't believe it."

"What was his name? The Buchanan guy?"

"Brandon. I can't remember his last name."

She shook her head to signal her lack of recognition. "I don't know him. He must have joined Buchanan directly. Not coming from Richmond, I mean. Did he say anything else?"

I thought back to our conversation, but nothing else came to me beside the headline points. *Russians. Crypto. Money laundering.*

"Just that, like you just said, he didn't think Michael would do anything illegal. But then, one of his bosses joined us, and he clammed up. It makes me wonder if the reason no one from Buchanan showed up today was because they didn't want anyone saying anything to my family."

"No, I don't think so," Arielle said. "Today's a workday and Buchanan is as profit-driven a place as they come. The powers that be at the firm probably figured that attending the wake was sufficient to show their respects and they had to get back to making money."

That made sense. I wasn't a total devotee of Occam's Razor, but I didn't resist the theory either.

"I'll call him tomorrow, I guess," I said.

"Don't waste your breath. He's not going to tell you anything and they might be monitoring his calls. All you'll be doing by calling is get the poor guy fired."

"What if I just show up at the firm?"

"That's even worse. You'll have to check in at the front desk. And I'm certain he works in a cubicle in the middle of the trading floor. You might as well draw a bull's-eye on his back."

I was stymied. The one lead I had was now a dead end.

"Look, like I said, I don't know what this Brandon was talking about," Arielle said. "But I truly don't believe that Michael would have done anything illegal. I used to joke that he couldn't have been any more straight of an arrow if he'd tried. Please don't let office gossip cloud your memory of your brother. Michael was a good guy. A very good guy."

"You should be ashamed of yourself. That girl was half, well, maybe not quite half your age, but still too young for you, Sean Kenney."

I turned in the speaker's direction, even though I knew who it was without visual confirmation. I'd never forget the timbre of Rachel Fischer's voice.

Her embrace thrust me back in time. To two years before, when I thought we were in love, but found out, much to my chagrin, that only I was.

I can't say that I was surprised to see her, but I wasn't sure she'd come either. Not necessarily because Rachel held hard feelings toward my brother, although she hadn't taken their breakup well, and for a while she told anyone who would listen that Kick's relationship with Jenny had overlapped with hers by a not insignificant amount of time. But all of that was ancient history. What I thought might keep her away were the much more recent events having to do with me.

"You haven't changed a bit," she said.

"I wish. You, on the other hand, look even more beautiful. Am I allowed to say that?"

Our two years apart had not weakened the effect Rachel had on me. If anything, she looked even more captivating than in my memory. Hers was a smoldering beauty comprised of olive-complexioned skin, with round light-brown eyes and full lips, all atop a perfect hourglass figure.

"There are no rules that govern seeing your ex at her ex's funeral," Rachel said. "I'm so sorry about Michael. I . . . just can't believe it."

"Had you spoken to him?"

"No," she said. "Not since we were . . . us. Jesus. That was fifteen years ago. More, actually. I was wondering if it was even okay that I came here today, to be honest. I know that I'm not Jenny's favorite person on earth."

That was something of an understatement. Rachel had been even more blindsided by my brother's switch from her to Jenny than I'd been, and she obviously took it much harder. In the aftermath, Rachel resorted to petty acts of harassment—texting screeds, keying Kick's car, that kind of thing. It seemed juvenile to me, but Jenny thought that Rachel was dangerous, to the point that I remember some talk about obtaining a restraining order, although, as far as I knew, it never came to that.

"Well, I'm very glad to see you," I said. "I just wanted to put that out there, in case you were wondering."

"I was, so thank you," she said, seeming somewhat relieved. "And I know it's a silly question under the circumstances, but how are you?"

"You mean, other than that, Mrs. Lincoln, how was the play?"

"Yeah, I guess I do."

I'd worn a brave face with everyone else who inquired about my well-being. Katie. Meghan. Even Coach Pal. With Rachel, however, I was determined to speak my truth.

"Well, I'm not doing great. I haven't been anything other than god-awful since . . . well, since you, if you want to know the God's honest truth."

I braced for her to tell me that she had gotten over me. That like a normal person, she'd moved on in the last two years. Maybe even, God forbid, found love.

"Well, if we're having a pity party, and with respect, because I know you're the guest of honor and all, but right back at you, Sean."

I couldn't deny being pleased that my misery had Rachel's company. I was about to ask if she was seeing anyone, but before I could, she said, "How long do you think you'll be staying in East Carlisle?"

"I don't really know." I chuckled. "I got a job offer today. To be the assistant coach of the East Carlisle track team. I suspect it doesn't pay anything, though."

She didn't react to my effort at levity. Instead, with some urgency, she said, "I'm going to throw caution to the wind and just put it out there . . . Do you think we could get a drink? Maybe Saturday night? There's some stuff . . . that I'd like to talk to you about and now obviously isn't the time or the place."

"That doesn't sound ominous at all," I said with a smile.

"It's nothing bad. Just things that I've been thinking about that I'm hoping you'll give me the chance to say."

I held her in suspense for a few seconds, but I'm certain she knew that I was going to accept her invitation. After all, I'd never been able to resist Rachel Fischer.

As had been the case at the wake, the last attendees at Jenny's house were once again my sister, her husband, and me. Jenny asked Ben to pour us all something to drink, and he retreated into the kitchen for a minute or two before returning with four empty tumblers and a bottle of scotch.

"I hope this is okay," he said to Jenny.

"Very fitting. It was one of Michael's favorites."

Jenny had reverted to her Jackie Kennedy in Dallas persona, which I was growing more and more convinced was an act. In her unguarded moments, Jenny seemed to be unfazed by her sudden widowhood. In my head I heard Katie's admonishment that everyone grieved in their own way, but my sister hadn't so much as smiled all evening. Then again, I won't deny that I was happy talking to Rachel. So perhaps I was being unfair to Jenny in thinking that her outward suffering was not sufficient.

"To Michael," Jenny said, without more, as if she feared she'd once again fail to get through a longer toast. Or at least that's what she wanted us all to think.

Our glasses all touched in the center, after which we each took a mouthful of scotch in honor of my brother. No one said anything after that, but Jenny started to sob. Ben, who was sitting next to her, brought my sister-in-law into his embrace, just like he had the night before.

10.

Later that night, Katie offered to make us both some tea. I settled onto one of the stools around the kitchen island while she filled the kettle.

"It's hot," she said after pouring in the water, as she pushed the mug in front of me.

I disregarded her warning and paid the price, recoiling when my mouth made contact with the lip of the cup.

"I told you."

"But you know me, always having to find things out the hard way."

She blew lightly on her cup, after which she took a small sip. "God, today was bad," Katie said as she placed her mug back on the kitchen counter.

After I agreed, we talked a little about our father, with me sharing that he seemed pretty out of it, and the two of us concurring that it was probably for the best. From there we segued to how our children were reacting, and concluded that they were doing as well as could be expected.

"So now that we've convinced ourselves that it's all good for all of us that our brother shot himself in the head last week," she said with that sarcastic tone I knew all too well, "I guess there's nothing else for us to do."

I was trying to think about how to share that I still had things to do. Things that I hoped would provide me with proof that our brother had, in fact, not shot himself in the head.

Before I could say that, however, my sister said, "What?"

I chuckled. "It's like you're a mind reader."

"Not like. Am. What's on your little mind, Sean?"

"Something I heard about Kick. Did you know he was in some legal trouble at work?"

She reacted inscrutably. I wasn't certain if that was because she was embarrassed she hadn't known our brother as well as she thought or because she was fully aware of Kick's work issues.

"Who told you that?"

"One of the guys who worked with him told me at the wake."

"What kind of legal trouble?"

That answered that question. I was imparting new information.

"I'm not sure. He said something about Russians and crypto and money laundering. But I spoke to someone else who worked with Kick and she said that the Russian part couldn't be true because of the sanctions against them. So now I just don't know what to believe."

Katie's expression turned on a dime. Now she looked at me as if she already knew she was going to vehemently disagree with whatever I said next.

"To believe about what?" she said.

That was the question I'd resisted answering since Katie first told me about Kick's death. I knew that once I did, everything would be different about how Katie viewed Kick. And me.

But it was time. I couldn't keep Katie in the dark about my suspicions any longer.

"Was the trouble at work a reason for him to . . . do what he did? Or was it a reason for someone else to do it?"

Katie winced, as if she'd been struck by something sharp. "For the love of God, Sean, don't start going down some conspiracy rabbit hole. The police said it was a suicide."

Rather than respond, I took a sip of my tea, which caused Katie to do likewise. But after she did, my sister looked at me with sad eyes that told me she wasn't yet done with this subject.

"I one-hundred-percent know how much you don't want to believe Michael did this to himself. But he did. For reasons that even if we knew them, still wouldn't make any sense to us. He decided that he could no longer go on living. I think of it this way. If Michael had suddenly died of a heart attack, we'd say, that makes no sense, right? He's young and in great shape. But if the doctors told us that they'd examined him and that he had some defect that no one knew about, and it killed him, it would be very hard to accept, but we'd have no other choice. This is really the same thing when you think about it."

I could no longer hold my peace. "But it's not, Katie. It's not even close. There's no medical professional pointing to a faulty aorta."

"Yes there is. The police concluded it was a suicide, and they're the experts here."

"Do you even know why they reached that conclusion? What the autopsy said, for example?"

Katie looked at me like the way you would a mental patient. "No, I'm not Columbo. I haven't conducted my own homicide investigation. When the police tell me that my brother committed suicide, I don't tell them they're wrong. They know how to do their jobs. And no offense, I'm not sure where you get off thinking that you're suddenly a criminologist."

"He didn't leave a note, Katie. Don't you find that telling?"

This elicited a loud sigh. *The breath of contempt*, Kick used to call it when it came out of our mother.

"I know it's strange to people like us who have no experience other than what we see on TV to think that everyone who kills themselves leaves a note," Katie said, now speaking in a measured tone, as if she was talking to a five-year-old. "But I'm sure you've Googled it, just like I did, and you saw that a lot of people don't leave notes. It's hard to get your head around, I know. But that doesn't mean it isn't true. Because it is."

I wasn't being fair to Katie by withholding that I'd spoken to Kick right before his death. No wonder she couldn't understand why I refused to believe that our brother had taken his own life.

"Kick called me. That day. The day he died."

My words stopped Katie in her tracks. Still, she didn't offer any immediate comment. Instead, she waited for me to explain what my brother and I had shared in our final call.

"We hadn't spoken since I'd left," I said. "Not once. But he called me that day. After he got off the ferry, because the call came in a few minutes after four. It was a short call, under three minutes. He said that, it being his birthday and everything, we needed to bury the hatchet. He told me that he loved me. That he wanted us to be brothers again."

I was tearing up, which had the effect of making my sister cry too. She rubbed her eyes, and then looked hard into mine.

"I'm sorry, Sean, but that sounds to me like he was saying goodbye. He wanted to make sure that you and he were on good terms because he knew that he wasn't going to get another opportunity to set things right."

I was shaking my head in disagreement. "No. It wasn't

goodbye. It was . . . the opposite of goodbye. Kick told me that he needed my help."

"With what?"

"He didn't say. Not exactly. What he did say, though, was that he was in some trouble. He told me that it was of his own making and he was going to own up to it. He wanted to make sure that when the smoke cleared—that's a direct quote—that I'd be there for him, which was another direct quote."

"What things?"

"Given what his coworker said at the wake, it seems pretty obvious to me he was talking about this criminal investigation. I think these Russian-crypto-money launderers killed Kick to keep him quiet."

Katie stared at me grim-faced. "That's an awfully big leap, don't you think?"

"No, I don't think. I—"

"I'm sorry, Sean, but Michael having work problems just makes it that much clearer that he took his own life. He didn't want to deal with the consequences of . . . I don't know, going to jail, maybe, and so . . ."

"No," I said rather declaratively.

I was about to say more. To press my case harder about why Katie should adopt my conclusion, or at least help me get to the bottom of my suspicions, when my sister shook her head just like our mother often had to suggest I was barking up the wrong tree.

"I didn't tell you this because I didn't want you to feel badly," she said. "But you're not the only one who got a goodbye phone call on the day Michael died."

It was my turn to look shocked.

"Yeah. I thought he hadn't called you and so I saw no reason to share that I'd spoken to him."

"What did he say?"

"The truth is that I don't really remember. Unlike you, talking to Michael was a pretty regular occurrence in my life. And it was his birthday. What I remember thinking was that it was weird that he called me. You know, usually I call him on his birthday, right? But now I know he didn't want to wait for me to call him because . . . well, because."

"What time? What time of the day did he call?"

"I don't know, afternoon."

"You haven't checked your call log?"

Katie looked annoyed at me now, like I was missing the point. With a harrumph, she pulled out her phone and ran her index finger across the screen. "4:14, okay?"

"How long did you speak?"

Still looking at her log, she said, "Three minutes, forty-two seconds."

I did the quick math. Kick got off the phone with Katie at 4:18. He called me a minute later.

"As best you can remember, tell me everything he said. Don't leave anything out."

Katie sighed to convey she didn't appreciate being interrogated, but then she told me what I wanted to know. "We joked a little about him being almost forty and how it all goes downhill from there, so he needed to make the most out of the next twelve months. I asked about his birthday plans and he said he was going to spend a quiet evening with the family. I think—but I honestly can't swear to this part—that we talked about when I'd get to celebrate with him, but I know that we didn't actually settle on a date, which I see in hindsight was because he knew it was never going to happen."

She came to a stop, as if she'd exhausted her recollection. But it made no sense that was everything they'd discussed. How could it be that just one minute later, Kick had reached out to me in order to bring me into his confidence, if he hadn't shared a word of concern with Katie during their call?

"Is that it?" I asked.

"No," Katie said. "There was one other thing."

She faltered, doing her utmost to hold back emotion. I should have let her collect herself, but my impatience overtook me.

"What?" I said, too sharply.

"When we said goodbye, Michael said, *I love you. Thanks for being such a wonderful sister.*"

Katie could no longer hold herself steady and she began to cry. I reached over to put my arm around her shoulder, but she pushed it away.

After a few seconds, she came back to me. Through tears she said, "He was saying goodbye, Sean. You need to accept that and move on with your own life. Not just for Michael's sake, but for your sake too. For all of our sakes, actually."

She'd said it suppliantly, as if she was begging me to adopt her point of view. But her plea fell on my deaf ears.

It was already becoming something of an article of faith that my brother had been murdered. For me to believe otherwise would mean that he wasn't actually asking for my help. Or worse, that after I'd sworn to always be there for him, no matter what, and he promised to see me soon, he still decided to end his life.

II.

In my sophomore year at Villanova, I got an invite to the NCAA championships. I'd already won the Big East championship, but this was my first opportunity to compete against the best collegiate 1500-meter runners in the country.

My strategy was to run near the lead from the gun. That way, I could ensure a relatively fast pace. In the third lap, I'd settle into a rhythm and either hold the lead or stay within ten meters of it until I turned it up to full throttle in the final two hundred meters.

I'd been assigned an outside lane, so as soon as the starting gun fired, I maneuvered into lane one. A runner from UCLA filed right beside me, while his teammate held the lead, with a cluster of runners to my rear.

In the straightaway, when the pace usually quickened, the UCLA tandem took it down a notch. Not only did that put the kibosh on my strategy of going out fast, but it was apparent that their race plan had been to box me in to maintain a slower pace.

Unable to break free, we ran like that through the first four hundred meters. At the starting line, I caught sight of my collegiate coach standing in his usual position in the infield.

Whenever I completed a lap, he'd flash the number of fingers on his hand to show how many seconds above or below one minute I'd run that leg. His digits pointed up when I was above sixty seconds and down when I had a run a sub-one.

Four fingers were pointing straight up.

I hadn't posted a time that slow since high school. Realizing that desperate times called for desperate measures, I suddenly slowed down even more than the pace required, allowing nearly half the field to pass me. When the coast was clear, I moved to the outside lane, and from there I was finally able to accelerate.

Then I started to fly. I blew past the UCLA runners and maneuvered back into lane one, never looking back. As I headed into the penultimate lap, my coach had two fingers waiting for me, pointing straight down.

In the entire season, I had only once run a faster third than second leg, and I'd never run the third quarter in less time than I had the first. That was about to change.

I turned on my jets, going in an all-out sprint into the first turn and didn't slow down.

When I heard the bell signifying one more lap to go, I was greeted by three of Coach's fingers hanging straight down. Usually he held that position until I ran by him. This time, however, he turned his three digits to point right at me, like he was firing a gun.

I had a consistent strategy for the last four hundred meters in my races: the turns and the back straightaway each in about thirteen seconds, and then the last hundred meters in a dead run.

Into the first turn, however, I was already going my sprinter's pace. That familiar pain from my finishing kick, overwhelming me. I'd always been able to quell it for a hundred meters, but now I was asking my body to ignore that distress for three times that long.

I didn't let up in the straightaway. To the contrary, I continued to accelerate, picking up speed in the third turn and churning even harder exiting the fourth.

By the time I could see the finish line, I was running so fast that there was no way I was going to be caught. In my head, I heard Coach Pal's Prayer.

Legs fast; mind faster; heart unstoppable.

It was like I was a young child, reciting the Lord's Prayer before sleep to ward off my fear. Except, unlike then, now I had faith that the words were true.

―――

I won the NCAA championships by more than three seconds. As I accepted congratulations from my competitors, I saw a skirmish in the crowd. A security guard was preventing a fan from coming onto the field.

I made a beeline toward the commotion. Once there, I hugged Kick over the railing that separated the spectators from the field.

In his hand was a notebook and our old family stopwatch.

None of the members of our family had ever before traveled any further than Philadelphia to see me compete. Kick, however, had flown cross-country and kept it a surprise.

"I can't believe you're here!"

"I wanted to see the fastest collegiate 1500-meter man in the country kick some ass." He waited a beat. "Because I wanted to tell everyone that I kicked his ass once upon a time."

―――

Kick and I went to a steak house for dinner. The kind of place that priced the food by the ounce, so I wasn't sure what anything actually cost. Kick saw my apprehension.

"I got you covered, little brother."

"Good. Because I get twenty-five dollars for meals per day, so tonight's dinner would cause me to go hungry for a month. But since when did you get so rich?"

"Working on it," Kick said. "I got accepted into this trainee program at Harrington Brothers, and although they're not paying me much now, I can see some big numbers in my future."

We caught up on everyone, which amounted to little more than him saying that Mom and Dad were *the same*, Katie was *Katie*, and Rachel remained *batshit crazy* as ever, but the kind of crazy that he just couldn't get enough of, if I caught his drift. I smiled at him that I did, but batshit crazy was about the last thing I ever would have said about Meghan, so I could only imagine.

"I'm thinking of asking Meghan to marry me," I said.

What I'd thought was good news brought a look of concern across my brother's face. "What's the rush? I mean, there's no rush, right?"

"No. We don't have to get married. I want to get married."

"So I say again, why?"

"What do you mean, why? Because I love her. Because I want to live my life with her. You don't feel that way about Rachel?"

"I don't know what I'm going to want tomorrow, no less in fifty years."

"Maybe that's the difference between us," I said. "I've got a plan and I'm sticking to it."

He laughed. "Tell me the master plan of Sean Thomas Kenney. I'd love to hear it."

I knew he was mocking me, but I answered him as if his question had been posed in good faith. "Step one, win the NCAAs. Done that. Step two, win them again next year and the year after that. Graduate. Marry Meghan. Train for the Olympics. Make the team. Win a gold medal."

Kick was no longer smiling. He now understood I couldn't have been more serious about how I expected my future to unfold.

"And then?"

Now I didn't understand. "What do you mean?"

"So if everything in your life works out exactly as you've planned, you'll be . . . what, twenty-seven years old, married to your high school sweetheart, and have a piece of metal around your neck. Then what?"

It was a fair question. Of course, I had some thoughts on the matter, but those seemed too embarrassing to share. International stardom of some type . . . even though I understood that was almost nonexistent, even for gold medalists.

"I don't know what happens after that."

"Doesn't sound like too good a plan to me, then," Kick said.

12.

The man behind the bulletproof glass read total law enforcement. Fortysomething, beefy, bushy black hair—on his head, under his nose, above his eyes. The wooden nameplate in front of him read, "Desk Sergeant."

Katie had been reluctant to join me on this fact-finding mission. I suspect she agreed to come solely so she could prevent me from doing something stupid.

"We'd like to speak to the detective who handled the investigation into Michael Kenney's death," I said.

"Are you family?"

"Yes. I'm Sean Kenney. This is my sister, Kate Whitting. Michael was our brother." Although it wasn't necessary, I added, "Still is our brother."

"Please have a seat," the desk sergeant said. "Someone will be with you shortly."

Katie and I did as instructed. For about ten minutes we sat in uncomfortable wooden chairs arrayed against the wall until a woman in uniform, probably under thirty, appeared.

"Mr. and Mrs. Kenney?" she asked.

"I'm Sean Kenney. This is my sister, Kate Whitting."

"My apologies," the cop said, although I wasn't sure if it was for making us wait or getting Katie's surname wrong. "I'm Officer Signorille. I understand that you have some questions about the death of Michael Kenney?"

"We do," I said.

"If you would follow me, please."

She led us to a small interior conference room illuminated by too-bright fluorescent bulbs. Inside was a round, wooden table and four metal chairs.

I'd hoped that a detective would already be seated there or that once we were situated, the uniformed officer would go fetch one. But Signorille closed the door behind her and then joined us at the table.

Katie said, "Are you the person who handled the investigation?"

My television viewing told me that she wasn't. Detectives wore civilian clothes.

"No, ma'am. I assisted Detective Montedesco. She's not available today. But hopefully I can answer whatever questions you have. Let me begin by expressing how very sorry I am for your loss."

"Thank you," Katie and I said in unison.

How many times had people expressed sorrow for my loss? Must have been dozens by that point. I'd always accepted it at face value, but when uttered by the police, it angered me. The officer was sorry my brother had killed himself, but she should have been apologizing for the way the cops mishandled the matter to have reached such an erroneous conclusion.

"So, how can I help you?" Signorille asked.

"I suppose the main way would be to tell us why the police reached the conclusion that our brother died by suicide," I said.

The officer nodded to indicate she had expected that question. "I appreciate that it's difficult to accept that someone you loved took his own life, but I can assure you that we reviewed the matter very carefully."

She stopped there, as if it were an answer to my question, rather than a defense of the police department's work.

"We're not here to accuse anybody," I said, "but we are looking for answers that would put our minds at ease. Our brother didn't leave a note and there were no signs he was even depressed, and certainly nothing to suggest he was contemplating ending his life."

I hated the smile Signorille provided in response. Not hers, necessarily, but when flashed by anyone to foreshadow that something patronizing was to follow.

"The reality is that many people do not leave notes. Also, with respect, a loved one is often able to hide his or her true mental state."

I knew from hard experience that nothing is ever gained by giving a police officer attitude. So as calmly as I could, I said, "We understand that, but what we want to know is the evidence that led the police to conclude that our brother did, in fact, take his own life. We have lots of questions. Was the gun he used registered to him? Because his wife said they didn't own a gun."

"It was unregistered," Signorille said. "No way to trace it. But also not very difficult to procure."

"What about gun powder residue?" I asked, omitting that this knowledge was also based on my television viewing.

"Yes. There was evidence that your brother had fired the gun."

That took the wind out of my sails. I'd expected to be stiff-armed on that information or at least for the evidence to be equivocal. But if Kick had fired the gun, that went a long way to concluding he'd killed himself.

Officer Signorille continued, "The key card to your brother's hotel room was only used once. When your brother initially entered the room."

"Did you search his phone for clues about what was going on in his life?"

The cop shook her head. "We couldn't do that. It was password-protected."

"Didn't his wife know it?"

"No, she didn't."

I looked at Katie, but her expression didn't suggest that there was something odd about Michael keeping that information from his wife.

"Can't you use his face to open it?"

"I know that they do that in the movies, but it doesn't work like that. You need the person to be alive. That's why a photograph or an extremely lifelike sculpture won't work either."

Katie shifted beside me. She'd obviously heard enough.

I hadn't though. Not yet, anyway.

"Someone told me that my brother might have had some legal issues concerning his job. Did you know anything about that?"

"We are not at liberty to divulge certain specifics of our investigation, but I can assure you both that we considered all relevant information in reaching our conclusion regarding cause of death."

That was a no, then. The police hadn't investigated the possibility that Kick's death had something to do with Russians, cryptocurrency, and money laundering.

"May we see the autopsy report?" I asked.

I expected Signorille to repeat the same party line about confidentiality. But she hesitated for a moment, as if unsure how to answer.

"An autopsy was not conducted," she finally said.

I looked to Katie, asking with my eyes whether she knew. She stared back at me blankly, which told me she did not.

"Why not?" I asked.

"Your brother's wife declined."

The ride back to East Carlisle was largely silent. Right about the time Katie pulled off the Garden State Parkway, I asked the question I'd been thinking about for the last half hour.

"Did Jenny tell you that she declined an autopsy?"

"No," Katie said, as if there was nothing unusual about our sister-in-law not sharing this information or her underlying refusal, even though an autopsy might have proved that Kick had been murdered.

"Don't you think that's . . . strange? If it was me, I'd want to know everything about how my spouse died."

"Spoken like someone without a spouse. Speaking as someone with one, I wouldn't want Ben cut open for no reason."

An autopsy room entered my mind's eye. Kick on a cold metal table, the Y-shaped scar on his chest, his private parts exposed, the blood or whatever bodily fluids circling a drain on a cement floor. I couldn't disagree that Jenny might have wanted to spare Kick that indignity.

"I'm not sure what an autopsy would have shown anyway," Katie added. "There's no question that he was shot in the head at close range, right? Besides, if the police had any suspicions, they would have done an autopsy no matter what Jenny wanted. So the fact they left it up to her means they didn't think they needed one."

"And you're telling me that it's not strange that Jenny didn't know Kick's phone password?"

"That's what I'm telling you, Sean. I don't know Ben's."

Rather than dissuade me away from my theory, Katie's claim actually supported it. Your spouse looking at your phone was the easiest way to be caught cheating. If Katie didn't know Ben's password, and Jenny didn't know Kick's, that was likely because their spouses didn't want them to be able to see with whom and about what they were texting.

Nevertheless, I let Katie have the last word, at least for the time being, and we rode a few more minutes in silence. When she pulled onto Route 18, Katie engaged me again.

"I saw you talking to Rachel Fischer at the wake," she said.

"Yeah. We're going to see each other Saturday night."

"You do know the definition of insanity, don't you? It's doing the same thing over again and expecting a different result."

This confirmed that Katie was privy to the sordid details of my prior relationship—and breakup—with Rachel. I shouldn't have expected otherwise. Kick had every right to share with our sister the literal blow-by-blow of our final fight, in which Rachel had played, if not a starring, then at least a pivotal role.

"And here I thought that was called 'living your life.'"

Even in profile, I could tell that my sister wasn't at all amused. "Seriously, what good is going to come from seeing her?"

"I'm not marrying her," I said. "We're just getting a drink."

"I'm not sure how to say this exactly, but I think it needs to be said."

She still wasn't looking at me, her eyes firmly on the road. Not that it mattered, she had my full attention.

"It's hard not to wonder about the mental health of everyone you love after you realize that you really have no idea about what someone else—even someone you love—is going through. And I'm not talking about Michael. I'm talking about you, Sean. For the last . . . I don't know how long, I've known you were in a terrible place and I didn't do anything about it. And, I'm sorry to put it this way, but I don't want to lose another brother and sometimes it feels like I'm the only one that cares about that. And now you're doing exactly the same thing you did that caused you to go off the deep end the last time."

I wanted to tell her that I wasn't at imminent risk by having a drink with Rachel. But we both knew that wasn't what she meant. Not entirely, anyway.

"Don't worry about my going off the deep end, Katie. I'm a really good swimmer."

My attempt at humor caused her to take her eyes off the road and look directly at me. "I'm serious."

"I know you are. I just don't know what you want me to say. I mean, it's not like I want to die, you know?"

"That's just the point. Sometimes . . . most of the time, I don't know that. It seems to me that if you did want to die, you'd do pretty much everything you're doing, including going back to dating Rachel Fischer and becoming obsessed with proving that Michael was murdered. Neither one of those things is going to end well for you and I'm terrified of what you'll do when that happens."

It terrified me too. Still, I was going to pursue them both. In each case, I felt as if I had no other choice.

13.

After Katie and I returned from the police station, I readied myself to see Rachel.

What I'd learned—and didn't—from the cops was still front and center in my mind. My list of suspects—which at first had been limited to Jenny, and then expanded to include Russian-crypto-money launderers, and maybe Ben too—remained fixed, but I was reluctantly allowing for another possibility: that Katie was right and Kick had simply decided that he no longer wanted to live.

I went over our last call for the millionth time. Was he saying goodbye? Could Kick have been telling me that he intended to take responsibility for his actions by taking his own life? And when he told me that we'd see each other soon, did he mean in heaven?

And if Katie was correct about Kick's cause of death, was she also right about the risks I ran by becoming involved again with Rachel?

I pushed the thought out of my mind. Not because Katie was wrong about Rachel and me, but because it didn't matter if she was right. The sad truth was that even if I knew for certain I was once again destined to crash and burn with Rachel, I still wouldn't be able to stop myself. It was more than just the heart wanting what it wants. It was the only way I could think of to turn back time.

If I could get Rachel to love me again, then the last two years wouldn't have been wasted after all. Rather than running away, my exile would have been necessary to put me where I needed to be—which was back to East Carlisle and reunited with the woman I loved.

Or at least that's what I told myself.

When I came upstairs, Ben was watching a college basketball game. One of the teams, I couldn't quite make out the name on the uniform, had just hit a three-pointer. Ben clenched his fist in solidarity.

"Is Katie around?" I asked.

"She's out. The Stop & Shop, I think," he said without turning away from the action on the screen.

"Any idea when she'll be back?"

"She just left," he said, still not looking in my direction.

It was a little past seven. I wondered if Katie had made herself scarce to deny me the car. It would take more than that to keep me from seeing Rachel, however. The Tavern was only about three miles away. I could easily walk it.

I was about to say goodbye to Ben when he finally looked at me. His redirected focus coincided with the game going to commercial.

"Hey, why don't you have a seat. There's something I've been meaning to talk to you about."

Ben had been a year behind Kick and a year ahead of me

at East Carlisle High. Neither of us knew him, though. It was a big place and we were both high school royalty and, to be charitable, Ben was not.

He and Katie had started dating after they'd graduated from college, when she went into Liquor-18 one night when Ben was working there. The plan had always been for him to inherit the store someday, and that turned out to be much earlier than anyone could have expected when Ben's father was killed in a car accident. Hit by a drunk driver of all things.

That was five years ago. Back then there was just the one store, which was located on Route 18, hence the name. When Ben's father had opened it, the drinking age was eighteen, so maybe there was that at play too. Either way, it made sense for residents of East Carlisle because there were a bunch of business that adopted that moniker—Lights-18; 18-Lumber; Route 18 Chrysler Dodge. The branding was a head-scratcher when Ben began to expand to other locations. Liquor-18 in Rumson was on Old Country Road. Liquor-18 in South River was on Main Street. Liquor-18 in Manalapan was on Route 9.

I sat down in the armchair beside him, turning it so I wasn't facing the television. Ben kept his chair where it was, but adjusted his body slightly so we were looking eye to eye.

"What's up?" I asked.

"I was wondering if you'd given any thought to how much longer we're going to have the pleasure of your company?"

I hadn't made any plans beyond seeing Rachel tonight and my daughters the next day. On the other hand, I also hadn't been planning to leave town anytime soon. Ben's question, however, suggested that I'd worn out my welcome, which created an immediate problem because I didn't have anywhere else to go.

"That sounds like you're about ready to have your basement back," I said.

"The opposite, actually. I was thinking, if you're open to it, of finding some hours for you at the store."

That was a relief. I not only wasn't about to become homeless, but I was being offered gainful employment. My joy was tempered only by the fact that it was common knowledge in our family that Ben considered the business to be his private fiefdom, to the point that I could scarcely imagine a presence he would find less welcome than his wife's brother.

"My sister strong-armed you into this, right?"

He laughed. "No. When it comes to my stores, if nowhere else, I call the shots. I'm not going to lie to you, if she was against it, I wouldn't have done it, but I proposed the idea to her, not the other way around."

"That's very generous of you, Ben. Thank you."

"Not that generous," he said with a smile. "I'm only going to pay you minimum wage. And you're going to work hard. Stocking shelves, cleaning up, carrying wine to people's cars. All the glamour of being a liquor store employee, I'm afraid. But it's what I did for a lot of years too, and still do when we're shorthanded."

I viewed the manual labor as a selling point. As much as I cursed my existence down in New Orleans, I found some semblance of peace on a jobsite. There was something about the strain of the work that reminded me of my running days, and rather than cause discomfort, it soothed me.

"Yeah, that sounds great," I said. "Which store do you have in mind?"

"I thought we'd keep you close to home. So East Carlisle. I got a guy there named Carlos, but he could use some help."

"Okay, when do I start?"

"No time like the present. I figured on Monday. Unless that's too soon for you."

"I do have a lot of very pressing matters up in the air at the moment," I said in a deadpan tone, "but I think I can shuffle them around so my schedule is free on Monday."

"Monday it is, then," he said, in a way that made me uncertain if he knew I was joking. "I think this will be good for you. Give you something to do and put some money in your pocket. Besides which, it'll be good for the rest of us, and I include myself in that group, to have you close by for a little while longer."

The game came back on and the roar of the crowd diverted Ben's attention away from me and toward the television. I thanked him again and then told him that I was going to head over to the Tavern to meet Rachel. I expected him to offer me a lift, or at least ask if she was going to pick me up, but he just told me to have a good time.

14.

The Tavern was an East Carlisle institution. A no-frills place with five brands of beer on tap and a decent burger. The décor was roadhouse joint, right down to the sawdust on the floor.

Even though I'd gotten there under my own steam, I still arrived before Rachel. Feeling nervous, and a little thirsty from the walk, I decided to get a jump on things and ordered myself a shot of whisky. After I'd thrown that back, I asked the bartender for a beer.

Despite what my family might have thought, I never considered myself a bona fide alcoholic. I know that's what bona fide alcoholics always say, but I don't mean it in the *I can stop whenever I want* way, which I knew I couldn't. I meant it in the *I don't drink every day* way, or *I don't drink to get drunk* way. At least not usually. But I did imbibe more than I should have and considered alcohol necessary to get me through certain times in my life. That evening being no exception.

I was midway through my beer when Rachel came through the door. Her coat was open, revealing a yellow dress with a modest neckline that fell slightly above the knee. Her hair was loose, and she wore small gold hoop earrings and an equally tasteful necklace.

It made me feel slightly underdressed in my flannel shirt and jeans. Then again, aside from Kick's suit, I didn't own anything dressier.

I'd first met Rachel in high school. She and Kick had already been a couple for a few months when my brother invited me to be his third wheel on their date to the movies. After seeing *Pet Sematary*, we went to the Orchard, a place of high school lore to which I'd never been. Part Shangri-La, Atlantis, and the Bermuda Triangle all rolled up into one.

I'd never gotten high before. I suspected Kick had because that's what cool kids did, not to mention that my father was always accusing him of being stoned. For some reason it surprised me that Rachel got high too, as I had thought of it as a guy thing, although I don't know why.

"Here," Kick said, putting the joint in front of my nose.

"How do I do it?" I asked.

"Put it up to your lips, take in the smoke, keep it in your mouth for a second, and then suck it into your lungs."

I didn't do it right. Instead, the smoke immediately left my mouth, followed by a cough.

Kick and Rachel laughed at me. But it didn't make me feel bad. They weren't making fun of me; my effort had been pretty pathetic.

"Everybody does that their first time," Rachel said. "Try it again, but when you do, inhale more slowly."

I made the most of my second chance. "Good," Kick said.

I handed the cigarette to Rachel. She took two puffs and then passed it to Kick, who did likewise. It was my turn again, apparently.

This time I was better, or at least felt more natural. I also took in probably twice as much smoke.

"You feeling it yet?" Kick asked.

"I think so," I said, by which I meant no. But almost as soon as I said it, a wave overtook me, which reminded me of the split second after I awoke, when I was uncertain whether I was still in a dream.

Rachel noticed the change of my expression. "There it is," she said with a laugh.

I heard music, which I hadn't recalled from before. Britney Spears. I wasn't sure if it was only in my head, however.

Rachel ended the mystery. "I love this song." She grabbed Michael by the hand. "Come dance with me."

When the song ended, Rachel came over to me. "Your turn, Sean."

I didn't have any moves. Instead, I shuffled my feet, first one and then the other.

Rachel put my hands on her hips. "I'm going to move and then you move like me."

I don't know if I was any better with her help, but I was enjoying it immensely. I felt weightless, certain I would have floated away but for my fingers on Rachel's waist.

"Sean, have you ever kissed a girl?"

I didn't answer because I was positive it was all in my head. Rachel repeated her question.

"No," I said, or at least I think I did.

"Close your eyes," she said with some urgency.

I didn't have to be asked twice. Apparently, I was so eager that I was clenching them shut.

"Relax. It's not going to hurt," she said with a laugh.

Her lips lingered on mine. How long I couldn't say, but it felt like forever and yet not nearly long enough. And then her mouth slowly opened, just a bit, and the tip of her tongue made contact with mine. That was all it took for my eyes to roll back in my head. I was that far gone.

When I opened my eyes, Rachel had the most beatific smile I'd ever seen.

Later that night I told Kick, expecting him to be angry. He laughed. "It was my idea, little brother."

Rachel's kiss upon greeting me that evening could not have been more different than that first one. It was a peck on the cheek, befitting old friends rather than past lovers.

"Let's get a table," she said, even though the stool beside me at the bar was empty.

The hostess led us to the back. The TV overhead was muted, so our corner of the restaurant was quiet.

I wondered what my brother would think about my being with Rachel once again. I regretted that I'd never shared with him anything about our first go-around, other than to use it to hurt him during that final fight.

It had been Rachel's idea to keep our relationship secret from my family, which I'd understood given the way things had ended between her and my brother. Even though it had happened a lifetime ago, Jenny still referred to Rachel as "Fatal Attraction" on the rare occasion through the years that her name had been raised.

Shortly before we'd broken up, I was pushing for a coming out. I wanted to introduce Rachel to my daughters and once that cat was out of the bag, there was no reason not to reintegrate her into my extended family too.

I've since wondered if that was the reason she ended things. Sometimes I think it was the realization that we had a future that was too much for her. But at others, I couldn't rule out that she just didn't want to be with the little brother of the man she truly loved.

The last time I'd seen Rachel, not counting the funeral, was the night she dumped me. I'd been completely blindsided. Her reasons sounded almost like a recording of what Meghan had said years earlier, which boiled down to the charge that I'd never gotten over my past failures and therefore couldn't find happiness in the future.

That the only two women I'd ever loved had reached the same conclusion about me should have been enough for me to change. Instead, I ran away, which I suppose proved their point rather emphatically.

My two loves could not have been more different. Meghan was thoughtful, both in the common parlance of the word in which she considered the feelings of others, and also in the literal sense that she thought about everything. Rachel, on the other hand, seemed to act on instinct more than out of any design. They both made me laugh, although again in different ways. With Meghan it was because she could be sincerely funny with a turn of phrase or quick-witted comeback. I laughed with Rachel because I was happy to be with her.

During our time apart, I'd often given thought to what alchemy Rachel performed to bring out a feeling of joy within me. I managed to bury that emotion deeply when I was around virtually anyone else. Sometimes I thought it was a sexual charge, but while that was undeniably present between us, it sold our relationship short to attribute the depth of my feeling to something solely carnal. The best I could do to explain it was that being with Rachel conjured the same feeling as I once had on the track. Something about how I liked myself better when I was in her company.

After the waitress returned with our beers, I held mine aloft in toast. "To Kick," I said, and then clinked the glass to Rachel's.

She offered a sad smile, one that suggested she not only

empathized with my loss, but felt it acutely herself. And perhaps she did. Her breakup with Kick had been toxic enough that I couldn't imagine either of them wanting anything to do with the other ever again, but I now realized that, although the circumstances were very different, she'd also loved and lost my brother. And like me, she'd been estranged from him at the time of his death, albeit for much longer, and for a very different reason. Even so, neither time nor circumstance lessened the pain of losing a loved one.

"I miss you calling him *Kick* . . . *Inky*," Rachel said, invoking my high school nickname.

Over our burgers, she told me that not much had changed in her life since I'd last seen her. She still worked as a bookkeeper for that same New Carlisle law firm, still lived in the same house, and drove the same car.

"And your romantic life?" I asked.

"What's that?" she said with a laugh.

"No, really. I can take it."

"Believe me, I'm not playing coy. There's no one. I mean, don't get the wrong idea. I haven't been celibate since you left, but . . . like I said, no one."

I smiled a bit too broadly. "Now, now, no reason to gloat," she said.

"Believe me, I'm not. I'm just glad that you didn't make anyone else leave town, is all."

Her face contorted. I'd obviously struck a nerve.

"I don't recall it that way," she said.

The issue had been joined. I paused for a moment, a last-second opportunity to stop this train. Once I engaged, I knew I'd be back to where I'd been before, two years earlier. And yet, even armed with this knowledge, and the sense of forbearing that accompanied it, I couldn't help myself.

"What I remember is that I was in love with you and you told me that we had no future."

Rachel's eyes narrowed. "I was in love with you too. And terrified that I was in love with you. In equal measure."

"But the terror won out because you ended it."

"Yeah, but I regretted it right away. You know I called you. And texted. And would have maybe even gotten on a plane if I knew where to even go. But it was too late, I guess."

Too late. Was there really such a thing? As I asked the question in my head, I realized that the answer was obvious. Yes. Sometimes you missed your chance and the window closed, making what could have been no longer possible. The very definition of *too late*.

That's what had happened between Kick and me. I told him that I never wanted to see him again and then he died, transforming what I'd considered an empty threat into a promise.

"I told him about us." I said.

"Who?"

"Kick."

This was clearly news to her, which stood to reason. My brother and his ex were not on speaking terms, after all.

"The last time I saw him, in fact. A few hours after the last time I saw you."

"I take it, given that you vanished off the face of the earth shortly thereafter, that it didn't go well."

"No, it went great," I said with a smile. "I tried to punch his lights out. He, needless to say, kicked my ass, and I ran away. Hollywood ending."

"And that was really the last time you spoke to him?"

There was sorrow in Rachel's voice, maybe because she realized that my estrangement from Kick was, at least in part, about her. I might have relieved her of that guilt by coming clean that my brother and I had made amends right before he died, but I wasn't prepared to share that. Not yet, anyway.

A part of me was already regretting telling Katie. Not only because my sister had shot down my interpretation of what it all meant, but also because those two minutes and nineteen seconds I spent on the phone with Kick were all that I had of my brother now, and I was holding on to it for dear life, not wanting my final memory of my brother to be possessed by others.

"Yeah," I said.

"I'm so sorry, Sean," she said.

"Yeah," I said again.

It had begun raining while we were inside. Rachel and I stood under the Tavern's awning, listening to the downpour.

We made a mad dash to her car. It was locked, which Rachel hadn't remembered. The few moments it took her to find her key fob was long enough for us to both get drenched.

As soon as we were inside, Rachel turned the car on, ostensibly for the heat, but when she did, the radio came on too. We made out like high schoolers through the next few songs. From the moment our lips made contact, I knew I'd fallen for Rachel all over again.

As much as I believed I'd died and gone to heaven in Rachel's embrace, a very real part of me wondered if I had my location wrong. I'd barely made it out alive when we'd broken up, and there was no reason to think that I would fare any better this time.

15.

"Wake up."

I thought I was dreaming and my mother was telling me I was late for school. After a few seconds, my mind cleared enough for me to register that my sister was speaking. And that it was Sunday morning.

"What time is it?" I croaked.

"There are two cops here to see you," she said.

The words no one wants to hear. Also a sentence no one ignores.

"They just had me go over my last call with Michael. When I was finished, they asked to speak to you."

"What did you tell them?"

She looked at me as if the question made no sense. "The truth, Sean. I told the cops the truth."

I got out of bed, brushed my teeth, splashed some cold water on my face, and used my wet hands to smooth out my hair. Then I pulled on the same clothing I'd worn for my date with Rachel the previous night and headed upstairs.

Two men were standing in the living room. Both were wearing suits and stony expressions.

"I'm FBI Special Agent Jason Liu," the shorter man said as he flashed his badge.

Katie had said cops. Or at least I thought that was what she'd said. But these guys were FBI. Which meant that my initial assumption that my visitors were here to follow up on Katie's and my visit to the police station from the other day was wrong.

"I'm Brian Walsh with the Securities and Enforcement Commission," the other guy said. He also had a badge.

It was then that it clicked. They'd made this visit because of the Russian-crypto-money laundering investigation. So much for Arielle's take that it was all nothing more than office gossip.

"Can I get you some coffee, Sean?" Katie asked. "I already offered the two gentlemen, but they declined."

"Yes, please," I said, thinking that coffee would definitely help me navigate what was to come.

Katie excused herself and headed for the kitchen, at which time Liu said, "We're very sorry for your loss, and we apologize for being here so soon after you laid your brother to rest. If you would please sit down, Mr. Kenney. We'll explain the situation."

We'd been having this discussion standing in the center of the living room. Even though it wasn't his house, Liu pointed to the club chair, and he and his partner lowered themselves into the sofa facing it.

Once we were all seated, Liu said, "Through your brother's phone records, we know that you were the last person to have spoken to him. We're here to understand what he said to you."

They were vultures, feeding on my brother's dead carcass. Even though Kick had already been punished beyond the law's reach, they apparently still weren't done with him.

"Before we talk about what my brother said to me, I'd like to know what crime or whatever you think he committed."

"We're investigating the possible commission of securities fraud," Liu replied.

He might have substituted *bad shit* for *securities fraud* for all the clarity his statement provided. I still didn't have the first clue about Kick's work problems.

"Can you explain what that means? What do you think he did, exactly?"

Katie, who had never had a knack for timing, entered the room. After handing me my coffee, she took the chair beside mine.

"I'm sorry, Ms. Whitting, but we need to speak to your brother alone," Liu said.

My sister apologized for sitting in her own living room and left. When it was once again just the three of us, I said, "I'm still waiting. What actual crimes or whatever do you think my brother committed?"

Liu looked at his partner. It was only then that I realized that the younger guy from the SEC was the one in charge. Walsh looked to be barely thirty, clean-shaven, short hair, probably never got anything lower than an A- in his life and cried when he saw the minus.

"Our investigation is still in its early days," Walsh said, "and it's confidential, to protect people like your brother from false accusations."

In other words, he wasn't offering me even ice in winter. "Why should I tell you anything then?" I said, a challenge to my voice.

"Because if you don't cooperate with us today, you'll be subpoenaed to testify to the contents of the phone call, which will be under oath, on pain of perjury," he replied.

That didn't sound too painful to me. "So you don't have to go through that trouble, you know, subpoenaing me and everything, why don't you tell me what I want to know, and then I'll tell you what you want to know. Win-win, right?"

There was a momentary standoff until Walsh's pronounced sigh revealed that he was capitulating. A moment later, he said, "As I said, this is confidential and so we ask that it not go outside this room."

I nodded that I understood, even as I was determined to remember every word so I could repeat them verbatim back to Katie.

"Are you familiar with the term 'front-running'?"

It meant going full tilt from the starting gun. The opposite of a sit-and-kick racing strategy, which was my brother's forte.

"Yeah. I ran track. So did my brother."

Liu and Walsh both seemed confused. "I meant in the securities context," Walsh said.

Now I was confused. "No. I'm not a finance guy."

"Front-running is a form of insider trading," Walsh said. "Under SEC rules, trades must be executed as soon as practicable after the client places the order. The evidence suggests that before your brother executed certain large trades placed by his client, he informed a fund manager at another institution. The other fund manager then purchased that same stock ahead of your brother's client's order, and then reaped a tidy profit after your brother's order pushed up the stock price. In the aggregate, it amounted to several million dollars."

I wasn't certain that I got all of that, but what I did glean pointed in the direction of the Russian-crypto-money launderers. So I pressed that angle.

"A guy at my brother's wake told me that your investigation involved crypto trading that my brother was doing for some Russians."

"We can't divulge the identities of the clients involved, as I'm sure you can understand," Walsh said.

"No, I can't understand," I said, my anger getting the better of me. "Why would you be protecting the people who may have killed my brother!"

"Hold on there," Liu said. "You've got this wrong. We don't think for a second that our investigation has anything to do with your brother's death."

"Are you kidding me with that? You were going to send my brother to jail and do the same with his Russian clients. And then he ends up with a bullet in his head. And now you're telling me that you never stopped for a second to think that those two things might be connected."

"Please, sir," Walsh said, trying to calm me. "Let me explain to you who we are and what we do." He stopped, perhaps to allow me to settle down a bit before he continued. "The SEC is not a criminal prosecutorial agency. That means your brother was not at risk of going to prison. We do, however, have the authority to revoke the licenses of regulated persons, of which your brother was one. If it had gone that way, your brother would have been ineligible to work in the securities industry. The Commission is also authorized to impose fines and civil penalties, and those can be quite substantial. So I'm not saying that this was not a serious matter, because it was. We consider all matters investigated by the SEC to be serious in nature."

Nothing he said changed my view that their investigation might well have been the proximate cause of my brother's death. Losing millions of dollars was more than enough motive to commit murder, after all.

"That said, we do not believe that your brother's death and our investigation are at all related." Walsh caught himself and added, "At least not directly," as if to suggest that he couldn't rule out that the prospect of being broke and unemployed might have led Kick to take his own life. "You must understand that your brother's clients have no motive to harm him. To our knowledge, they're unaware of our investigation or even that they've been financially harmed."

That made absolutely no sense to me. How could someone lose millions and not know about it?

"I don't understand," I said.

"Let me try to explain it to you this way," Walsh said. "Suppose, hypothetically speaking, a stock is trading at five dollars a share. Your brother's client puts in an order to buy a million shares. That's going to push the price up to six dollars. So the client knows they're going to be paying five and a half as a blended average for their million shares. But, before your brother fills the order, he calls a friend at another fund. That other fund places a smaller but not insignificant buy. Maybe for a hundred thousand shares. They probably get all of that at five bucks, or a tick above, because it's not large enough to move the market very much, if at all. But after your brother places his big order, the stock starts to go up in price, and after the full million shares are purchased, the stock is now trading at six. Which means the other fund has made almost 20 percent on their investment in about two seconds. The reason why the scheme works, why your brother can keep doing it, is that his client expected their order to move the market price, so they have no reason to think that the price wouldn't have been six after their million-share order. As a result, they don't think they've lost any money. And if the stock keeps going up after the buy, then what does the client really care so long as they're making money, which more often than not, they did."

I could now see how Kick's clients might be none the wiser, but it still eluded me why my brother would engage in such reckless conduct. Obviously, money was the usual answer to that question, but that didn't track in Kick's case. He had more than enough money. And although this front-running seemed to be lucrative, to be sure, it paled in comparison to the millions that his employers were shelling out to him on a regular basis.

I was still considering what it all meant when Liu said, "Are you familiar with a woman named Arielle Taylor?"

That's why. Kick wasn't doing it for money. It was for a woman.

I might have said she told me that she knew nothing about the investigation and didn't believe Kick would ever do anything wrong. But the mere fact that they'd mentioned her name meant everything Arielle had told me had been a lie. I also didn't need a pen to connect the dots. Arielle was the other fund manager. My brother's co-conspirator.

The less I said, the better, however. At least until I could see the shape this was going to take.

"No. I met her for the first time at my brother's wake."

"What did she tell you about her relationship with your brother?"

There was something untoward about the way he said the word *relationship*.

———

As soon as my uninvited guests left, Katie told me everything she'd shared with them. Her rendition provided nothing new, as she merely repeated to Liu and Walsh the same thing she'd previously told me about her last phone call with Kick—how it was a run-of-the-mill birthday call, but for the fact he made it and not her, and his *I love you* at the end.

When it was my turn, I told her how the FBI had disabused me that Russian-crypto-money launderers had played a role in Kick's murder.

"Good," she said. "Does that mean that you're finally ready

to accept what we've all already come to terms with about Michael's passing?"

The answer was *No*. Or at best, *Not yet*.

But rather than tell Katie we still didn't see eye to eye on this most critical issue, I deflected.

"The FBI guys think that Kick was having an affair with this woman, Arielle, the other fund manager. The one who I spoke with at the wake."

"Do they have any proof of that?" she asked.

"Not that they shared. But, why else would he be engaged in criminal conduct with someone who's . . . you know, Jenny 2.0."

"Money?"

"He had more than enough of it, don't you think?"

She shrugged, as if to say that no one ever has enough money. Or maybe she was suggesting that Kick could never have enough.

"It's not fair to Kick for us to be speculating about the state of his marriage when he's not here to defend himself," Katie said.

"What if he told Jenny about it? Or she found out some other way?" I said, engaging in precisely the kind of speculation Katie had just said was unfair. "That gives her a pretty strong motive, don't you think?"

"Jesus Christ, Sean," she shouted. "You know you sound insane? Let's say you're right about Kick and this Arielle—and I don't think you are—when your husband cheats on you, you divorce him. You don't murder him."

"Not if you're going to lose millions of dollars, you don't," I said.

"What are you even talking about? You just said a second ago that Kick had more than enough money. Even if it was halved under your divorce theory, Jenny would still have more than she could spend in two lifetimes."

"You know about the loans, right?"

Katie shook her head. "No, what loans?"

"Kick told me that whenever he joined a new firm, they'd give him this enormous loan that was interest-free, and he was supposed to pay it through the commissions he'd earn over the next ten years. The last one he told me about was like for $30 million. Since it was a loan, and not income, I'm not sure that Jenny would have any right to that money in a divorce. But more importantly, Kick would have to pay back every penny if he was fired—which he might have been because of the investigation. But not if he died. If that happened, he kept it all."

"Stop it," Katie said sharply. "I'm not going to listen to another word of this. Don't get me wrong, Jenny has never been my favorite member of the family, but she is a member of our family. She didn't kill our brother. She just didn't."

I could see that I was upsetting her, and should have left it there for that reason. But I couldn't help myself.

"So you're telling me that you think Kick is more the type to kill himself than Jenny is the type to commit murder?"

Katie didn't answer, which I first took to mean that she agreed with my conclusions that Jenny wasn't above murder to keep herself living in luxury. But after I smiled in a self-satisfied way, my sister disabused me of that.

"Yeah, I do, actually," she said.

16.

The Colonial Diner was located at nearly the precise geographic center of East Carlisle, and in my romanticized view of my hometown, served as its beating heart. On Sunday, it was the go-to after-church brunch spot, which was why I arrived before noon, fearful that otherwise I'd have to wait for a table.

A girl, who must have been an ECHS student, led me to a booth. I asked her if I could get a coffee, and she told me that she'd tell the waitress. A woman who looked old enough to be the hostess's grandmother came by a minute later and asked if I wanted any coffee. When I told her that I did, she said she'd be right back.

While I waited to be caffeinated, Phoebe walked through the front door with Harper a step behind. I'd expected Meghan to be accompanying them and hadn't ruled out asking her to join us. But out of the diner window, I spied Steve in his car, alone. He was, no doubt, waiting for a text from one of my daughters to confirm that I'd actually shown up.

I waved my hand overhead until Harper's eyes fell upon mine. She poked her sister and pointed in my direction. Phoebe then sent a text, and when I looked back to the parking lot, Steve was reading it. A moment later, he drove away.

The waitress returned with my coffee and asked my daughters if they wanted anything to drink. Phoebe ordered a coffee. I wondered if it was her way of telling me that she'd grown up since our last meeting. Harper requested a hot chocolate with whipped cream, which she might have selected for the opposite reason.

It reminded me of the other moments when my children suddenly announced they were no longer little girls. The first time Phoebe climbed into the passenger seat as if nothing out of the ordinary had occurred, after a lifetime of being relegated to the back. When Harper nonchalantly informed Meghan and I that she was going to be a scary witch for Halloween after a long string of Disney princess costumes.

"Thank you both for coming," I said.

They each smiled. Harper's was less forced than Phoebe's, but only marginally so.

"Before I say anything else, I want to again tell you that I'm sorry. Even though I wasn't physically with you, you were both always at the front of my thoughts every single day. And I missed you. More than I could ever put into words. But I know that's not the same thing as being here. Not even close. And for that, like I said, I am very sorry."

For the better part of twenty years I'd been chasing the feeling I had when winning a race, and had always fell far short. It was much easier to conjure the sensation I experienced whenever I lost. Facing down my daughters, I once again contended with the excruciating pain of failure.

"I wish I could provide you both with some explanation for why I left," I continued. "But I just can't. And I'm sorry for that too. I can tell you that it had nothing to do with not loving you. Or anything you did or didn't do. Or Mom or Steve. Or anyone else for that matter. It was all about things I had to deal with that were only about me."

Harper interrupted my monologue. "What things?"

I shook my head, and then pushed back an emerging tear with my finger. "The saddest part is that I'm not really sure. I just felt like . . . that everyone would be better off if I wasn't here for a little while. Does that make any sense?"

Phoebe said, "Are you going to stay now?"

"Yes. I'm going to live at Aunt Katie's for now. But soon I'll get a place of my own. And when I do, I'd really like if you came to visit me there. How's that sound?"

"Good," Harper said.

Phoebe didn't offer her opinion. I didn't know if that was because she was uncertain whether she wanted to let me be her father and risk being hurt again, or if she doubted that I was going to stay.

"So tell me. I want to know positively everything about each of you."

Crickets. I should have remembered that teenage girls do not rush forward with information about themselves. At least mine never had.

"Let's start with you, Phoebe. What's your favorite subject in school?"

"Lunch," she said, which would have been my answer back in the day too.

"Fair enough. How's basketball going so far?"

"One and one," she said.

"You know, when I was in high school, they didn't let freshmen compete in varsity sports."

"Fresh people," Harper said.

It took me a second. "Yes. Of course. Fresh people."

"They do now," Phoebe said.

"Still a big accomplishment to start on varsity as a fresh person."

She didn't respond. I got the sense she was enjoying making me work for every bit of information I could extract.

"Any boys in your life?"

"Or girls," Harper corrected again.

"Or girls," I said.

"No," Phoebe said.

I clearly wasn't getting anywhere with my eldest. So I decided that discretion was the better part of valor.

I turned my focus to my youngest. "Your turn. Tell me about Harper Clare Kenney."

"You need to ask me questions like you did Pheebs."

"Okay. What's your favorite subject at school?"

"Math."

"Really?"

"Yes."

"Any boys—or girls—in your life?"

She giggled. "No."

"Are you playing any sports?"

"Softball maybe."

"Did either of you ever think about going out for the track team?" I asked.

"No," Phoebe said, as if she had not only thought about it, but soundly rejected the idea as repugnant. Harper shook her head from side to side. "Me neither."

It gave me a taste of how my father must have felt when Kick rejected football. I knew now, in a way I hadn't fully comprehended then, that both Kick and my father were speaking a language I didn't understand. Whereas I took their positions on the issue at face value, they were communicating about something entirely different than what sport my brother would be playing in high school.

Kick was rejecting what our father thought made him who he was. It was my brother's way of saying that he didn't want to be anything like our old man. And my father heard that loud and clear.

Just like I did now by my daughters' rejection of track and field.

———

I drove the girls back home in Katie's SUV. They both sat in the back seat, as if I was an Uber driver. I spied on them through intermittent glances in the rearview mirror.

Most of the time they were on their phones, but occasionally one would lean over to the other, either to point to what was on her screen or to whisper something, and I'd hear giggles in response. Seeing them together reminded me of how Kick and I had been once upon a time. As if nothing could come between us.

"My mom wants you to wait when you drop us off," Phoebe said. "She just texted."

I still referred to Meghan as *Mom* when talking to my daughters. *Go ask Mom. Mom said you have to do your homework.* But after Meghan and I separated, first Phoebe, and then Harper, started using *my*, to distinguish Meghan from all the other mothers out there to whom they might be referring. I supposed it was their way of making clear to me that Meghan was now theirs, and only theirs.

After what Meghan had said at Jenny's house, I was not eager for another tongue-lashing. But declining wasn't an option either, not if I wanted to continue enjoying our newly reached détente. So, when the girls got out of the car, after I told them that I had a great time and hugged them goodbye, I leaned against the car door awaiting Meghan's arrival.

She jogged toward me wearing a green East Carlisle High School girls basketball hoodie. "Nice," I said, pointing to the sweatshirt.

"It's Phoebe's."

"I assumed. So what's up?"

"Did you have fun with the girls?"

"Yeah. I hope they did too."

"I'm sure they did."

I was less certain about that, but not much interested in engaging in further small talk. I knew Meghan had something on her mind, and I wanted her to get to it already.

As if she could sense my anxiety, she put me out of my misery. "So, anyway, I was thinking about what I said the other day, and I might have been a little harsh, especially given that it was your brother's funeral."

"No, it's fine. You said something that needed to be said. I appreciated your honesty."

"I don't know if that's true, but thank you for saying it. The reason I wanted to talk to you, though, is that I thought that maybe I'd left out the most important part."

"Which is?"

"That I think you can do it. Re-engage with the girls and be the father that I know you want to be. And I know even more that they want you to be. Need you to be, if I'm being honest. I guess, I also want you to know that I'm rooting for you to do it."

"Story of your life, right? You cheering me on."

"Maybe. But this isn't some stupid race, Sean. This is real life."

That was the crux of it. This was real life. Like I'd said to Katie the other day, what Meghan said cut deep because it was true.

"Well, it means a lot that you've . . . forgiven me, I guess."

Meghan shook her head, as if she disagreed. That she, in fact, didn't forgive me. I felt myself deflate at the prospect that no matter what I did from now on, I'd never make it back into her good graces.

"The truth is, Sean, that I don't even know what forgiveness means in the context of you and me," she said wistfully. "I know it doesn't mean amnesia. Not a day goes by where I don't curse your stupid name. For the time you weren't here. For what the girls lost by not having their father present in their lives even before you physically left. And, if I'm speaking my truth here, for what went wrong in our marriage."

I started to say something, even though I didn't really know what. Something I hoped conveyed that I wasn't that awful a father. Or husband.

Meghan wasn't ready for me to get a word in edgewise, though. She held up her hand, like a traffic cop, instructing me to keep quiet and let her finish.

"Listen to me, will you?" she said with a laugh. "I wanted to talk to you because I thought I might have been too harsh the other day, and here I am heaping even more blame. So here's what I think about the whole forgiveness thing, because believe me, it's something I've given a lot of thought about. Recently I read something that suggested that every day we wake up as different people. That's because the events of the preceding twenty-four hours have changed us. You can't tell in real time, of course. You still look the same, feel the same. But you know that at forty you're not the same person as you were at thirty. To say nothing of twenty, right? And when did that change happen? Not all at once, but all the time."

"Okay. I'm with you."

"So, the Sean that needs to be forgiven, the Sean that you think I *have* forgiven, who is he, really? The Sean who left? The

Sean who wasn't really there even before he'd left? Or the Sean standing on my lawn right now?"

I knew the question was rhetorical, but I answered nonetheless. "All of the above?"

I'd said it with a hopeful smile. She offered me a weaker one in return.

"Well, the truth of it is that I've never really forgiven those first two guys. But you, the Sean of right now, I'm willing to give him the benefit of the doubt. Is that forgiveness? Or is it just withholding judgment when you meet someone new?"

After leaving Meghan's house, I called Rachel.

"I just finished having brunch with my daughters and I was in your neighborhood and wondered if you might want some afternoon company."

"That's quite serendipitous because I was just thinking to myself that there was nothing I wanted more right now than to have your afternoon company."

"So can I take that as a yes?"

"You can take that as please get here as fast as you can."

"I'm not going to say that I'd forgotten how nice it was with you," Rachel said, "because I thought about it all the time while you were gone. I will say, however, that it's even nicer than I remembered it being."

"Yeah, for me too."

The musty scent of the last hour's activity filled the room. It had been a long time for me, and I was pleased it hadn't shown.

The pleasure was short-lived, however. I felt shame that I was experiencing any emotion other than grief. It wasn't time for me to get back to living my life when I had so many unanswered questions about what ended my brother's. Beyond that, I hadn't been truthful with Rachel about how things were between Kick and me at the end. I justified keeping it to myself before, but I couldn't resume a relationship with her without coming clean now.

"I need to tell you the truth about something," I said.

Rachel pulled her head off my naked torso and sat up. She wore a concerned look that suggested my truth wasn't something she was ready to receive.

"I lied to you before. When I said that the last time I spoke to Kick was when we had our fight before I left."

"Okay," she said noncommittally. "So you were speaking with him?"

"No. We hadn't spoken since I'd left. But we did on the day he died. On his birthday."

Her expression widened. "What did you talk about?"

I'd started down this path prepared to reveal all, but now that the moment was at hand, I faltered. I still wasn't ready to share that I believed Kick had been murdered. When I considered the reason for my reluctance, I knew it was because I feared that Rachel would agree with Katie's assessment that I'd lost my grip on reality.

"That we loved each other and forgave each other," I said.

She nodded. "Anything else?"

"That was the important part."

She smiled in a way that made me smile too. "Well, that's good, right?"

"Katie thinks it was his way of setting things right before he . . ."

"Yeah, that makes sense. I've heard people do that sometimes."

"I guess I have another confession too," I said. "I told Katie about us."

"Not the worst sin."

"I know, but the last time you were pretty clear that you didn't want my family knowing about us until we had taken root—"

"That was the last time, Sean. This is this time. So, did Katie curse my name?"

"No, she told me about the definition of insanity."

Rachel nodded, apparently familiar with the expression. "What's the definition of learning from your mistakes?"

"Is that what you think this is about?"

"I do, Sean. I truly do."

17.

Ben usually spent Mondays in Rumson, but he accompanied me to the East Carlisle store on my first day so that he could give me the orientation spiel himself.

"I can't thank you enough for the opportunity," I said on the drive over.

"You can thank me by doing a good job," Ben replied.

I was truly grateful. I've always been at my best when I've had something to occupy myself with, and I knew that sitting in Katie's basement obsessing over the failure I'd become or how to prove someone murdered my brother was not good for my mental or physical well-being.

"It's weird," Ben said, apropos of nothing, "but you know the way when you're a kid people tell you that you can be whatever you want when you grow up?" He didn't wait for me to agree before continuing, "No one ever said that to me. As long as I can remember, my father made it clear that I'd take over from him someday, although he had no idea someday would come so soon, obviously. But I think he saw this store as a way for him to live forever." Ben laughed. "I thought it was insane back then, but I get it now."

I thought about how my father once upon a time wanted to live vicariously through Kick. Ben's father never wanted a football hero for a son, but he pressured his boy to follow in his footsteps all the same.

"Anyway, after my dad died, it was really important to me to build the business into something that was mine, not just a continuation of what he'd left me. That's why I've expanded so aggressively in the past couple of years. And why this restaurant deal in New Carlisle is so important to me."

A restaurant in New Carlisle was news to me. "I'm sorry, did you say that you're opening a restaurant?"

He laughed. "Didn't Katie tell you?"

"No."

"Figures. Your sister's not, how shall I say this? She's not fully on board. But she'll come around. Anyway, I've got this line on a great space on Main Street. It used to be an Italian restaurant and it has this amazing bar. Twenty feet of solid mahogany. My plan is to divide it into two spaces, so there's a restaurant and a liquor store right next door."

Ben was practically bursting with pride. He didn't smile that broadly when discussing his children.

"That sounds very exciting. Why does Katie think otherwise?"

"Because it's a huge capital investment, that's why. You can't imagine the up-front costs that go into a restaurant these days. And, of course, most of them fail in the first year. But I just feel it in my bones that this thing is going to be a huge success."

Liquor-18 was your typical strip mall liquor store. Racks of wine, arranged by region, hard liquor in the back, a wall of refrigeration off to the side housing beer.

"This is where we keep the Italian reds," Ben said as he walked me down the aisles like a monarch surveying his lands. "If someone asks for a recommendation, act like you've sampled every bottle in the store. Then give them any bottle in their price range and tell them it's an excellent value. If you really want to sell it, refer to any red as having *notes of cherries* and any white as being *crisp*."

As his last act before leaving, Ben introduced me to my co-worker. Carlos looked to be in his early twenties, tall and lean, with a goatee that I suspected he thought made him look tough.

When Carlos and I were alone, I thought it wise to put him at ease that I was no threat to his job. "I know that no one dreams to work side by side with the boss's brother-in-law, so let me apologize in advance for that."

"I'm actually happy to have the help," Carlos said. "I've been working here for four years now, and it's always been a two-man job. Then about . . . I don't know, maybe four, five months ago, the guy I was working with got axed. Ben just couldn't afford to pay him anymore. I've been by my lonesome ever since."

Not being able to pay employees didn't exactly jive with Ben's plans for expansion into the restaurant business. Then again, I doubted Carlos had any real insight into the decision-making that led to his buddy being fired. And he certainly had even less visibility into my brother-in-law's finances. Still, it seemed a bit odd.

"Is that right?" I said.

"For real. I don't want to put you in a tough spot or anything because, you know, he's your family and all—"

I interrupted him. "By marriage, so . . ." He didn't seem to get the joke, so I said, "Ask. If I don't want to tell you, I won't."

"Okay, well, Leo—he's my buddy in the Manalapan store—he heard that the stores were all going to close, and that's why

Ben fired half the staff and the inventory was running low. But now we're fully stocked, the stores are back to two guys each, and Rumson has three, and here you are."

"I don't follow you."

"Like what's going on?"

"Nothing's going on. I'm sure that Ben just thought he could run the stores with one person and then realized that was a mistake. I don't know anything about the inventory, but maybe it was a supply chain problem or something."

"Okay. I guess it's all good, then," Carlos said.

His face told me otherwise. He was trying to hide it, but Carlos didn't think it was all good. It was also apparent that he wasn't going to say another word on the subject. It reminded me of the way Brandon clammed up. Like he knew he'd overstepped and wished he could go back in time and undo our last exchange.

With little choice now, I decided to table any further discussion about Ben. So I asked Carlos to tell me a little about himself, and he seemed more than happy to oblige. He was originally from Trenton, moved to East Carlisle for high school, and started working at Liquor-18 after graduation. He said that he was thinking seriously about joining the military, but he wasn't sure which branch of service best suited him.

When it was my turn, I provided a bullet-point version of how I'd spent the past two decades. "I grew up in East Carlisle, college at Villanova. After a stint out West, I came back home. I lost my job during Covid and spent the last two years in New Orleans doing construction work. And now I'm here with you."

Hearing the words come out of my mouth, I was reminded how my one-time life plan didn't bear the faintest resemblance to my actual life. But then I realized that wasn't my entire story. In fact, it wasn't even the part that truly mattered.

"I have two daughters. Phoebe is fifteen. She plays on the ECHS basketball team. And my youngest, Harper, she's thirteen."

"Cool," Carlos said with a smile.

I'd thought that working in a store would be a cakewalk compared to my construction jobs, but by four o'clock my back was feeling the effects of being on my feet all day, not to mention a burning in my biceps from lugging those cases of wine. Shortly before closing time, I finally had reason to smile. Into Liquor-18 walked none other than Rachel Fischer.

"May I help you, madam?"

"Madam? Not even a ma'am?"

"I assumed you ran a brothel."

"Clever. I like my liquor salesmen clever."

I glanced over at Carlos. He'd heard every word and looked as if he was about to faint.

"Carlos, this is my friend Rachel. Rachel, this is Carlos, who's been showing me everything I need to know about the operation here."

"Nice to meet you," he said, before going back to pretending to ignore us.

"So, how's it going so far?" Rachel asked.

"I haven't broken anything yet."

"You're obviously a natural."

"I am at drinking it, so how much harder can it be to sell the stuff, right?"

"That's good to hear because I was hoping you could recommend a nice bottle of red to go with pasta with crushed tomatoes and prawns that I'm going to be cooking for this guy I just started seeing. Actually, we were a couple about two years ago, but then he . . . kind of went crazy a little bit, but thankfully, we're back together again."

"Is that right?" I said. "He must be a very handsome man and an incredible lover to have a woman as beautiful as you be so forgiving."

She laughed. "Well, he certainly thinks he is at least. So, what wine do you propose I serve my rather conceited friend?"

I pretended to consider the issue, stroking my chin with my fingers as if I was giving the matter deep thought. In reality, I had no idea what I was going to recommend, but in keeping with Ben's prior instructions, I figured any fifteen-dollar bottle would do the trick. I walked over to the Italian red aisle and pulled a bottle of Chianti in that price range.

"I think you will enjoy this one very much. It's got notes of cherry."

When I came home, I provided Katie with an abbreviated version of my first day before telling her that I wasn't staying for dinner because Rachel had invited me over.

"You're certainly not wasting any time, are you?" she said.

"What's that supposed to mean?" I said, even though I knew.

"It means you've been back in town for a minute and you're picking up exactly where you left off. Need I remind you, it didn't end very well the last time."

"Maybe I'm learning from mistakes," I said, mimicking Rachel's explanation.

Katie didn't respond. Not verbally, at least. But that didn't mean I didn't hear her loud and clear.

I'd been on the receiving end of that same withering expression in that very kitchen countless times a generation ago.

Rather than defend myself against her unspoken criticism, I went back in time too.

"Okay if I borrow the car?"

The moment I stepped inside Rachel's home, she offered me a glass of wine from the bottle I'd selected for her. Then she asked me to join her in the kitchen, where she was still preparing dinner.

"This is actually very good," I said after taking a sip of the Chianti. "That guy in the liquor store really knows his stuff."

"About some things," Rachel said without turning to look at me. She lowered the flame beneath a skillet to a simmer and poured a tube-shaped pasta into a larger pot beside it. "We're almost there. The sauce is done, and it's quite delicious, if I do say so myself." She joined me at the kitchen island and, in a world-weary tone, said, "So, how was your day at the office, dear?"

"Same old, same old," I said, playing my part.

"Look at us, like an old married couple already."

Rachel had gone all-out to set the mood. The fireplace was lit, the dining table set with linen napkins, candles flickering in the center. Adele sang softly as the soundtrack.

As we ate, I recalled the feeling of domestic contentedness—sharing my day, having someone share theirs with me—from my prior life with Meghan. Back then, whenever I experienced that type of tranquility, I rebelled against it, as if accepting that existence would be further proof that I'd failed in my prior one.

I hoped that I could be different this time around. That with

Rachel I'd be able to finally slay my demons and find happiness and meaning in my life again.

"I saw Meghan and the girls the other day," I said.

"How'd that go?"

"Better than I feared, worse than I wished."

She smiled. "It'll take some time to integrate yourself back into everyone's life."

There was that word again: *time*. The bane of my existence but also my only hope at salvation.

"I always got the sense that Meghan didn't like me much," Rachel added.

"If anything, she was jealous of you. Prom queen and all."

The reference to Rachel's glory days made her grimace. I understood that reaction more than most. Sometimes I thought of myself as two different people. The Olympic hopeful I'd been a long time ago and the failure I was today. I hated that first guy for turning me into the second, which had the cyclical effect of making me detest myself even more for letting that happen. Rinse and repeat.

"Trust me, that wasn't it," Rachel said. "It was because Meghan knew I'd picked the wrong Kenney brother and I think she was always a little worried that I'd eventually figure that out."

The last time we were a couple, Rachel told me about her high-school-through-college relationship with Kick. Nothing graphic, of course. The same kinds of things that she likely shared with all her new boyfriends about her first one, except that, if anything, she probably portrayed her time with my brother through a more rose-colored lens for my benefit. That he was her first love. That she lost her virginity to him, which I already knew from Kick. That she thought they were going to get married, and then he dumped her for Jenny, which made Kick her first heartbreak too, and that, like with the passion of first love, the pain of that loss was also far more intense than any that would follow.

"Meghan wasn't wrong, though," Rachel continued. "I mean, yeah, it didn't end up being happily ever after till death do you part for the two of you, but you loved her and gave her two beautiful daughters. Michael, God rest his soul, on the other hand, moved on from me to Jenny like he was changing his underwear."

Her reference to Kick brought me back to thinking about my brother. Rachel must have noticed the change in my expression because she said, "What?"

"I was just thinking about something. Something else. Not us."

"Care to share with the rest of the class?"

I had to come clean. I simply couldn't hope to start off on the right foot without telling Rachel what was weighing most heavily on my mind. Besides which, I needed someone to talk to about my suspicions, and Katie had made clear that she was not a receptive audience.

"I don't think Kick committed suicide."

I expected Rachel to react the same way as Katie, with a horrified look that she was in the presence of a crazy person. But she kept a neutral expression and asked, "What makes you say that?"

I recounted the evidence to support my hypothesis—the securities investigation, Jenny's rejection of an autopsy, her claim she didn't know Kick's phone password, Kick not leaving a note. Before Rachel could respond, I offered the counterargument—the gunshot residue on his hands, the absence of evidence of anyone else in the hotel room, the fact that the Russians didn't know about the investigation.

"The big thing, what ties it all together, is that I think Kick was having an affair with this woman Arielle."

I knew that Rachel, of all people, would be quick to believe that Kick could be unfaithful. It was likely the first thing she thought about whenever my brother's name was uttered.

As expected, she didn't claim it couldn't be. Instead, she nodded to confirm that everything I was telling her made perfect sense.

It emboldened me to go further. "There was also more to my final call with Kick than I told you before," I said.

In response, Rachel looked at me suspiciously. I got the sense that she would accept my omissions, but not a deliberate falsehood.

"The part about our making up was right," I said quickly, a bit defensively, "but then Kick told me that he was in some type of trouble and needed my help. He didn't say what that trouble was, but he did say that he was going to take responsibility for it, and he expected that when he did, things might get, he said, very real, very fast. He wanted me to be there for him when that happened. But it's the last thing he said to me that I keep thinking about. He said we'd be together soon. There's just no way that he would have hung up the phone with me right after saying that to put a bullet in his own head."

Once it was all laid bare, Rachel was still. I got the sense she was still weighing the evidence. But then her expression changed, and by the way she lightly bit her lower lip, I knew I wasn't going to like the conclusions she'd drawn.

"You're grieving, Sean. It's only normal that you'd question everything."

"It's not just that I'm questioning," I said. "I feel . . . lost not knowing. I was hoping that by going to the Rumson PD they might take a second look at things, but now I'm not so sure. I was thinking that maybe I can figure out how to access Kick's phone. I've read on the internet that there are people who can do that."

Rachel's smile reflected a sense of pity. Even if she didn't agree with my conclusions, I got the sense she at least understood how I felt.

"Can I help you?" she asked.

I wished she could. That anyone would come to my aid. But I imagined this as a path I was destined to travel alone.

"I don't see how. Unless you have the skills to open a locked iPhone. And maybe investigate Arielle's whereabouts on the day Kick died."

"No, but I have the next best thing. You forget that I work at a law firm. I can introduce you to this private detective who does some work for my firm. This guy, he's the real deal. Former Israeli intelligence. He'll be able to figure out what happened."

"I can't pay for that."

"You won't have to. He'll do it pro bono. A favor to me."

"Are you sure?"

"I wouldn't have offered if I wasn't. Let me call him and then we can all meet and he'll tell you what's doable and what's not. No commitment necessary. Just a getting to know each other thing. How does that sound?"

It sounded like manna from heaven.

18.

Upon entering East Carlisle High School, visitors passed in front of the school's Wall of Fame, which was little more than a trophy display case. Back when I was a student, front and center sat a picture of my father along with the rest of the '79 East Carlisle Bears, on a plaque denoting they were New Jersey state champions.

Whenever Dad had to show up at the high school, for parent-teacher conferences or some assembly, he almost always made some reference to it. But even when he didn't say a word, he never walked by the damn thing without looking at it, like a beauty queen who couldn't pass a mirror without admiring her reflection.

Dad's team photo was now relegated to the very back. In the place of honor was a different wooden plaque, one etched with gold letters that proclaimed:

> NEW JERSEY STATE CHAMPION
> BOYS 1600 METERS
> SEAN T. KENNEY
> EAST CARLISLE HIGH SCHOOL

Beside it was a photograph of me crossing the finish line. My white shirt and green shorts amid a cloudless blue sky.

The photo wasn't taken at that state meet, however. It was on the ECHS field, and I was reasonably sure it was from the first meet of my junior year. That was the day that I broke the school record for the 1600 meters. Kick's record.

I called Kick that night to tell him that I'd beaten his best time.

"Times are for suckers," he'd said. "What matters is who finishes first when you're running head-to-head. Until you beat me on the track, you'll always be second-best, little brother."

I knew he meant it good-naturedly, which was enforced every time he refused to grant me a rematch. "I run 1500 meters now," he'd say, because in college and the Olympics that was the metric mile, while high schoolers ran 1600 meters for some reason. "I mean, if you want to race where I do 1500 and you do 1600, okay, but even though you're fast, I don't think you're that fast."

The truth was that there came a time when I could have spotted Kick the hundred meters and still beaten him. Kick was a very good runner—good enough to secure a spot at Rutgers, just as Coach Pal had predicted—but I was an elite runner, such that anything short of the Olympics was a failure.

———

The teams were still in shoot-around practice when I entered the gym. The bouncing balls and squeaking sneakers providing a staccato rhythm. I scanned for Phoebe and spotted her when her back was turned.

As I started climbing up the bleachers, I saw Meghan. "Fancy seeing you here," she said as she scooted over to make a little more room beside her. "Phoebe's going to be so happy you came."

Meghan laughed, although I hadn't said anything.

"What's so funny?"

"I was just thinking that it sometimes feels like I've lived half my life in bleachers. I don't think you have any idea how many hours I've spent on wooden slabs watching you run."

Midway through the first half, my phone vibrated in my pocket. I wouldn't have answered except for the fact that the caller ID displayed *Rumson PD*.

"Hello?" I said, getting up to find somewhere quieter to talk.

"Is this Sean Kenney?" a woman's voice asked.

"Speaking. Can you hold on just one second?"

The caller said, "Sure," and then nothing further.

By this time I'd already made it off the bleachers and was leaving the gym. I found the first classroom door locked, which led me to assume that they all were, so I resigned myself to having this discussion in the hallways.

"Sorry about that, but I can talk now."

"This is Detective Montedesco of the Rumson Police Department. I'm sorry it took me a little bit to get back to you, but I've just been swamped. I know you came into the station a few days ago and met with Officer Signorille. She told me that you might have additional questions, which is the reason for my call."

I heard Katie's voice in my head saying that I should let it go. That I should tell the detective that I appreciated her getting back to me, but I'd made peace with the police department's conclusion that my brother took his own life, and there was no longer any need for me to take up her valuable time.

But just like I told Rachel, I couldn't do that. I needed to see this to the end, wherever it led.

I returned to the gym just as the first half was ending.

"Everything okay?" Meghan asked.

"Yeah, fine," I said.

Meghan looked at me in that way she had when she wanted me to know I wasn't fooling her. I decided to deflect by mentioning two other things I hadn't yet shared.

"I've been working some shifts at the liquor store. For minimum wage, but it keeps me out of trouble."

Meghan lit up at the news. "I think that's great."

"And I guess, while I'm filling you in about my life, I should tell you that I've started seeing Rachel Fischer."

"As in Kick's girlfriend? That Rachel Fischer?"

Meghan's question confirmed that she didn't know about my prior involvement with Rachel. Or that Rachel was, at least in part, the reason for my self-imposed exile.

I saw little upside in sharing the details about Rachel's and my past relationship with Meghan. So I said, "As in the girl who back in high school, which was almost twenty years ago, dated my brother before he got married. Yes, that Rachel Fischer."

"How'd you get so lucky?" Meghan said in a way that made crystal clear that, unlike my future employment, she didn't think that my dating Rachel was *great*.

"We saw each other at the funeral."

Not a lie. Not the truth either. An in-between place that I so often occupied with Meghan. Or maybe with everyone.

"So you picked up your brother's ex-girlfriend at his funeral," she said, shaking her head.

"Don't make me sorry I told you, Meghan. It's still really early. I've seen her like twice. But I like her."

"You always did," Meghan replied.

"What's that supposed to mean?"

She shook her head again. "Nothing. I'm sorry I said anything. It's really none of my business."

I couldn't leave well enough alone. "Tell me. I want to know."

She sighed, loudly enough that I sensed it was for my benefit. Meghan's way of reminding me that I was asking for it, and she was going to give it to me, both barrels' worth, for that reason alone.

"I think it's time for you to grow up, Sean. I get why Rachel is so alluring for you. A reminder of a time when you were on top of the world. The track star and the prom queen, right? But nobody cares about those things anymore. And that means you shouldn't either."

19.

Katie was sitting on the living room sofa wearing her Sunday best when I returned from the game.

"Am I that much of a lapsed Catholic that I'd forgotten that they do church on Thursday nights?"

She rolled her eyes. Even doing that, she reminded me so much of our mother.

"I've got to go meet with Ben and the lawyers about this new store slash restaurant," she said.

"Yeah, he told me about that. Also that you aren't a fan of the idea."

"Don't get me started. Instead, tell me about the game."

I joined her on the sofa. "It was good. We lost by ten."

She chuckled. "Sounds really good."

"Meghan was there too."

"Keeps sounding better and better. How's Meghan doing these days?"

"She seemed good. You know, for Meghan."

Katie came to her feet. "So, the kids are all out for dinner and Dad's already down for the night, although you should check in on him in about an hour. We're going to be back around nine. You can forage for dinner. There's some leftover chicken that you can microwave." She held her hand out. "Car keys, please."

I reached into my pocket and dropped the keys into Katie's waiting palm. As she closed her hand around them, I said, "Can we talk for one more minute before you go? It's important."

"Okay, but I truly only have one minute." Then she sat back down.

"While I was at the game, I got a call from Detective Montedesco."

Katie's face registered her usual opposition to my refusal to leave well enough alone. I thought she wasn't going to even ask what I'd learned, but curiosity must have gotten the better of her.

"And?"

"She told me that there were two gunshots."

Katie looked at me as if I might be joking. "That doesn't make any sense."

"Detective Montedesco tried to tell me that it does. She said that sometimes there's a practice shot or the person flinches and misses. Apparently that guy who played Superman killed himself and he fired three shots."

"That's not right," Katie said, as if she knew better about what Detective Montedesco had told me. "Christopher Reeve had that horse riding accident that left him paralyzed. He died like ten years after that."

"No, the actor who played Superman on TV. Like in the 1950s."

Katie didn't seem to care that we were talking about two different actors portraying the Man of Steel. Nor did it seem to register that the police had concluded that our brother had fired twice in order to shoot himself in the head once.

"What else did the detective say?"

"Same stuff the other cop had. About the gunshot residue being on Kick's hands, how the only prints on the gun were his, and that no one else entered or exited the hotel room," I said in a somewhat monotone to convey that I was merely passing on information but didn't accept the conclusions the cops had drawn based on it.

I thought the fact that two shots had been fired would have given Katie pause to think that perhaps I wasn't crazy to believe Kick hadn't killed himself. I could tell just by the look in her eyes that wasn't her take on it, however. Katie was never going to question the police's determination that Kick died of a self-inflicted gunshot wound without hard evidence to the contrary.

Alone in the house, I walked through the rooms that I had once crawled as a baby, ran through like a banshee with Kick and Katie as a child, and prepared for a glorious future during my teenage years. Now everything seemed smaller, but also more precious, as if time had transformed what I'd always considered fairly ordinary objects into priceless artifacts.

Our family photographs hung on the staircase wall. Most of the ones I remembered from my childhood were still there, supplemented by some pictures of Ben's parents and a few depicting him as a boy, as well as more recent images of Katie and Ben's family through the years.

I stopped at a photo of the Kenney siblings taken at my wedding. I'm in the center, smiling as if the world was truly my oyster. Kick's looking at me, nothing but pride in his eyes. Katie's focus is toward the camera, but her hand rests upon my shoulder.

Back then I believed with every fiber of my being that my brother and sister would always be there for me. I doubt that they ever had the reciprocal faith in me, however. If they had, I'd proven them wrong. And now I had a taste of that medicine. I was alone too. Neither would help me uncover the reason for Kick's murder.

The bedroom I shared with my brother was at the top of the stairs. During our residence, it was painted a light blue, with two twin beds under each window. When we were children, it was football-themed, decked out with Giants paraphernalia. Over time, it took on our personalities, although more Kick's than mine. In the last iteration that I can remember, there was a Hoobastank (Kick's favorite band at the time) poster peeking out between my brother's medals and trophies on his side of the room, and one of Pamela Anderson (also Kick's choice) on the other, behind my trophies and medals.

Katie's eldest daughter had transformed the space to be more suitable for a nine-year-old girl. Pale pink walls, a white desk and dresser. Stuffed animals covered the bed and a short bookshelf extended the length of the window. Katie's old bedroom, which was now her youngest's domain, was decorated in almost precisely the same fashion.

My parents' room always seemed like a fortress when I was a kid. Perhaps that was because they had imposing furniture, in the 1960s style, which I think they'd inherited from my grandparents. Katie and Ben had a more minimalist approach, which left the space somewhat cold.

The green room, as my father's study was called, because its walls were Kelly green, was off-limits to anyone but my old man, my mother included. It was where he went at the end of the workday to have a drink, or two, before he was ready to face his family at the dinner table. Once Dad caught Kick and

I inside and not only did he mete out disproportionate punishment for our transgression, but when we attempted to gain entry the next time, we were thwarted by the installation of a lock.

The walls of the green room were now white and adorned with needlepoints Katie had done of the four Liquor-18 stores in their respective strip malls, each encased in a wooden frame. A photograph of Ben looking like he couldn't have been older than twenty-five, standing in front of the cash register with his father beside him in the East Carlisle location hung beside a framed newspaper article about Ben's old man entitled, "The Wine Merchant of East Carlisle."

Ben's desk was glass and he had the same ergonomic mesh chair you'd see in start-up tech companies. I took the opportunity to pretend I was Ben for the moment and sat in the chair, my eyes glancing over floor plans scattered across the desk. Closer inspection revealed they were the architectural drawings of the New Carlisle space, as it currently existed and how Ben planned to remodel. The design was to separate the square footage in sort of a funnel configuration, so that each part had somewhat equal street frontage, but then the restaurant became much larger in the back.

A mock-up menu was under another sheaf of papers. I laughed when I saw that he was considering naming the place the Liquor-18 Restaurant, which sounded to me like where drunks would congregate. The food would be family-style Italian, pastas and pizzas. A few pages underneath, however, I happened upon a different menu. It had the same name, but this one offered burgers and more comfort-oriented food.

I figured if I kept searching through the piles there'd wind up being a menu of seemingly every type of cuisine. But I only had to dig a little deeper before finding something much more meaningful than appetizers and entrees: a notice from the Internal

Revenue Service. At the top, in large font, it proclaimed it was a levy.

Liquor-18, Inc. was in arrears with back taxes to the tune of $379,818.55.

Or at least that was the debt as of a month ago.

That's why Ben was cutting expenses at the stores. He had an IRS problem. A serious one.

Something had changed, obviously. He was now flush, which meant that the IRS must have been paid off. Not only that, but he had enough left over to open a restaurant.

There was only one way that I could imagine Ben climbing out of that financial hole so quickly: Kick.

It suddenly dawned on me why Katie had been so insistent that I stop my inquiries and accept the police's conclusion that Kick committed suicide. She was protecting her husband.

20.

Meghan was sitting in the same spot in the stands as we had for Phoebe's last game. This time, however, Harper was beside her. It took a beat for me to realize that Steve was on Meghan's other flank.

The tip-off went to East Carlisle, and then bounced to Phoebe. She dribbled upcourt and passed off to the corner. The ball found its way back to her hands behind the three-point line. She took a step to her left before launching it toward the basket. A perfect swish.

"All right, Pheebs!" Harper screamed, rising to her feet.

"Let me show you something," I said to my daughter after she sat back down. "Do you have a piece of paper, a pen, and a hard surface to write on?"

Harper reached into her backpack, pulling out a loose-leaf binder. She clicked open the rings and handed me two sheets of paper. After closing the notebook, Harper retrieved a pen from elsewhere in her bag and then handed it all to me, including the binder for me to lean on.

I drew an upside-down U starting from the bottom of the page and turning at about the one-third mark.

"What's that?" Harper asked.

"What does it look like to you?"

"A doorway."

That hadn't occurred to me, but she was right. Along the vertical red margin line, I drew a second upside-down U that was about two inches from the edge of the paper.

"Now what?"

Harper shrugged. "Two doorways?"

I nodded toward the gym floor. She turned to see what I saw.

"The court?"

"Very good. So whenever Phoebe touches the ball, I'm going to mark on the map of the court that sort of does look like two doorways, where it happens with a dot. If she passes and it leads to an immediate basket, I'm going to put down an *A*, for assist. If she shoots and misses, I'm going to signify that with an *X*. A basket gets a star. That way, when the game is over, I'll have a pretty good diagram of Phoebe's performance."

"Fire," Harper said.

"When I was your age, I'd watch Uncle Michael's track meets and record his times in my notebook."

"Uncle Michael ran track too?"

I was surprised that Harper didn't know this about my brother. I'm sure I'd told her through the years, and she'd undoubtedly overheard Kick and I joking about it too. But like all kids, perhaps, Harper likely didn't consider anything that occurred before she was born to be very important.

"He did. Your uncle was an excellent runner. Captain of the team when I joined it. You know the way I always called Uncle Michael *Kick*?"

"Uh-huh."

"It's because he had a great finishing kick, which is a running term for being the fastest at the end of a race."

"Want to guess what they called your father?" Meghan asked, leaning in to join our conversation.

"What?" Harper asked.

"Inky," Meghan said, smiling at me.

"But now, for the tougher question. Can you figure out why?" I said.

"Because you have black hair?"

Meghan offered her a hint. "No. It has to do with Uncle Michael's nickname—*Kick*."

"Tell me."

"So, when I joined the team, they called me *New Kick*. But then they abbreviated that to its initials. N.K.," I said.

Harper still didn't get it.

"Say it out loud," Meghan said.

"N-K."

"Now say it three times fast," I said.

"N-K, N-K, N-K." She broke out into an oversized smile. "That is soooo funny."

I smiled back at her. The kind of smile that made me realize that my muscles didn't usually work that way.

"Anyway, before I was on the team with that funny nickname, I was in middle school, like you, and I would go to Uncle Michael's track meets and sit in the stands with your grandfather's stopwatch and I'd record his times in my notebook. When we got home, Uncle Michael and I would go over the race. Then, after I joined the team, your aunt Katie would do the same thing for him, and after Uncle Michael graduated, she did it for me. And if you can believe it, when I was in college, Uncle Michael would sometimes come to my meets and use that same stopwatch."

On the court, Phoebe had a fast-break lay-up for an easy bucket. I scribbled a star on the diagram.

"Let me do it," Harper said, taking the pen, paper, and notebook.

———

When I got back to Katie's, she was alone in the living room, watching a home show. It was the kind where they take some abandoned, ramshackle house and turn it into a palace. Her needlepoint was in her hands, about 20 percent more complete than the last time I'd seen it, now with the foreground stitched, but the house remained blank. The home on the television also had not yet begun its renovation, the rooms still piled high with garbage.

"How was the game?" Katie asked.

"Good. They won. I showed Harper how to keep stats of Phoebe's game, which I think she liked."

"Sounds like a nice night."

"What's been going on here?"

"Same old, same old. Dad's asleep. Kids are . . . doing whatever they do up there, and Ben is out checking on the New Carlisle place." She laughed. "I swear, sometimes I think that man's worried space aliens are going to lift the building clean off the earth and take it back to their mother planet by the way he stands guard over it."

Her reference to Ben and the restaurant poked the elephant in the room. I hadn't been certain about when or how to raise their money issues with Katie, but now and however it spilled out seemed like a good enough plan.

"There's something I wanted to talk to you about," I said, "but I don't want you to get mad at me."

"I think if you really didn't want me to get mad, you'd keep whatever's on your little mind to yourself. So it's pretty clear that you've already decided asking your question is worth earning my wrath, so you might as well come out with it."

She was right about that. I wasn't sure if their family finances fit into Kick's death, but I was certain that it might, which meant I wasn't going to ignore it. Still, I was going to tread carefully by not mentioning the IRS levy, which would have required admitting to snooping around Ben's office.

"I had this strange conversation with my coworker, Carlos. He said that he'd heard from another guy—I can't remember what store that guy works in—that Ben was in some financial difficulty."

"It's worse than a sewing circle in those stores," Katie said. "The way everyone gossips."

It wasn't lost on me that she hadn't denied the claim. "Is what he said true, though?"

"That's kind of a personal question, don't you think? I'm not asking you what you have in your bank account."

"I don't have a bank account."

"Right. How could I forget, *Mr. Please Pay Me In Cash.*"

"I'm not trying to pry into your family finances, Katie. But Carlos also said that about four months ago, Ben fired half the staff and up until recently, he wasn't restocking the inventory. Then, all of a sudden, everything gets reversed. He hires more people and the shelves are filled again. Not to mention all the cash going into this New Carlisle place. I mean, don't go telling me that I'm crazy for wondering if Ben got some money from Kick."

"You ever hear of a bank, Sean? Place that lends money to businesses? Our brother was rich, but last time I checked, he wasn't Bank of America."

A bank didn't loan people money to pay off the IRS. Or maybe they did. I really didn't know.

"So you're telling me that Ben got a bank loan?"

Rather than answer me, Katie expressed her displeasure with a pursed lip. Once again, she looked exactly like Mom. Mom when she was furious, I should add.

"What are you not saying that you think is going on?" she asked.

I had ventured onto the thinnest of ice. The last thing I wanted to tell Katie was that I considered it a very real possibility that Ben murdered Kick, or that a part of the reason I'd reached that conclusion was because I suspected he was having an affair with Jenny.

"Nothing. I'm just asking if Ben borrowed some money from Kick. That's all."

She gave me Mom's classic church lady look. "You're going to be the death of me, Sean. Hand to God."

"You know, back in my day, we played offense and defense," I said in a gruff voice.

"What?"

"Oh, I'm sorry. I thought we were doing imitations of our parents. Yours was good, but you need to put your hand on your hip when you say 'Hand to God.' And also, never use just my first name. It's always, *You're going to be the death of me, Sean Thomas Kenney*. And then the Hand to God thing."

"Very funny."

"Seriously, Katie. Just tell me if I'm barking up the wrong tree here about Kick and Ben."

She sighed. "You are. And not that it's any of your business, but Ben took a mortgage on the house to get the money he needed for everything."

I had a rough idea of the value of the house, and 80 percent of it might have netted them enough to cover the IRS lien, although not very much more. Certainly nowhere near enough to fund a restaurant. Or at least I didn't think so. But maybe they had other resources on top of that. Ben probably had life insurance from his father, or maybe he tapped into the kids' college funds.

"I appreciate your concern about our finances," Katie said, turning off the television and gathering up her needlepoint. "I'm sure Ben does too. But don't worry, we're going to be able to keep the house that you live in and buy the food you eat, not to mention employ you. And on that note, I'm going to go upstairs and I'll see you tomorrow."

She was at the foot of the stairs when she turned back to me and said, "Have a good night, Sean. Although, I sometimes wonder how you can sleep at all."

I didn't think I was the one who should be tossing and turning with guilt, however. If Ben had gotten bank financing, I suspected there'd be some proof of that in his office. Loan applications, for example. But my search hadn't revealed anything like that. Besides, it didn't make sense that Ben would let things become as dire as an IRS levy and firing people if he had a ready access to cash.

Our father always told us that he picked our mother, while he had no choice in who became his children. It was his way of saying that he'd always side with his wife over us kids. Katie had apparently taken that lesson to heart, believing the bonds of matrimony were thicker than blood.

21.

Carlos had an outsized grin stretching across his face when I showed up at the store the next day.

"That coffee have crack in it?" I said. "Because your smile is kinda freaking me out."

He took a sip of the coffee, as if to test for himself whether a controlled substance lurked within. After he placed the cup down on the counter again, Carlos flashed the same stupid-ass smirk as before.

"Nah, just coffee."

I'd seen Carlos's expression before. Usually on women, though. I steeled myself for what was about to come.

"Why didn't you tell me that you were once the fastest man in the world?" he said.

"I think you're confusing me with the Flash."

"No, for real. How can you not tell somebody you're working with that you're actually famous when they think you're just a regular guy?"

I took a moment to consider how to disabuse Carlos of the notion that anything he'd read about me on the internet actually mattered. Because it didn't.

"A very long time ago, I used to run 1500 meters very fast. It doesn't mean shit now, and I'd appreciate it if you stopped looking at me like it does, thank you very much."

Carlos put on a more serious expression, befitting that he now understood he'd struck a nerve. I was certain he wouldn't drop the subject, however. Prior experience had taught me that few people left well enough alone in such circumstances.

"So what happened?"

That was what everyone wanted to know. Not what it felt like to succeed, but why I'd ultimately failed.

Invariably, I cited an injury. Knee or hip was my usually go-to. Once I told a woman that I lost my pinky toe in a freak accident and went on for a few minutes about how most people take their pinky toe for granted because it doesn't occupy much room in the shoe, but for a runner it's the most important digit because without it you can't make the turns. Even after we had sex, she never noticed that all my toes were present and accounted for.

After lying for so many years, I'd come to almost believe it was an injury that had ended my running career. Almost. Deep down, of course, I knew all too well the actual reason.

"My running career ended because I just wasn't good enough," I said. "That's what happened."

It was the first time I'd heard myself say aloud what had previously been screaming in my brain for more than a decade. That it was my own damn fault that everything crashed and burned around me.

Not just running, either. My marriage. My job. My connection to the ones I loved.

Carlos, however, didn't seem to realize I'd just made a heartfelt confession. In fact, quite the opposite. He laughed at me.

"You're crazy, man. I wish I was that good at something, you know? I played a little baseball in high school. Had a great glove, couldn't hit for shit. But man, to be good enough to compete with the best. I would have killed for that chance."

Ben came into the store at about ten minutes to noon.

"Carlos, can you hold down the fort for a few while I talk a little with Sean," he said, not a question as much as a directive.

I followed Ben past the aisle of reds, beyond the refrigerated wall of beer, and through the door marked *No Entry*. On the other side, Ben had a little office. By little, I mean tiny. It was probably a closet at one time, but he'd wedged in a desk and the same mesh chair he had in his home office.

It was the only chair there, so we both stood. Ben shut the door behind him, which made me feel like I was in an elevator.

"What's up?" I asked as if this was all casual.

It felt anything but, however. My best guess was that Katie had shared with her husband my inquiries about their finances and Ben decided to retaliate by firing me.

Just as I braced for that hammer to fall, Ben said, "I just wanted to check in to see how it's going."

I tried not to look too relieved. On the other hand, it made no sense that was the reason he was meeting with me in the store's tiny office. I lived in the man's house, after all.

"It's all good. I'm getting the hang of everything. Carlos has been great, showing me the ropes. No complaints."

"Glad to hear it. There is one more thing I wanted to talk to you about, actually."

"Okay. Shoot," I said while thinking—*here it comes*.

"The New Carlisle place is definitely going to happen, so I'm on to next steps. The remodel, staffing, hiring a chef."

"I'm sorry, but I can't cook, Ben," I said with a smile.

He laughed. "No, I actually had another position in mind for you. I want you to be its general manager."

I hadn't expected this tête-à-tête to result in good news. Few of my one-on-one interactions ever did.

"Wow. Thanks. I wasn't expecting that."

"What did you think this was about? That I was going to fire my sister's brother after a week?" Ben was laughing and I joined in to signify that such a thought was outside the realm of possibility. "Anyway, the GM job is going to require you to stay in East Carlisle for a while. At least a couple of years. So don't accept unless you're willing to make that commitment."

Once upon a time, I thought living in East Carlisle was a prison sentence. But now, being close to family, and Rachel, it seemed like a godsend. Not to mention that I was being handed on a silver platter a job with responsibility and challenges that paid a wage a grown-up could live on.

All I had to do was say yes.

Yet the words wouldn't come. Something just didn't seem right about suddenly being the beneficiary of such good fortune. Especially with it coming on the heels of my accusation the previous evening.

"I don't want to sound ungrateful, but I don't have any experience running anything other than myself around a track. And let's be honest, the last couple of years, I've hardly been the model of responsibility. So, I got to ask, why me?"

"Okay, that doesn't instill me with a hundred-percent confidence," Ben said with a laugh. "But to answer your question, here's why you. You're good with people, Sean, and this is a people job. And, even though you might not know it, I believe in you. So, that's why you."

I wanted all of that to be true. But another justification

crowded it out of my brain. Was this Ben's way of slapping on the golden handcuffs? Maybe he figured that if I had something to lose if he went down for playing a part in Kick's murder, I'd be less likely to take him down.

22.

I had a distinctively inauspicious start to my track career. I fell in my very first race. Aside from the acute embarrassment, a twisted ankle kept me sidelined for the next several meets. When I returned, Coach Pal suggested that I run the 800 meters, thinking that the shorter distance might be easier on my still not one-hundred-percent ankle.

My times were never more the middling, as I lacked the speed required to excel at that distance. But as luck would have it, Tim Pittman, who had run the second fastest 1600 meters besides Kick, came down with mono and Coach Pal gave me his spot in the Group IV championships.

The Group IVs brought together New Jersey's best runners in high schools with student bodies greater than two thousand. The state championships were more prestigious, but no one from East Carlisle was of that caliber, Kick included, so the Group IV title was the achievement that Kick coveted more than any other.

He'd come within a hair's breadth the prior year, only to lose to Eric Sheffield. It had been Kick's only loss in his entire high school career, and the Group IVs and Eric Sheffield had become my brother's white whale. Kick had told me more than once that if he never won another race, he'd consider his running career a success if he were able to avenge that loss and win the Group IVs.

While waiting to be called to the starting line, as my brother entered pre-race mode, doing his high leg lift, the straddle stretches, and rocking his neck back and forth, I caught sight of my mother in the stands (my father had been true to his word to boycott Kick's meets) with Katie beside her. My sister's composition notebook appeared to be in her lap and by the faint reflection of the sun, I assumed that our father's stopwatch was in her hand.

When the starting gun fired, Kick went off like a shot, running in a full-out sprint. It took Sheffield a moment to figure out what was going on, but then he revved into top gear too.

My instinct was to try to stay with them, but I quelled it, opting to blend into the second pack with four other guys. A runner from Thurgood Marshall led the way, his red shorts conjuring the image of a bullfighter's cape for me to chase.

Soon enough, it became clear that Sheffield couldn't maintain my brother's pace, and he was ceding ground with each step. By the time I finished the first loop, Kick was out in front by a good ten meters. Despite falling off the lead, Sheffield was still at least that far ahead of my pack.

Midway through the second leg, the guy who had been glued to my side since the starting gun fired broke stride. I didn't know if it was because the pace had gotten too much for him or if he developed a stitch or something, but my first impulse was to do likewise and put an end to the fire that I could feel in my lungs, which I knew was going to get much worse before I reached the finish line.

But it was as if my mind and my legs were not connected.

No matter the messages my firing neurons were sending me to stop, I kept going.

Heading into the final lap, the Marshall guy sped up. I did my best to keep pace, but couldn't and he opened up about a five-meter lead on me, maybe more. Although I didn't dare check, I could no longer hear footsteps behind me, which told me that the rest of the pack was falling even further off my pace than I was lagging behind the red shorts ahead of me.

In the backstretch, I could see Kick was about twenty meters ahead of Sheffield, who was that far in front of Mr. Red Shorts, while I was maybe slightly closer to third place than that. Nobody ever chased Kick down at the finish, which meant that the race was as good as won.

As soon as I took comfort in that thought, I realized I couldn't have been more wrong.

The kid from Marshall began to accelerate and in a matter of seconds had shot into second place, overtaking Sheffield as if his feet were in cement blocks. If Mr. Red Shorts kept his pace, he'd pass my brother with equal ease.

Like I was the cavalry rushing to Kick's aid, I started to gain on the leaders. Within no time at all, I ran by Sheffield and set my sights on catching the red shorts still a few meters ahead of me.

Entering the third turn, I did exactly that. The Marshall runner had started his kick too early and was now out of gas.

As strange as it was to find myself in second place, odder still was that I felt stronger than I had at any other time in the race. Kick's body was coming into sharper and sharper focus with my every stride.

With a hundred meters to go, he was within arm's length.

With fifty, I could almost feel his hair touching my nose.

At ten, we were neck and neck.

My momentum pushed me forward for another hundred meters past the finish line. When I turned around, Kick was bent at the waist with Coach Pal's hand on his back.

Monday, in homeroom, the morning announcements mentioned my name for the first time.

"At the Group IV track and field championships, East Carlisle placed fourth overall and won four of the individual events," the disembodied voice said through the loudspeaker. "Junior Olive Hester won the girls' 200 meter hurdles; senior Matthew Caine won the boys' long jump; senior Greg Pavin won the discus; and East Carlisle placed one-two in the 1600 meters with senior Michael Kenney narrowly defeating his brother, sophomore Sean Kenney."

The whole class applauded, although I suspect it was more for the winners than my second place. Still, Bonnie Rudnitsky, who hadn't uttered one word to me that entire year, made a point of saying, "Congrats, Sean," when we left homeroom for first period.

In the hallway, other kids, including some I didn't even know, said, "Nice race," or "Way to go" as I passed them.

Third period was my lunch. I never complained about having to eat lunch at 11 a.m. because I had company for my misery in the form of Jake Marshall, who'd been my best friend since third grade.

"Glad to know that you're not too big a track hero to still have lunch with the likes of me," Jake said when I joined him at our table.

"I am, actually," I said as if I was serious, and then pretended to look around the cafeteria for cooler kids to sit with.

Jake laughed. "Nice try. But face it, you came in second. That means you lost. In fact, if I were you, I'd be embarrassed. You're the slowest guy in your family, right?"

I sat back down and considered flicking at Jake the noodles smothered in orange whiz sauce that was my lunch. Before I could load it up, however, Ms. Lentz, who I had for seventh period social studies, put her hand on my shoulder.

"I'm sorry to interrupt your lunch, Sean, but Mr. Palomino asked that you visit him in his classroom. It's S.110."

"Did he say why?"

"I'm just his messenger, not his confidant," she said.

When I arrived at S.110, the door was closed. Looking through the small, square window, I saw Coach Pal eating his lunch at the teacher's desk.

I knocked but apparently did so too lightly because Coach Pal didn't even look up. So I rapped the door harder, twice.

"Come," Coach Pal called out.

S.110 was your typical social studies classroom, which was what Coach Pal taught when he wasn't coaching track. A map of the United States was on the back wall, a collage of US presidents hung beside the window.

"Sean, thank you for coming. Sit down, take a load off."

The only chairs were attached to desks, the beige Formica kind that were shaped like kidneys, with a hole on the right or left side for you to get in. I grabbed the one nearest him and pushed it closer to Coach Pal's desk, the process making a god-awful screeching sound as the chair legs scraped the floor.

"I pulled you out of lunch, didn't I?"

"Yeah. Ms. Lentz said you wanted to see me."

"I did, but I didn't want to starve you. Want half?" He waved the sandwich toward me. "It's turkey and Swiss and some mayo."

"No thanks."

"You sure?"

"Yeah, I'm good."

He bit into the sandwich and seemed to be enjoying it. I momentarily regretted turning down a bite, as I hadn't done anything with my mac and cheese apart from considering staining Jake's shirt with it.

"That was quite the race yesterday, wasn't it?" he said while chewing.

Coach Pal must have considered his question rhetorical because he didn't seem to care that I didn't answer it. Instead, he took another bite of his sandwich. I watched him chew and then swallow, not certain if our conversation had run its course.

"So, I imagine that right about now a smart guy like yourself is thinking, *Why did Coach Pal pull me out of my nice lunch period to offer me his weak-ass turkey sandwich?* Am I right?"

He was, but somehow it seemed rude for me to confirm that, so I continued to keep quiet.

"It's because I had the clock on you for the last lap."

This was news to me. I thought all eyes were on Kick all the time.

"Care to venture a guess at your last split?"

According to Katie, my brother ran his final four hundred meters in 1:05:42. I knew I'd run faster than that because I'd been gaining on Kick the whole loop.

"I don't know. One-oh-two. One-oh-three?"

Coach Pal smiled. "Fifty-nine flat."

"Really?"

"Really. And call me crazy, but I think you had even more at the end."

He stopped cold, as if challenging me to respond. It was the closest anyone ever came to suggesting that I'd let my brother win. I wasn't going to come clean to Coach Pal, however. The moment I crossed the finish line I'd promised myself to take the secret to my grave.

"So, here's the reason I took you away from your lunch period, Sean."

He was staring right at me, focused like he was really trying to make me understand that what he was about to say was significant, monumental even.

"If the good Lord came into this room right this very second, I would swear to him that your brother was the finest runner I ever had the privilege to coach, bar none."

It filled me with pride that Kick held that distinction. Yet I could tell by Coach Pal's pregnant pause that what was still to come would please me even more.

"But, I'm prepared to say right now that by the time you leave East Carlisle High School, I'm going to be telling people that Sean Kenney is the finest runner I've ever seen, bar none."

It was the first time anyone had ever suggested I might be better than Kick. My parents never had, and until that moment, I'd never for a second thought such a thing was even possible.

23.

I was the first to arrive at the Dunkin'.

I ordered myself a coffee and one for Rachel. She entered as I was returning to the table. Her private investigator friend stepped through the door a moment after that.

I hadn't expected him to be so large, but he was easily six foot four. For some reason, I also had in my head the image of an older man, but he seemed to be about my age, or at least not much older. He was fit too, which stood to reason given his line of work. Attractive, but not in a pretty way, which might also be an occupational plus. Dark-complexioned with a nose that gave his face character, and a full head of curly black hair. His facial hair was somewhere between scruff and beard, which made him look dangerous, which I once again assumed was a professional asset.

"Dolev Attias," he said, extending his hand.

He spoke with an Israeli accent. Not heavy, which caused me to believe that he'd emigrated a while ago, but his words had a trace of that guttural noise in the back of the throat.

"Good to meet you," I said.

"Let me get a cup of coffee and then we can get down to business," he said.

In addition to a coffee, Dolev returned to our table with a glazed donut. He took the seat with his back to the door, beside Rachel.

"I filled Dolev in over the phone about what's going on," Rachel said, "but you should go through everything again, in case I missed something."

After taking a bite of his pastry and a slug of coffee, Dolev pulled out a leather-bound notepad. It looked like the kind that cops used to write parking tickets except it was a little smaller, about the size of a large iPhone.

"First off, I wanted to say that I really appreciate you doing this," I said. "I wish I could pay you, but I—"

Rachel interrupted me. "Don't worry about Dolev getting paid. He owes me big time. If you total up all the questionable expenses he puts through my law firm that I reimburse, he should be paying us."

Dolev smiled. "I'm not sure that I should be paying you, but Rachel is right that you shouldn't worry about my fee. Just tell me what's going on."

"Okay," I said, as I watched him take another bite, reducing his donut to a semicircle. "Last week, my brother's body was found in a hotel in Atlantic Highlands, about ten minutes from the ferry he took from Wall Street to commute home from work. A gunshot wound to his head. The police concluded it was a suicide."

"Rachel told me that you think your brother was murdered. Is that right?"

Hearing how stark the allegation sounded, and knowing how little, if any, evidence I had to support it, gave me pause, so I quickly filled in the details, such as they were. "There's a lot that just doesn't add up. For one thing, there were two shots fired. The cops said that maybe one shot was for practice or that he missed the first time. Another suspicious thing is that my brother didn't leave a suicide note."

"And he didn't own a gun," Rachel added. "At least not one that was registered in his name, and his wife claims that she'd never seen a gun in their home."

"Okay," Dolev said, noncommittal-like.

"The biggest reason I don't believe it was a suicide is because I spoke with him right before he died," I said. "We'd been estranged for a couple of years, but he reached out to me on the day he died. Probably less than an hour before. He said that he needed my help with something. It was a problem that was of his own making, he said, and that he was going to own up to it, but when he did, he thought it might get worse."

Either Dolev had a world-class poker face or nothing we'd shared was reason for him to doubt the police's conclusion that my brother had taken his own life. "That all he said?" Dolev asked. "Just that he had a problem and wanted help if it got worse?"

I pulled out the crumpled piece of paper on which I'd jotted down my recollection of the call. "I wrote this two days after he died, but it's my best recollection of what my brother said."

Dolev took a moment to scan the words. "Can I keep this?"

"Yeah. I know it by heart."

"Okay. Thanks. This is very helpful."

"Also, Michael made a lot of money," Rachel said. "He was a banker type and most recently worked at Buchanan Partners. At his wake, one of Michael's coworkers told Sean that Michael's clients were these Russian-crypto-money launderers and there was a criminal investigation into Michael's trading. So we thought, you know, maybe a Russian mob thing."

Rachel had overstated it, so I felt the need to dial it back a bit. "I met with the FBI a few days ago. They told me that the thing my brother was being investigated for—it's actually called front-running—do you what that is?"

"Yeah. I know what front-running is," Dolev said.

"Okay, then you know that it's not criminal, but some type of securities thing. But it could have resulted in his being barred from the securities industry and fined a ton of money, so it was definitely serious. The guy from the SEC said that my brother's clients didn't know he was even doing it, though, which means that the Russians, or any of Kick's clients, aren't suspects. He also said that my brother was doing this front-running thing with a woman named Arielle. She used to work with him at his prior firm. She's . . . you know, twenty-seven or so, beautiful, looks like a younger version of my brother's wife. Red hair, green eyes."

"Her name is Arielle, and she has red hair," Rachel interrupted with a chuckle. "How'd you not mention that until now?"

"I know, right."

Dolev seemed not to be following. I filled in his apparent knowledge gap regarding Disney princesses.

"There's this cartoon mermaid. It's a Disney movie. She's young and has red hair."

"I know about the Little Mermaid," Dolev said without a smile.

"Yeah, right," I said. "So, I asked Arielle about the investigation and she lied right to my face. Claimed she knew nothing about it. And the more I think about my last call with my brother, the more it makes sense that, you know, he was having an affair. Maybe that's the thing that he needed to own up to."

"Okay. Last name on your mermaid?" Dolev asked.

"Taylor. She works at Richmond Partners. My brother used to work there, before he left to go to Buchanan."

"I'll do a little digging on this. But to state the obvious, if she's a mistress, that puts the wife in play too. Always works that way."

I nodded, conveying that I understood that this might come closer to home in the form of Jenny being Kick's murderer. It seemed that from whatever angle I looked at it, my suspicion always landed hardest on her.

"Anything else I need to know?" Dolev asked.

There was one thing. I wasn't sure I wanted to go there, however.

And then, after taking a beat, I did.

"My brother-in-law is named Ben Whitting. He owns Liquor-18. There are a bunch of stores."

Dolev nodded. "Yeah, I know them."

"Anyway, it seems like, until recently, he was in some financial difficulty. I found an IRS levy notice for close to four hundred grand. A coworker told me the place was heading for bankruptcy. But now, Ben's flush again. He's hired everybody back, shelves are filled, and he's opening a restaurant that's got to be costing him, I don't know how much, but I figure at least a hundred grand. My sister claims that he took out a mortgage, but I . . . I just don't know. I think that maybe my brother gave him the money. I also have this strange feeling about Ben and Jenny, my brother's wife. Just . . . I don't know, like there's something going on between them."

Rachel looked at me wide-eyed. "You think Ben could have killed Michael?"

"No," I said quickly. "I'm not saying that. But I guess I'm not, not saying it, either."

———

That night, as I was helping Katie clear the dinner table, handing her the dishes that she then rinsed off and put in the dishwasher, I told her that I'd hired a private detective. She looked at me with the same wide-eyed amazement as if I'd said I could fly.

"I'm not paying the guy anything," I was quick to add, although I'd already surmised that the cost of Dolev's services was not the chief basis for Katie's opposition to his engagement. "He does work for Rachel's law firm and he owes her, so she decided to cash in that chip."

Katie cast the same expression as she did when she first laid eyes on me in New Orleans. Like then, all I saw was her disapproval.

"So, you don't believe the police when they say that Michael committed suicide. Or me, when I tell you the same thing. But the second Rachel Fischer says that Kick was murdered, you go out and hire a private investigator. Do I have that right?"

"No. You don't. This is my doing, not Rachel's. She just offered to help."

"Look, I understand why you're so enamored with her. I mean, I have eyes. I also know that, if I'm being all Freudian about it, there's the whole you and Kick competition thing that seems to be the motivating factor in so much of what you do. But I don't think she's good for you, Sean. And I wouldn't much care about whether you get your heart broken again—I mean, you're a grown-up and you can make stupid-ass decisions about your love life if you want—except that I'm terrified that when it's over, you're going to run away again."

I wanted to disabuse Katie that there was any risk of that, but I couldn't. I had no idea what would happen if Rachel once again dumped me. All I did know was that I'd fallen hard for her. Again.

24.

The last time I'd worn Kick's suit, I was unemployed, alone, and wondering who had murdered my brother. When I donned it again on Easter Sunday, two of those three things had changed. But I was still no closer to finding my brother's killer.

Jenny. Ben. Arielle.

―――

Father Cavanaugh had led Easter services throughout my childhood, but he'd since gone to his reward. The head priest was now Father Cleary. He'd only been at St. Bart's a year or so. Katie said she liked him, although it took some getting used to calling someone her own age *Father*.

"On the Sunday before his death, Palm Sunday," Father Cleary told the parishioners, "Jesus entered Jerusalem on the back of a donkey welcomed by massive crowds waving palm branches and shouting, 'Hosanna to the Son of David! Blessed is he who comes in the name of the Lord! Hosanna in the highest!' Within a matter of days, however, he was betrayed by Judas Iscariot. He was arrested and then betrayed again, this time by Peter's denials. He stood trial, was convicted, and sentenced to death."

Father Cleary paused for emphasis.

"But Jesus's story—our collective story—which only hours previously had seemed to have ended in unimaginable suffering had, in fact, only just begun. Three days after he was put to death, Jesus rose triumphantly to assume his place beside the Holy Father in the Kingdom of Heaven."

I'd never believed in a higher power. My time on the track had drilled home that I was the only one responsible for whether I won or lost. If I couldn't blame the man upstairs when things went bad, I saw no reason to thank him when things turned out well.

As little as a week ago, hearing about Jesus's travails would usually have caused me to roll my eyes. Three days from agony to ecstasy. Give me a break. I'd been traveling that road for the better part of a decade without feeling as if I was getting anywhere.

But on this day, wearing Kick's suit, I felt my brother with me, telling me that I was close. That if I persevered, all my questions would be answered. And it felt a lot like faith.

It had been two years since I'd last been at a family Easter dinner. I suspected today's had the same guest list as those during my absence—Jenny and her kids, Katie, Ben and theirs, and Dad. The only difference was I was here but my brother was not.

Jenny still looked the part of a grieving widow, teetering on the verge of tears. I studied her as I might a painting's brushstrokes, looking for some flaw to reveal the forgery. There was no subterfuge about her children's grief, however. They sat on either side of their mother with a hollow look in their eyes, as if they were not actually at that table, but had only sent a pale imitation to fool the rest of us.

Ben led us all in grace, mentioning that this Easter we knew a tiny bit of God's pain when he lost his only son. Like my thoughts about Jenny, I wondered how much of my brother-in-law's demeanor was performative.

For the most part, Ben seemed unaffected by Kick's death. Instead, alone among all of us in the family, he'd seemed absolutely giddy in the last few weeks about the opening of his new restaurant, which he referred to as the crown jewel of the Liquor-18 empire.

A jewel that I suspected had been bought and paid for by my brother, no matter what Katie had said to the contrary. That made my brother-in-law's motive as strong as Jenny's. Maybe more so.

There was no denying that Liquor-18 meant everything to Ben. His identity, his financial support, his family's legacy. If that was threatened, I had very little doubt that Ben would take extreme measures to protect it. If he was having an affair with Jenny too, killing Kick was the ultimate win-win.

The conversation flowed in the usual way it did during our family functions. Compliments to Katie on the meal, questions to the children about their current interests and aspirations, some discussion of current affairs, the listing of movies we'd seen or TV shows that we'd binged. Katie liked to ask what people were reading, but hardly anyone in our family did other than her.

"I've been talking with this chef who works down at the Shore who might be interested in coming aboard the New Carlisle place," Ben said at one point. "He invited us to visit his restaurant and check out the menu. So, I was thinking, maybe we could all take a family trip on Saturday night."

Katie smiled politely, but her views regarding Ben's business expansion clearly hadn't changed. It wasn't apparent to me whether Ben was oblivious to Katie's opposition or he just didn't care, but it was beyond question that, whichever it was, he was moving full steam ahead with the project.

Turning to Jenny, Ben said, "Why don't you and the kids meet us there? It's not too far from your house."

He said it hopefully, almost like he was asking her out on a date. Jenny's smile revealed that, unlike Katie, she was supportive not only of the Saturday night outing, but the opening of the restaurant too.

"That sounds like fun," she said.

"And of course you too, Mr. General Manager," Ben said to me. "In fact, bring Rachel."

"Rachel?" Jenny asked in my direction.

I felt a wave of guilt, as if I owed an allegiance to Jenny, or maybe to Kick, not to be involved with Rachel. I quickly cast the feeling aside, given that Jenny might well have committed a far worse transgression.

"I've been seeing Rachel Fischer," I said.

"Again? Since when?"

It sounded accusatory. As if no response would be satisfactory.

"Since the funeral. So not very long."

Jenny offered me a full-on smile, suggesting she recognized her initial reaction had been off, and she was actually fine with me resuming a relationship with her dead husband's former girlfriend. It brought home that my sister-in-law had perfected the ability to display false emotions. There was no way Jenny could have been pleased at the prospect of Rachel returning anywhere near her orbit.

"You should definitely bring Rachel next weekend and we can all spend some time together," she said.

At first I thought Jenny was shining me on, but then another possibility entered my mind. Perhaps Jenny had softened about Rachel because she had long ceased believing Kick's high school girlfriend posed any risk to her marriage, and my sister-in-law's ire was now fully directed toward Arielle, who did. Or maybe, she didn't care anymore about ex-girlfriends or current mistresses now that Kick was dead.

After the dinner plates had been cleared, the men—Ben, my father, and I—adjourned to the living room. Katie and Jenny did the dishes, and the kids vanished to the basement to begin a movie marathon.

The plan was to serve dessert after Jenny's sister and her family arrived. They were having their Easter dinner in the town over and Katie had been kind enough to invite them to stop by.

Dad was in his recliner, where he spent most of his time when he wasn't in bed. In both, he mainly slept. Katie and I had discussed how much longer the current situation could be maintained before our father required professional care, with the decision being that we would take it day-to-day. He was still awake, or at least his eyes were open. Sometimes my father seemed to be in a trance and so it was never clear whether he was actually lucid.

"You doing okay, Dad?" I said.

"Yeah," he said. Then he said it again. "Yeah."

"Did you enjoy dinner?"

"Yeah," he said for the third time. Then he asked, "Do you know where you mother and Michael Junior are?"

"They're together, Dad," I told him.

"Good. I was worried that maybe they couldn't find us."

"They always know where we are," I said.

He smiled, placated, if not fully comprehending what I meant. A moment later, Jenny came out of the kitchen and headed up the stairs, which prompted Ben to jump to his feet.

"I'll be back in a second," he said.

Right after Ben left my sight, I heard the sound of a door closing. He returned a few minutes later, looking somewhat uneasy, while Jenny hurriedly made her way back to the kitchen.

I was about to ask Ben if something was wrong, but before I could get the words out, he said, "There's something I've been meaning to talk to you about, Sean." He looked at my father, who was oblivious to us. That apparently wasn't enough privacy for whatever Ben wanted to talk to me about because he said, "Do you mind if we go upstairs for a second?"

It again felt like I was being called to the principal's office. I reminded myself that the last time Ben wanted a private audience, he'd offered me a job.

Ben's demeanor this time—his jaw was rigid, his brow furrowed—sent the opposite message, however. I was getting the clear signal that his tête-à-tête was not going to end in smiles.

I followed him upstairs and into my father's former green room. Ben closed the door tightly behind him, but remained standing. He apparently didn't expect this meeting to last very long.

"Okay, you have my attention. What's going on?" I asked.

"So, look, Katie said you heard some things from Carlos about the stores from before you started."

I felt the need to defend my coworker. "Carlos wasn't—"

"That's not what this is about," Ben interrupted. "Carlos isn't going to get in any trouble. The opposite, actually. I'm glad he said something because I should have told you way before this."

I wondered if it was possible Ben was building up to a

confession. Perhaps he believed I'd keep his secret, just as my sister had. Like her, I was dependent on Ben for food and shelter, not to mention the big new job he'd just given me, so it might have made sense to him that I'd be reluctant to give all that up in the name of obtaining justice for my dead brother.

For a flicker it made me think about what Meghan said about forgiveness. Could such absolution ever apply to murder?

After his preamble, Ben came to a stop, as if he was unable to get the rest of the words out. When his silence became awkward, I nudged him along.

"Okay, so what did you want to talk to me about?"

"Your sister and I, we're not rich. I inherited the Route 18 store, as you know, and like I told you the other day, it was really important to me to build the business into something bigger than my father's version of it. But what I didn't tell you, what I'm kind of ashamed about, actually, is that the new stores are all losing money. Not a lot, but still. Rumson, though, that was a huge mistake. I thought, rich people, top-shelf booze, right? But the rent there is astronomical and the competition is pretty entrenched. That one store was threatening to bring down all the others. And I owed a shitload of taxes, and that's serious business. I didn't see any way out of the hole I'd dug for myself, so I went with my tail between my legs to ask your brother for help. I didn't even tell Katie I was doing it. I told her that I got a bank loan. But in reality, I just called Michael up and asked for $500,000. Just like that. *Michael, can you give me half a million bucks? Thank you.* And of course he did. Didn't even ask me why I needed the money."

Kick had offered me money in the past too. But when he had, he'd always made clear it was a loan, not a handout. I had little doubt that the money he'd sent Ben's way also came with repayment terms. A condition that Ben would not have to fulfill now that Kick was dead.

"I used that money to pay Uncle Sam, and then I replenished the inventory and started hiring to bring the stores back to full strength. And then this New Carlisle opportunity came along. I know Katie thinks it's too soon. That we should take a breath before taking on more expenses. But I think that in business you're either expanding or contracting. But that's off topic, I guess. What I mean to say is that when you asked 'Why you?' about the general manager job, I should have told you the truth then."

I wasn't following him. It seemed clear he wasn't confessing to murder. Beyond that, though, I didn't understand how what he'd said connected back to me.

"What truth?" I asked.

"That a big part of the reason I offered you the job is because I owe your brother. I was kind of hoping that I could repay some of my debt to him by helping you."

Neither of us said anything after that for a good thirty seconds. I suspected Ben's silence was because he'd said his piece. Mine was because I was still considering if it was possible for him to have murdered my brother.

"I'm going to ask you one question. If I think you're lying to me, I swear to God, Ben."

"Anything."

"Did your money problems have anything to do with Kick's death?"

He seemed shocked by the allegation, which struck me as odd. What other question could he have possibly expected me to ask?

"No. Sean, I swear. Absolutely not."

Ben looked sincere, but of course he did. His life depended on it.

"You never thought it was a little too coincidental that Kick gave you half a million dollars and then he died?"

"Jesus Christ, no. No, Sean. Not for a fucking second."

I didn't know whether to believe him. He must have realized that because he started to explain.

"Michael gave me the money a month before he died. It never even occurred to me that one thing had anything to do with the other. I mean, how could it?"

"I think you know how it could," I said, staring at him like he was a bug.

Ben's eyes twitched. He finally realized I suspected him of murdering my brother.

"Okay, okay," he said.

For the second time I thought he might confess. And for the second time he didn't.

"It's not that I never thought about the fact that he died after he gave me the money," Ben said. "But I thought the reason Michael was so generous was because . . . well, because he'd already been thinking that he wasn't going to need the money."

There was some sense to that. The way people with terminal illnesses start giving away their possessions. Maybe Kick knew that the end was near for him, and he wanted to make sure Ben and Katie were taken care of when he was no longer around.

On the other hand, maybe Ben decided that he'd never be able to true-up with Kick. Rather than try, he eliminated his debt by killing his benefactor.

"But now that Kick's dead, you're not going to repay it, right?"

Ben was vehemently shaking his head, as if I couldn't have been more wrong. "Jenny knows all about the loan. I told her all about it at the wake. She told me that she didn't want me to repay it. That it was what Michael would have wanted too. But I told her no. It would feel like blood money that way. I wanted to repay her. In fact, I just handed her the first check two minutes ago."

25.

Jenny jumped up from her chair in the living room. "That must be them," she said.

I hadn't heard anything to signal the arrival of visitors. But right after she'd said it, car doors began to slam in the driveway. A minute later, three people entered the room.

"Everyone, this is my sister, Jane, and her husband, Gregg," Jenny said. Then she added, "And their daughter, Arielle."

I wasn't listening to a word of it. Instead, my eyes were glued to the person whom I'd previously thought was a younger model of Jenny. How had I been so stupid to have concluded that Kick had a type rather than see the family resemblance?

Jenny pointed at Ben. "Jane, you remember Ben, Katie's husband, right?"

"Of course," Jane said. "Thank you for letting us crash your Easter."

"And Sean, Michael's brother," Jenny said, now in my direction.

"The runner, right?" Jane said.

"Once upon a time, yes," I replied.

"All the kids are downstairs, doing God knows what," Jenny said, "and I was helping Katie with some cleanup. Gregg, why don't you join the men. And Arielle, you and your mom can follow me into the kitchen."

Arielle did as requested without looking back at me.

As everyone indulged in dessert, I half-listened to Jenny's sister talk about their earlier morning church experience, while devoting most of my focus on Arielle. She seemed to be assiduously avoiding eye contact with me, however. I could hardly blame her. We both knew that she had some serious explaining to do.

When the dessert plates started to be cleared, after Jenny and her sister had made it into the kitchen, in a stern whisper, I said, "I need to talk to you."

If she was surprised by my request, Arielle didn't show it. "Outside, okay?"

Arielle was waiting for me on the porch. She showed no outward sign that she knew why I'd asked for this private audience.

"Why didn't you tell me that you were Jenny's niece?"

She seemed confused by the accusation. "I don't go around advertising I'm a nepo baby. But I certainly wasn't trying to hide it from you, if that's what you're implying."

It was a weak excuse. "Are you going to tell me that you also weren't trying to hide that you and my brother were engaged in securities fraud when you looked me straight in the eye and lied that you knew nothing about the investigation?"

That smacked the smile off her face. Still, she didn't break character.

"I don't know what you're talking about."

"Wrong answer, Arielle. Since we last spoke, I've had a

discussion with some folks from the FBI. So, no more lies. You either tell me the truth or I tell the FBI . . . well, I guess I can tell them whatever I want and claim that's what you said to me."

My threat created a momentary standoff. Arielle was undoubtedly considering whether I was bluffing.

She must have concluded I wasn't because she finally said, "You don't understand."

"Then explain it to me."

She looked at me with desperate eyes. I stared back at her without forgiveness in mine.

"Okay. Okay." She drew a deep breath. "So the fund I run at Richmond, it's not in the traditional model. Our investors are charitable organizations and we only invest in entities that benefit humanity. Climate cleanup companies, for example, and one of our big holdings in the portfolio is this agricultural firm that devotes 50 percent of its yield to the hungry, that kind of thing."

"Right. You're a regular Mother Teresa, except you work for an investment bank. I get it."

She didn't react to my sarcasm. Instead she said, "The whole idea for my fund came from Michael. It would have never happened without his pushing it to management. And then, right after the fund was up and running, he left Richmond to join Buchanan. I wanted to go too—I mean, Michael took our whole team over to Buchanan. But Buchanan wouldn't allow me to operate the fund there. They're a profits-at-all-costs kind of place, and the purpose of my fund wasn't to outperform the S&P, but to provide a vehicle for charities to do well by doing good. Michael said he wanted me to stay at Richmond and keep operating the fund. He said that it was important work. That he believed in the fund's mission. So I stayed. But then the market turned. In good times, people are willing to pay a little more to feel good about themselves, but when things get tight, the hell with the planet or the hungry."

I had no interest in her proselytizing. "I assume that this story is going to connect to you and my brother engaging in criminal conduct at some point, right?"

"Did you even know your brother?"

I'm sure Arielle meant it rhetorically, but I considered the query at face value. Did I know Kick? I had once. I'd swear to that on a stack of Bibles. But did I know who he was at the end of his life?

"I'm sorry for lying to you," Arielle said. "But the last thing I was going to do is admit to someone I just met that I'm guilty of securities fraud. For all I knew, the SEC had you wearing a wire. I shouldn't be telling you now either, if you want to know the truth. But I won't be able to live with myself if I let you think the worst of your brother. What I told you when we first met I stand by 100 percent. Michael was a very good man. He wasn't like a typical investment banker where all he cared about was how expensive his car was or flying on a private jet. It was important to him that his life be more than the size of his bank account. What he always said was that he wanted to use his knowledge of the dark arts to bring people into the light. He found a way to do that with my fund. That's why he was so committed to its success."

"So committed that he was willing to lose everything for it?"

She flinched at the suggestion that their little scheme led to my brother's death. I assume she thought that I was implying that it was the cause of his suicide. But I meant it in a far more sinister way. It was the reason he'd been murdered.

"What we did was a pretty victimless crime," she said. "None of the clients lost any money and charities made money."

"The FBI obviously disagrees," I said.

"Look, I'm not saying it isn't serious. I've been freaked out of my mind since I first got wind of the fact that the SEC was involved. But for the life of me, I just don't understand why Michael didn't let it play out. After we learned about the investigation, we decided it was best not to have any contact unless there was some real emergency. So I hadn't spoken to him in . . . I don't know, a month, probably longer, before he died. But my lawyers have told me from day one that it was going to be all right in the end. I'm sure his lawyers told him the same thing."

"I don't understand. How could it turn out all right if you were guilty?"

"Nine times out of ten the way these investigations end is with the banks paying some fine and, worse case, maybe Michael and I would get a letter of censure or a short suspension, which we'd spend on a beach somewhere. A slap on the wrist kind of thing. Buchanan wasn't going to let Michael take a fall because he made a crapload of money for those guys. No way they were going to let somebody—even the SEC—kill their golden goose."

I tried to piece together what Arielle had just said. She was claiming that the SEC investigation wasn't dire enough for Kick to believe suicide was the only way out. She must not have realized that this newest bit of information convinced me that what I'd believed from day one was true.

My brother had been murdered.

———

Rachel and I had discussed a late-night rendezvous, but I'd texted earlier that I was too tired. When everyone had left Katie's, and I was alone downstairs, I Facetimed her.

Rachel was in bed, sans make-up, looking beautiful, as always. I wished I was with her.

"Hey, sorry again about canceling tonight," I said.

"It's fine. Family, am I right?"

I chuckled. "You have no idea."

"So give me some idea."

"I'm not sure where to even start. It's like an Agatha Christie novel, with all the suspects arranged, except I'm no Hercule Poirot, because I'm even more at sea now than I was before."

"Maybe this is more of a Sherlock Holmes, Dr. Watson type situation."

"Who am I in that scenario?"

"I believe that's elementary, my dear Sean. But seriously, what happened?"

"I guess the first thing is that Ben told me he borrowed five hundred grand from Kick. That's how he was able to stave off bankruptcy and have the seed money for the restaurant."

"Really?"

"Yeah, but he claims that he told Jenny all about it. So, I don't see how he benefits from Kick's death. If anything, he's in worse shape now because he's lost Kick as a safety net. Besides, I can't figure out how Ben would end up in a hotel room with Kick. I mean, what could Ben have said to get Kick to meet him in a fancy hotel room?"

"Maybe he said he had a fight with Katie and was staying there," my Watson offered.

"I thought of that too. But in that case, there's no way that Kick doesn't call Katie first."

"Okay. Maybe nobody invited Michael. Maybe something was going on between Jenny and Ben, and he went there to confront them."

"That doesn't track either," I said. "For one thing, I think Kick was in the hotel room when he called me. I didn't hear any outside noise to indicate otherwise. So that means he got there first. Besides, he told me that he was the one who'd screwed up. He wouldn't have said that if he thought Jenny was cheating on him. No, I think when I saw Jenny and Ben together, they were talking about the loan."

Dead air hung between us before Rachel said, "Your elementary logic has convinced me, Sherlock. But you said the Ben loan was the first thing. What's the other one?"

"Get this. Arielle . . . she's Kick's niece."

"What?"

"Yep. Kick doesn't have a type—or maybe he does—but Arielle looks like Jenny because she's Jenny's sister's daughter. That's how she got the job at Richmond in the first place. According to her, Kick was trying to help her with this do-gooder fund she runs that was his idea. She claimed the whole securities fraud thing was a Robin Hood type situation. Taking from the rich, giving to the poor."

"That sounds like Michael, right? He was always trying to help people."

"There's something she said, though. Arielle was adamant that no one was going to lose their job over the front-running. She said that the investigation would end with the banks paying a fine and everyone going on their merry way. That means Kick's career was safe. Or at least it wasn't in any imminent risk. Which means there's no way he killed himself."

Rachel hardly looked convinced by my logical deductions on this score, however. "Arielle is a liar, Sean. She lied to you about not knowing anything about the investigation. She's very likely lying about this too."

It was true that I didn't trust a word out of Arielle's mouth. But the evidence supported her version of events.

"She's still working at Richmond," I said. "And she wasn't half the moneymaker as Kick. If her firm is standing by her, Buchanan would have supported him. At the very least, the jury is still out. It doesn't make sense that Kick assumed the worst and made an irreversible decision. He just wasn't that way."

Rachel looked stymied. "Then what do you think happened?"

"I think Kick was having an affair with Arielle. And either she murdered him or Jenny did."

"There's absolutely no evidence to support that, Sean."

"That only means that I haven't found it yet."

"Yet? You're still going to try to prove that your brother was fucking his niece? Why?"

"Look, I'm not saying anyone should go pin a medal on Kick for cheating on his wife. Especially with his niece. But you always hear about people sleeping with their wives' sisters, right? This really isn't any different than that."

"Maybe not different, but disgusting all the same. Why would you want to prove that Michael was that kind of a person? I just . . . it doesn't make any sense. I'm sorry. I've tried to be supportive of you on all of this, but I think you're grasping at straws now. Your entire theory is based on the idea that Kick was having sex with his niece. Which may not be true. Probably isn't. There's certainly no evidence of it, at least. And based on that, you go to the next step and assume that either Jenny or Arielle killed him. But that's just too many unsupported assumptions on top of one another."

She was right that I had no proof of any of it. But that didn't mean I was wrong. It just meant I had more work to do. And as for which was worse, whether Kick killed himself or was murdered because of his affair with Arielle, I voted for the truth. The truth was better than a lie. Always.

"I understand if you want to . . . I don't know, let me go deal with this on my own," I said. "It's a lot to ask you to support me while I engage in what I know everyone thinks is some type of crazy obsession I have with proving the unprovable. But I can't give up. I won't. Not until I know the truth."

26.

As he had four years prior, Parker Swanson did the television play-by-play for the 2012 Olympic track and field trials.

"I first predicted today's winner in the men's 1500 meters four years ago," he said, "and there is nothing I've seen since to change my mind that Sean Kenney is the man to beat. He ran a very respectable fourth as a twenty-two-year-old, but now he's ready to capture the prize. Kenney's posted one of the fastest times in history at 3:28:09, and there's no one in the field with his combination of experience, speed, and heart. I'm going to go one step further and predict that we'll be hearing much more from this young man at the Olympic Games. I'm not going to say that gold is a lock, but I think Kenney has the best chance of any US runner in a generation to medal at this distance."

My chief competitor was Washington again. He was now the oldest runner in the field by a good two years and would need a slow pace to have any real chance. The other name mentioned in the same breath as mine was the youngest invitee, George Garcia, the reigning NCAA champion. The field also included Lee Williams, the world record holder in the 800 meters.

Williams was by far the fastest man on the track in a sprint, but the safe money was that he didn't have the stamina to go all-out for 1500 meters.

When the starting gun fired, I shot into the lead. My plan was to set a fast pace and therefore take Washington and Williams out of the equation.

Garcia stayed right with me, apparently following the same strategy. I assumed that the rest of the field was keeping pace, but wasn't entirely sure.

I held the lead through the first circuit, but Garcia took it back midway through the second. The barely audible rumbling behind me told me that Garcia and I were about ten meters ahead of the trailing pack.

Whenever Garcia amped it up another notch, I did too so as not to allow too much distance to open up between us. Entering the third lap, I finally allowed him to create some daylight, in order to conserve energy and ensure I had enough left in reserve to finish strong.

I didn't need to win. I only needed to make the team.

When the bell signifying the final lap sounded, I still thought I could catch Garcia but that was not my primary concern. Rather, I was focused on the lack of footsteps behind me, which meant that I was comfortably in second place.

In the back straightaway, the crowd started to roar, the usual din when the runners were accelerating into their finishing kicks. I imagined Meghan and Phoebe among the cheering throngs, and began to visualize a joyous family reunion after I crossed the finish line.

I caught Garcia just as we were exiting the final turn and took the lead, with less than two hundred meters to go. Unlike four year earlier, the wind was not a factor. There was nothing and no one who could stop me.

Legs fast; mind faster; heart unstoppable.

Just as I allowed that thought to take hold, Garcia went past me and into the lead. I reached for my reserve to run by him again, only to see Lee Williams slingshot past both of us at a sprinter's pace.

Even at my best, I couldn't run as fast as him for a hundred meters. To my shock, though, Garcia could, and the two of them ran neck and neck, distancing themselves from me with every step.

It was then that something happened that had never before occurred in a race. I started to panic. I needed to finish third and that was now the best I could do given that I was eating Garcia's and Williams's dust.

What happened next, I haven't a clue. Like the way people block out the aftermath of a car crash. I remember nothing from the moment after Williams blew by me until two hours after the race ended.

But from my countless viewings of the race on YouTube, I've relived the horror again and again. In the next ten seconds, not even, everything I'd worked for in my life ended when Washington passed me to go into third place.

Meghan later told me that she'd waited for two hours at the stadium, calling and texting nonstop. But I never went back to the locker room to retrieve my phone. Or even to change out of my race clothes.

Instead, I started walking aimlessly. After about ten minutes, I stopped and sat down on a stoop.

I hadn't cried in years. Funny how that is, that there is this period in your life when crying is not that out of the ordinary, and then all of a sudden you've cried for the last time. From then on, you might tear up at a funeral or a particularly sad movie, but you'll never have the same type of waterworks that you did as a child.

Unless you fail in the one thing that you'd dedicated your entire life to achieve, that is. There, with the sweat of my failure on my body, on a desolate street corner, under a flickering streetlight, I began to sob.

———

Meghan jumped up the moment I entered our apartment and threw her arms around me. She held me so tightly I thought she might never let go.

"I was worried out of my mind, Sean. You weren't answering your phone."

"I'm sorry. I . . . I don't have my phone, actually. I never went back to the locker room. I just needed some time to think."

"I'm just so glad that you're here now." She smiled at me, but it looked crooked, like it was sliding off her face. "And so is Phoebe," she added. Meghan's hands dropped to her belly. "And so is baby girl number two."

Even my wife's reference to our growing family wasn't enough to alter my desperation. Our lives had dramatically changed for the worse in the last few hours.

"What are we going to do now?" I said. "I've never had a plan other than going to the Olympics."

"That can still be our plan. In four years we can take *both* our children. Think about how great that's going to be."

I knew it wasn't going to turn out that way. We'd never go anywhere because of my running again.

After that, I stopped running. Cold turkey. Not for the

bus if I thought it was going to pull away or when crossing the street after the light turned against me. Not even to play tag or hide-and-go-seek with my daughters.

Any movement faster than walking reminded me that I was a failure. I knew, of course, that my anger was misplaced. My rage should have been directed against the runner, not the act of running. Then again, I hated him too.

27.

I got to the Dunkin' right as Rachel did, greeting her in the parking lot.

Dolev had called the night before, saying that there was a new development. I asked him to tell me about it over the phone, but he claimed that visual aids were involved, requiring an in-person meeting.

"I'll get the coffee. You get a table," I said to Rachel.

Rachel and I hadn't seen each other for three days. We'd spoken, of course, and when we did, Rachel didn't betray that anything was wrong. But I got the sense that she'd been rattled by our Easter night conversation. It had probably only then dawned on her just how hellbent I'd become with proving that my brother had been murdered.

I ordered Rachel a large coffee with milk and sugar and one for myself without cream. For our guest of honor, I purchased what he'd ordered the last time—a glazed donut and black coffee. Dolev arrived while I was in line.

"Thank you," he said before taking a bite of the donut and then washing it down with the coffee.

Neither Rachel nor I said anything as he indulged. I suspect that, like me, she was waiting for him to explain the reason we'd been summoned.

"Okay, I don't want to drag this out. I found out some stuff, but I think you'll find it's a mixed bag."

He took a second bite and a second gulp of coffee. For a guy who didn't want to drag things out, Dolev was doing a piss-poor job of getting to the point.

Finally, he said, "I was able to see the official police report. Got some buddies at the Rumson PD. Everything they told you checks out. The forensics are what you'd expect to see in a suicide. Gunpowder residue on the victim's hands. Only his prints on the gun. The ballistics prove that the bullet was fired at close range. I also watched the hotel's security tapes. They only have coverage in the lobby, so nothing in the hallways where the rooms are, and of course not in the rooms themselves. But there's no one there that shouldn't be in the lobby, at least as far as I could tell. The police, obviously, came to the same conclusion. So, like I said, it all adds up to make a pretty compelling case that this was a suicide."

"What about the second shot?" I asked.

Dolev took another donut bite. Then another. Then he sucked down some more coffee.

"Like the cops told you, sometimes it happens that way. They can't summon the nerve and shoot in frustration, only to regroup and get it right with the next shot. It doesn't mean that there was someone else pulling the trigger. And given that your brother's hand had gunshot residue on it, he definitely fired at least one of the shots."

"So that's it, then? You dragged me down here to tell me the cops had it right all along?"

"No," he said with a tilt of his head to suggest he didn't

appreciate my tone. "You were right on the money about the affair. Your brother was stepping out."

Dolev reached into his pocket and retrieved a manila folder. Reaching inside, he extricated three pages and carefully laid them upon the table.

They had the familiar pattern of a text conversation. My quick scan revealed that the exchanges were between lovers. Sex talk, words of longing, about being in love, and in lust.

There were no names identifying the participants, however. Before I could point out this hole in the case, Dolev filled it.

"I got these off your brother's phone. Don't ask me how." Dolev reached back into the envelope. "And this little beauty came from your mermaid's phone."

He slapped a photograph onto the table. In it, my brother was shirtless, in bed. The angle suggesting he had nothing on below the waist.

The reveal made me feel faint. Even though I'd told Rachel I believed that Kick was sleeping with his niece, a part of me couldn't fathom that Kick could ever have done such a thing. Of everyone I'd ever known, my brother always stood on the side of right. And yet, the proof Dolev was sharing unequivocally told a different story.

I was about to mention the family relationship, but caught myself. No reason for Dolev to be privy to just how twisted this had all turned out to be.

"There's something else," Dolev said. "Arielle's got an alibi for the time of your brother's death. She was in Boston."

"How do you know that?" Rachel asked.

"A hotel charge I got off her credit card," Dolev said, his mouth chewing. "Her driver's license is on file with the hotel too. So it's airtight."

I felt myself deflate. Arielle was the lesser of two evils, which was why I'd been secretly hoping that she was Kick's murderer. But this was going to be the worst-case scenario.

Even though I knew the answer, I asked the question.

"What about Jenny? Does she have an alibi?"

"No," Dolev said. "At least not as far as I could find."

Dolev said he was sorry it had turned out the way it had. Then he scooped up the text messages and the shirtless photo of my brother and placed them back in the manila folder. Before they returned to his coat pocket, I asked if I could keep them.

He hesitated for a moment. "Only if it's for your eyes only. You show them to the cops, I deny that I ever knew you. Then they're going to arrest you for hacking and invasion of privacy and a dozen other things. We clear on that?"

"Yeah," I said. "I hear you."

"Good."

He handed me the envelope. After we both came to our feet, I shook his hand and thanked him for everything he'd done.

"I'm not going to be any part of that," Katie said. "Absolutely not."

I'd just finished recounting everything Dolev had shared. By the dread that came over her face, it was apparent that Katie found Kick's affair stomach-turning. Still, she parted ways with me when I said it proved Jenny was guilty of murder. Katie was even more adamantly opposed to my plan that we confront her.

"If you could put your obsessive need to prove Michael was murdered aside for just one second," Katie said, "you'd realize that Michael must have thought that the affair was going to come out in the securities investigation. That's why the fact he wasn't going to be fired didn't matter to him. All he cared about was Jenny. Once she found out about the affair, she'd leave him for sure. Not to mention that this has Lifetime movie written all over it: Wall Street bigwig and his niece. Michael just couldn't live with that shame."

I couldn't deny that everything Katie said was true. That didn't mean I agreed with it, however.

When I tried to voice my objection, she talked over me. "Didn't Michael say that he knew the right thing to do was for him to own up to it? And that when he did, he'd make it worse?"

I nodded that she was right. That was what Kick had said.

"Don't you see? He was saying he needed to admit to Jenny that he was sleeping with her niece. Maybe even that he was in love with her. He wanted to make sure that when it all came out, when everybody else thought he was the worst person alive, that you'd still be there for him."

"Then why didn't he?"

"Why didn't he what?"

"Come clean, like you said. Tell Jenny about the affair?"

"Probably because when he got off the phone with you, he realized what coming clean would actually look like and just couldn't face it."

"Then why'd he bring a gun to the hotel?"

This momentarily derailed my sister. Then she said, "I don't know."

"Well, I do. It's because he didn't bring the gun. Jenny did."

We sat for a moment in silence. Katie seemed barely able to even look at me.

"Can you even imagine for just one second the harm you're going to do by, first, telling Jenny that her husband was cheating on her with her sister's daughter, and then accusing her of murder?"

"Jenny's not my concern. Preserving Kick's memory is. It should be yours too."

"You're beyond reason on this, Sean. I just don't know what to say or do anymore."

"You don't have to say or do anything, Katie. I know how to get to Jenny's house on my own."

Katie didn't respond to my threat to accuse our sister-in-law of murdering our brother without her. I suspected she was going through the same list of pros and cons that had ultimately caused her to accompany me to the Rumson PD. Back then, she didn't believe in my objective, but she wanted to make sure I didn't make things worse. When Katie's posture slackened, I could tell that she reached the same conclusion this time.

"I'll go, but only on one condition," she said.

Katie wasn't in a position to dictate terms. On the other hand, I didn't want to confront Jenny alone.

"What?"

"That, for Michael's sake, no matter what Jenny says, we let it end there. I don't care if Jenny admits she killed Michael and says she's coming after us next, I'm not going to be responsible for separating Jenny from her children. Michael would have wanted his kids to grow up with their mother. And shame on you if you think otherwise about our brother. You know what Jack and Molly meant to him and you know that them having a dead father and a mother in prison is the last thing Michael would have wanted."

I didn't answer her right away. But I could see that there was no way for me to get what I wanted without giving her what she wanted.

"Okay," I said.

"Swear to me, Sean," Katie said.

"I swear."

28.

Katie and I arrived at Kick's house early the next morning. It seemed like merely a minute had passed since we'd made this pilgrimage right after I'd returned home, and also a lifetime ago.

Then I was suffering from grief, but now I was consumed by anger. The emptiness of my brother's absence, which I'd filled with the need to prove everyone wrong about why he'd left us, had given way to a deep-seated hatred toward the woman who had authored my suffering.

I was trying mightily to keep that rage in check. For today's mission to succeed, I needed to maintain at least the veneer of open-mindedness.

Jenny met us in the foyer, looking as if she was about to go to brunch with friends, clad in a smart sand-colored sweater set. The only wearing black phase of her life had seemingly come to an end.

"Come in," she said without a smile. "It sounded like you had something important to talk to me about. Before you get to that, can I get you anything?"

"No, we're good," I said. "And we do have something important to talk to you about, so it's best we get right to it, I think."

We all took the same seats as we did the last time we'd met to discuss my brother. Once we were situated, Jenny said, "Okay, so what do you want to talk about?"

On the drive over I'd told Katie I wanted to do the talking. She said she was more than happy to let me take the lead.

"I should have told you this long ago, but on the day Michael died, he called me," I said.

Jenny looked surprised. Almost as if she considered my brother reaching out to me on his birthday to have been outside the realm of possibility.

"It was around—not around, I know precisely the moment he called and for how long we spoke because it's still in my phone log and I look at it all the time. He called me at 4:19 p.m. and we spoke for exactly two minutes and fourteen seconds. He told me that he was in trouble. He said that he knew the right thing for him to do was to admit to what he'd done, but he was worried that it would make things worse. He said that he wanted to be sure that I'd be there for him after he did."

"Okay," Jenny said, apparently not fully understanding the import of what I'd just conveyed.

"Do you have any idea what trouble Michael was in?" Katie asked.

I hadn't expected my sister to say anything until I was finished with my prepared speech. But now that she had, I waited to hear Jenny's response.

"No. I've told you, I had no idea anything was troubling Michael. Sean told me about the investigation into Michael's work, but that was the first I'd heard of that. What did Michael tell you was the problem, Sean?"

Jenny's ignorance looked sincere. Then again, I'd long ago discounted my ability to gauge her truthfulness.

"He didn't tell me, but whatever it was, I don't believe that he was contemplating suicide. The opposite, actually. He was focused on setting things right. On top of which, a bunch of other things never added up for me—the two shots fired, the fact he didn't own a gun. So what I'm saying is that I never believed that he'd killed himself."

"I don't understand," she said, again seemingly like she didn't.

"I think he was murdered."

All of a sudden Jenny looked to be on the verge of tears. "The police said it was a suicide."

"I know that's what they said," I replied coldly. "But I didn't believe it. So I hired a private investigator to see if there was something the police missed."

"You hired a private investigator without telling me. That's insane. Why would you do such a thing?"

Katie said, "Please, Jenny. This is going to be hard enough. You need to hear what Sean has to say. When he's done, we definitely want to hear what you have to say."

Jenny slumped back, her arms crossed. The posture I would have imagined she'd be in if she knew what was coming.

"Okay, just tell me already," she said.

"The private investigator showed me proof that Kick was having an affair."

Reaching into my coat pocket, I retrieved the manila envelope Dolev had provided the other day and arrayed the evidence on the table like a dealer in Vegas laying down the flop. For a moment Jenny's eyes glanced over the text messages, but not nearly long enough to read them in full. She only fleetingly glanced at the photograph of her husband's naked torso, and then returned her gaze to mine.

I saw nothing but anger. The very definition of if looks could kill.

"This is bullshit. There are no names here. The picture... it's been photoshopped."

"It's all real. The private investigator got them off their phones."

"Whose phones?"

"The text messages came from Kick's. The photo from your niece. Arielle."

Jenny's body tensed. She looked like she was fighting a losing battle not to lunge toward me and gouge out my eyes.

"You're out of your mind, Sean. You know that, right?"

"I'm not, Jenny. The proof is all here. He was having an affair with your niece."

Jenny brought her hands to her face, hiding from us. I wondered if, despite her rage a moment earlier, she might still come clean about the affair in an effort to buy some credibility for her ultimate denial of Kick's murder.

"Did Arielle... what did she say?" Jenny asked, now much more quietly.

"There was no need to confront Arielle because as clear as the proof was about the affair, it's equally strong that she was in Boston on the day he died," I replied. "Which means that she couldn't have murdered Kick."

"Don't call him Kick," Jenny said sharply. It was as if the pendulum had swung back to anger. "High school was a million years ago. His name was Michael. And no one killed Michael except Michael."

Before I could reply, Jenny jumped to her feet. "Get the fuck out of my house," she screamed at me. Then looking at Katie, she said, "Both of you. I never want to see either one of you ever again."

Katie said, "Sean, can you go outside for a second and let me talk to Jenny alone?"

Jenny didn't repeat her demand that Katie leave too, which meant she was receptive to further communication with my sister alone. So, I said, "Okay. I'll meet you outside."

After a few minutes, Katie emerged through the front doors.

"Let's get out of here," she said.

"What did Jenny say?"

"I'll tell you. I promise I will. But we need to get out of here first. I feel like I'm going to throw up."

As soon as we pulled out of the driveway, Katie opened the window for some air. I held my peace for a few minutes more, but by the time we were on the highway, I broke my silence.

"I need to know what she said, Katie."

My sister nodded and then took a deep breath. After quickly glancing in my direction to bear witness to my impatience, she said, "Okay, okay. So, I told Jenny that you were determined to go to the police and I swore on the lives of my own children that if she told me the truth, we'd take it to our graves."

"And?"

"And you were right. I'm sorry for doubting you."

"Tell me what she said. Every word."

In a monotone, with her eyes firmly on the road, my sister did just that.

"Jenny said that she found out Michael was cheating, but she didn't know with whom. She told Michael that the hotel room was a birthday present. I asked her about the two shots. She said the first was to scare him because he wouldn't tell her with whom he was having the affair. I didn't ask her how she found out or anything, but she said she'd known for about a month by then. When he told her it was Arielle, and that he was in love with her, she said she just snapped."

I had been expecting some type of relief from the closure, but it didn't come. If anything, I was overtaken by a numbness that I remembered from my heaviest drinking spells. As if I was barely even there and the place I did inhabit was one where nothing mattered.

Kick was still dead. I would never see him again.

Since the first moment I learned of my brother's death, I'd told myself that it was important that his loved ones knew that he didn't willingly leave them. But I'd failed in that objective too. Jack and Molly still believed that lie, and they always would, at least if I kept my promise to Katie. I, on the other hand, had never doubted that Kick had been taken from us, so Jenny's confession meant nothing to me on that score. At the end of the day, the only person whose mind was changed was Katie's.

"Was she . . . did Jenny show any remorse?" I asked.

"She was hysterically crying, so I guess that's a yes."

"What did you say?"

Katie again turned in my direction. She looked as angry as I felt.

"I said that we'd never forgive her for what she'd done and that it didn't matter that she wasn't going to jail." My sister looked back at the road and then quickly turned back to me. "And I told her that we took great comfort in the fact that her soul would burn in hell for all of eternity."

SEVEN MONTHS LATER

29.

Rachel and I were married on the first Tuesday of the first week of October.

We said our "I dos" before a justice of the peace in the township's municipal building. I wore Kick's suit, naturally, and my bride looked radiant in an off-the-shoulder, cream-colored dress that fell to her knees. The entire ceremony took all of twenty minutes. Only my daughters were in attendance.

For so many years I'd been unable to find happiness or purpose off the track because I'd wrongly concluded that living the life I'd been living made me a failure in my previous one. In fact, the two were unrelated. Or maybe, as I'd now come to believe, my difficulties in the first had actually paved the way for me to find success in the second.

The road to that salvation had been more difficult than any race, but my life with Rachel had brought me greater happiness than breaking the tape ever had. I not only believed I would love Rachel until death did we part, but also that I could be happy with who I was, and everything the future had in store.

Rachel's relationship to my brother, which once was a gulf

separating us all, now seemed like a bridge by which we were connected. I was certain Kick would not only have approved of our union, but be thrilled that I'd found love with his former flame.

Rachel and I decided to put off our honeymoon until after the restaurant could operate without the need for my daily presence. So the day after our nuptials, I was back at work.

It had taken some persuading, but I'd convinced Ben not to call the place Liquor-18, or even Restaurant-18, which, believe it or not, had been his second choice. He still insisted on some reference to the branding, so when you open the menu, right at the top, it says *The New Carlisle Kitchen* in big letters and then in a slightly smaller font beneath it—*A member of the Liquor-18 family*.

Everything came together—the remodel of the space, the hiring of the chef and the entire staff, the creation of the menu—at breakneck speed. Among Ben's first instructions after I took on the role of general manager had been not to pay rent on interior that wasn't generating income any longer than absolutely necessary, so I cracked the whip to get us open by Labor Day weekend.

Although it was still early, and more than one person told me that sometimes restaurants show initial promise due to neighborhood curiosity, and then fail to attract regulars, so far we had exceeded our grandest expectations. Our tables were filled for both seatings on weekend nights and above the 50 percent occupancy we'd projected for Sunday to Thursday and the bar area generated significant revenue, which is extremely important to a restaurant's success because the margins on alcohol are much higher than on food.

It was partly because of how successful we'd been that I was surprised Ben was willing to close on a Saturday night to host a wedding reception. But he and Katie insisted. They said they wanted to provide friends and family a happy occasion to congregate, given that the last time we'd seen everyone was at Dad's funeral, which was three months earlier, and then Kick's before that.

My father's death had come more quickly than anyone had imagined. I took some solace in the fact that his existence as a man unaware of his surroundings had finally ended. I also found strength in the fact that I was there for him in the end, doing my best to make up for all the time I wasn't.

In the last months of my father's life, before I left for work, we'd go on walks through the neighborhood. I'd do almost all of the talking, sometimes about races that I'd run and other times about our family. On rare occasions he'd say something back, although it never had anything to do with what I'd said. Still, I hoped that some of what I'd shared had gotten through and that when he took his last breath, my father knew that I loved and respected him, and that I would miss him.

Having the chance to say goodbye drove home how much I still, and always would, regret being denied that opportunity with my brother. But it also showed me that I could learn from my mistakes.

I'd wanted to ban Jenny from my father's funeral, but Katie insisted that it wasn't our place to keep her children from saying goodbye to their grandfather. Witnessing my sister-in-law once again in mourning clothes felt like a slap in the face. I seethed with the knowledge that Jenny was the reason all of my father's children were not there to say goodbye to him.

"Nice for her to attend a Kenney funeral that was not of her own making, I suppose," I said to Katie. Then I asked her the question I thought about every single day since the last time I'd seen my sister-in-law. "Do you have any regrets that Jenny's not going to be punished for what she did?"

"I don't think that's true," Katie said. "I can scarcely imagine any greater pain than living with the knowledge you'd done something terrible to someone you loved. To have taken from your children their father."

The restaurant was dimly lit, but the votives on every table provided a romantic glow. A torch singer, accompanied by a tuxedo-clad pianist, performed standards. The waitstaff circulated with silver trays atop which sat hors d'oeuvres or flutes of champagne.

The guest list was close to a hundred, and from the look of the restaurant, nearly everyone we'd invited was in attendance. I was once again wearing my brother's suit, even though my closet now contained several others of my own. Rachel wore her wedding dress, looking every bit as lovely as she had on the day we were married.

"Thank you both for coming," I said to Meghan and Steve. "It means a lot to me. Really."

"Thank you so much for having us," Meghan said. "Not everyone invites their ex-wife and her husband to their wedding, but we're very glad you did." Then she laughed.

"What's so funny?" I asked.

"You are, Sean. Wearing a suit, with short hair even. I swear to God, you've become an honest to God grown-up."

"It only took me . . . what, fifteen, twenty years longer to get there than most people."

"But you're here now. That's all that matters."

About an hour into the festivities, Coach Pal and George came up to me to say that they were leaving. "Don't ever get old, Sean," Coach Pal said. "You can't stay out past nine o'clock, I'm afraid."

"I'm just so glad you came. Thank you for that."

"Before I go, I'm going to beat my favorite dead horse, I'm afraid. Have you been running at all?"

"A little bit," I said. "Not for speed, though. Just around the neighborhood."

It had been Rachel's idea. She'd gifted me a pair of running shoes for my birthday and made sure I used them by jogging alongside me the first few times. When I competed, I'd always been completely focused on the race, but now running was an opportunity to clear my mind. To think about nothing and everything. Like Coach Pal had said at Kick's funeral, it was good for my soul.

Coach Pal's face lit up. "Good. That's good for you."

He extended his hand, but I brought Coach Pal in for a hug. I had every hope that he had a long life still ahead of him, but I'd come to realize it would be a mistake to take that for granted.

When we separated, I said, "Maybe we can find some time to get together just the two—or four—of us."

He looked sincerely pleased by my overture. "Yes. I would like that very much."

After I shook George's hand goodbye, Coach Pal said, "I've said it before, and I'll be saying it until the day I leave this mortal coil, Sean Kenney was the finest runner I've ever seen, bar none. But, and this is so much more important, he's also a very fine man."

I caught up with my daughters not long after. They looked not only beautiful, but grown-up. Part of that might have been that they each had on lipstick, but I couldn't deny the passage of time played a greater role. Phoebe had already secured her learner's permit. Harper was now a high school student.

Both of them were holding red-colored drinks with maraschino cherries floating on top.

Phoebe intuited my question. "It's just a Shirley Temple," she said.

"Are you having fun?"

"Yes," they said in unison.

Lost time with your children cannot later be found, but I took comfort knowing that at least I wouldn't squander any more. My weekends and weeknights with the girls were now sacrosanct, and I never missed one of their games or plays or anything else they'd let me share.

"I can't tell you how happy I am that you're both here," I said.

"Why not?" Harper said.

It took me a second, but I got the joke. "You're right. I can. And I should." I took a beat. "I am so-so-so happy that you're both here."

"We are too, Dad," Phoebe said. Harper nodded that she agreed.

A disembodied voice rang out in the distance.

"Everyone. Everyone. Can I have your attention?"

All eyes turned to the front of the restaurant. My sister was standing on top of a chair.

"It's time for toasts," Katie said. "For the sake of brevity, we're going to limit them to one per side. So, in the usual tradition of beauty before age, speaking on behalf of our bride is her friend, Alyssa Sanders."

I made my way across the room until I was beside Rachel. We held hands watching Katie step back onto the floor with Ben's assistance, and then Rachel's friend allowed my brother-in-law to guide her back atop the chair.

"Rachel and I met on our very first day of college," she began, "and we've been through a lot together." She went on to recount a litany of Rachel's dating mishaps before the predictable denouement that Rachel had finally found true love with me.

I drank along with the others in toast to Rachel and my future happiness, but only enough to wet my lips. I hadn't become a teetotaler, but in the past few months I'd reduced my intake to the point that I only imbibed in social situations and limited myself to one glass. Tonight, I'd been nursing the same flute of champagne for more than two hours.

When it came time for the best man's speech, my sister explained that I had elected to say a few words on my own behalf. To do so, I eschewed the chair, preferring to stand beside Rachel because what I had to say was for her more than anyone else.

"I know that this may be bad form because tradition holds that the honor falls to the best man," I said. "But the only person who could ever be my best man is my brother, Michael. He couldn't be with us today, but I know he's here in spirit, and so I thought I'd say some words that I believe he would have said if he were able."

I could feel the emotion trickle in my throat, the tears beginning to pool in my eyes. I steadied myself, not wanting to break down.

"But before I do that, though, I'd like to say something directly to my beloved bride."

I paused to inhale and exhale, as if for strength, like I sometimes did before the starting gun fired. Looking into Rachel's face, I said, "I was lost and now I've been found. Out of the very worst thing that has ever happened to me, sprang the best. I know now that life can be that way, and it's a lesson I plan to take to heart for the rest of my days."

Rachel kissed me on the lips. The assembled clapped and a few said *Aww*.

"Before everyone drinks," I said quickly, "allow me to return to my brother for just a moment. If he was giving this toast, I'm confident he would have begun by taking credit for me being with Rachel in the first place because he introduced us a very long time ago. He was even instrumental in our first kiss, although that, I'm afraid, is a story for another time."

The hint of lasciviousness brought the expected juvenile reaction. A few *Ooh*s, and one person shouted out, *Tell us*. But I went on with my speech.

"I'm also certain that my brother would have told all of you that he always believed that I could find happiness, even when I'd lost faith. Now that Rachel and I are married, I don't have the slightest doubt he wouldn't have been able to resist saying, *I told you so*."

Our guests laughed. And I smiled too, imagining those very words coming out of Kick's mouth.

"And then, with a smile like he'd just won the lottery, and in a booming voice, my brother would say, *Everyone, please drink a toast to the future happiness of Rachel and Sean*."

After I'd taken a second sip of champagne, Rachel put her arms around me. Into my ear she whispered, "Michael's with us now. I can feel him here. And I know he's so happy for us."

On the drive home Rachel commented for the thousandth time how generous it was for Ben and Katie to throw us such a lavish party. Then she lamented that she didn't feel like she spent enough time with her friends, and I assured her that they understood.

"I liked your toast," she said.

I chuckled. "Not the height of eloquence, but heartfelt, so I guess that counts for something."

"No, I'm serious. I like to think that we met when we'd each lost all hope about the future, and then, *presto!* happiness."

"I always think about it as just being my story. How I was at rock bottom until you came into my life. It's nice to know that you feel a little bit the same way."

"A lot a bit. I don't think you have any appreciation of just how . . . *desperate* may not be the right word, but it's close. That feeling like you're drowning and you're not going to be able to survive, but it may take a while before you finally go under for good, and so all you can do is fight to keep your head above water, even though it feels like a losing battle."

"Story of my life from my failure at the Olympic trials until I saw you at my brother's funeral."

"Me too. But now we have a different story. And it's a fairy tale come true."

"I love you, Rachel Fischer. I truly do."

"And I love you, Sean Kenney."

30.

The next day, I met Phoebe and Harper at the Colonial Diner.

By now, I was on a first-name basis with the hostess, who led me to what had become our usual table in Marilyn's section under the glass-enclosed atrium. My daughters were there when I arrived, sitting side by side.

Coffees had already been brought for Phoebe and me and a hot chocolate for Harper. As I slid into the empty booth, Marilyn asked, "Usual food orders?"

"Yes," Phoebe and Harper said.

I laughed. "We're getting way too predictable, but for me too, please."

"Do you think that Rachel will start coming to our brunches from now on?" Harper asked.

"Maybe sometimes. But, call me selfish, I like to have you two all to myself sometimes."

"Okay, you're selfish," Harper said, and gave me her smart-aleck smile.

By the time our food arrived, we were on to our usual topics. Phoebe had an English paper about *The Great Gatsby* due on

Wednesday and her first basketball practice on Thursday. Harper had a science test, although she couldn't remember which day.

"Any idea how the team will be this season?" I asked Phoebe.

"Probably about the same as last year. We lost three girls. Two of them weren't so good, but one was our top scorer, so that's going to hurt. But there's this really tall girl, I mean, she's probably six feet, who moved here from Arizona, and so maybe that'll make up for it."

"I can't wait," I said. "I've already put the entire schedule in my calendar and arranged coverage at the restaurant so I won't miss a single basket." Turning to Harper I said, "And the same is going to hold true for your softball games."

"I'm not going to play softball this season," Harper said.

"Really? Why not?"

"I didn't like it so much last year. But Mom says I needed to play a spring sport, so I figured maybe I'd go out for the track team."

I tried not to sound too excited by her choice, but inside I was bursting with pride.

———

After breakfast, I took the girls back to Meghan's. She came out to greet me.

"Thanks again for inviting us last night. We had a really nice time."

"Thanks again for coming."

"I hope you take this with the spirit with which it's intended, but having been divorced and then happily remarried, I can tell you that there's something wonderful about being given a second chance to get it right."

"Well, I hope you take this with the spirit with which it's

intended, but I'm hoping that I can be a much better husband this time around."

We both laughed for a moment. After which, Meghan placed her hand in mine.

"I think you will be. The truth is, I've always thought you could do whatever you set your mind to doing. The problem was that you never believed it."

From Meghan's, I headed over to the restaurant. We had just begun serving a Sunday brunch, and the place was bustling. After checking on the kitchen staff, and thanking them again for their work at the reception the previous evening, I made my rounds at the tables.

This was a people job, as Ben had said to me when he'd offered it. And I was pretty good at it, if I did say so myself.

Ben would never become a substitute for Kick in my life, but we'd grown exceedingly close in the past half year. So much so that I was ashamed I ever thought him capable of murder.

After Jenny's confession, Ben asked for my advice regarding how to repay his debt to my brother. Katie suggested he pay the money into a trust for the benefit of Jack and Molly, for them to use as they pleased when they reached adulthood. Ben hired a lawyer to set it up and made the payments directly from the restaurant's account to show me that he was making good on the debt, even though I'd told him that there was no need because I trusted him, which I did. If Jenny objected to the arrangement, no one told me. Nor would I have cared.

"Thanks again for the party," I said. "It was amazing. I hope you and Katie had a good time because I'm certain that everyone else did."

"Very glad to do it," he said. "And yes, it was great. You got really lucky with Rachel. So, you know, don't screw it up."

"I promise, I won't."

"Go, get out of here, then. Go home to your beautiful bride."

"You sure?"

"I think I can handle one day without you," Ben said with a smile. "But not more than one," he quickly added.

I thanked Ben for the dispensation and was kissing Rachel a half hour later. When she asked how brunch with my daughters had gone, I told her about Harper's decision to run track.

"Look at you. I don't think I've ever seen you look so happy," she said with a laugh.

"It's just—"

"I know what *it's just*, and there's no need to apologize for it. I love that for you. Do you still have your father's old stopwatch?"

I didn't know. "I hope so," I said. "I'll ask Katie."

31.

A month later, on the Friday night the week before Thanksgiving, the New Carlisle Kitchen was jumping. The bar area was two people deep, both seatings were booked by reservations, and the hostess was maintaining a waiting list forty minutes long.

I was making my rounds, going from table to table, asking if everything was to satisfaction, when one of the waitresses told me that a large party ordered multiple bottles of a particular vintage of Châteauneuf-du-Pape. I went next door to the liquor store and asked the kid who worked the register to retrieve the bottles out of the stock room, while I held down the fort.

I wasn't behind the counter for a minute when I heard my name sound like a question.

"Sean?"

I recognized him at once. "Jake Marshall, no way."

It had the sense of seeing a movie star in real life. The disconnect that they should be a certain way—either as the character you identify them as, or in Jake's case, still my high school best friend—and yet of course they're not that image in your mind at all, but the person standing before you.

"Yes, way." He laughed. "Hey, man, it's been forever. How the hell are you?"

"You mean, what have I been up to for the last . . . however long it's been?"

I tried to recall the reason we'd lost touch, but quickly realized there was none. As with so many things in my life, especially the ending of relationships that mattered to me, the fault was all mine. If the past year had taught me anything, however, it was that mistakes could be rectified. And there was no time like the present to do so.

"We have way too many years to catch up on while I'm at work," I said.

"I'm here all weekend, staying with my parents. They're still in East Carlisle, same house on Corona Road."

"Great. Can we meet up later tonight? How about at the Tavern at ten?"

"Are you sure you can get away from here?"

"Perks of being the boss," I said.

When I arrived at the Tavern, Jake was at the end of the bar. I'd been so surprised by his sudden appearance at the restaurant earlier that evening that I hadn't done a thorough physical inspection. As I made my approach, I took Jake's measure.

He was reasonably fit for a guy who had never been much of an athlete. During our friendship, Jake had always been rail thin, but the weight he'd added as an adult looked good on him. The few patches of gray in his hair gave him a touch of gravitas.

His smile hadn't changed, though. Not one bit. Goofy as ever.

Jake stood when I got to him and opened his arms for a hug. I entered his embrace, patting him on his back the same way he was doing on mine.

After we were both seated, Jake said, "So, who's going to go first?"

"You," I said.

The bartender interrupted him. "What can I get you?"

"Club soda," I said. Then to Jake, "You want another?"

"No, I'm still good." Which he was, his beer glass half-filled.

When the bartender departed, Jake said, "Alrighty, then. The Jake Marshall story in two minutes. Well, if you recall, I moved to Houston for a little bit, but too many Texans for me, and I came back East about ten years ago. I live in Brooklyn now . . . with my husband."

He stopped short, apparently thinking he'd dropped a bombshell. Truth of the matter was that, despite his string of girlfriends, I'd always suspected that Jake was fishing in the wrong pond.

"That's great. What's his name?"

Jake's smile told me that he was relieved that part was over. "Peter."

"So you and Peter, any kids?"

"No, just a cat. Her name is Maggie."

"Maggie the cat. Very cute. Job?"

"This is a bit embarrassing, actually—"

"More than naming your pet after a Tennessee Williams character?"

"Well, maybe not *that* embarrassing. I'm retired. Peter works long hours, and he does very well. What can I say, he likes coming home to a hot meal . . . and me."

"You can say that you're happy."

"I am happy," Jake said with conviction. "For a lot of years, I thought—not that it *wasn't* going to happen for me, but that it really *couldn't* happen for me. And then I met Peter. Now I wonder why I was so pessimistic for all those years, you know?"

I did know. He might have been describing my life.

"Okay, now I got to know about the one and only Sean Kenney."

The bartender spared me, placing my club soda before me.

"As you were not saying," Jake said with a smile after the bartender departed. "I'm still waiting to hear everything about Sean Kenney that I'm afraid to ask."

"Let's see. I have two girls. Phoebe, who's now sixteen, and Harper, who just turned fourteen."

I took out my phone. The most recent photo I had of the girls was of them sticking their tongues out. I turned the phone to show Jake my daughters.

"They're beautiful," he said. "You really dodged a bullet there, didn't you?"

I didn't follow. "How's that?"

"That they both look exactly like Meghan."

He flashed me one of his smart-ass smiles. We could have been back in third period lunch.

"Anyway," I said in an elongated fashion, "Meghan and I split up when Harper was five, so about ten years ago now. After we divorced, I'm sorry to report, I struggled a bit. I'm not going to give you the gory details, but I drank a lot and just tried to survive, usually doing so by the skin of my teeth."

"And yet, a club soda sits before you."

"Yeah, so like yourself, I've had a second act. Although in my case, maybe it's more like my third act. Either way, now is the happiest time in my life." I chuckled to myself. "You know, the way life is always unpredictable, it began with the worst part of my life. About a year ago, my brother died."

"I'd heard that," Jake said. "I'm really sorry."

I nodded to accept his condolences. "Thank you. That was truly rock bottom. But fast-forward a year and I'm managing that restaurant that is connected to the liquor store you happened into. I really enjoy it. My brother-in-law owns the place, but even though I'm quite clearly a nepotism hire, I'm actually pretty good at it."

"That's great. And your life outside of work?"

"Well, that's the other part of the story. Rachel Fischer and I are married. Just last month, in fact."

"Your brother's Rachel Fischer?"

I smiled, wondering when, if ever, that wouldn't be how people from my past referred to my wife. "Once upon a time, yes," I said. "But since we're married, she and my brother hadn't spoken in twenty years, I like to think she's more mine than his at this point."

Jake saw that he'd touched a nerve. "I'm sorry, that was stupid of me."

"No worries. You're not alone in saying it. It was the reaction of everyone in my family too."

All of a sudden there was an uneasiness about Jake. I didn't think it was due to his faux pas, which, like I'd told him, was the common reaction. There was something else bothering him about Rachel and me.

"What?" I asked.

"I don't know if I should be telling you this," he said.

"Now you have to. Those are the rules."

Jake didn't smile at my quip. Instead, he seemed even more distressed by my insistence he come clean.

"Really, Jake. It's okay. Just tell me."

He nodded that he would, but then took a sip of beer. "I saw your brother . . . I don't know when, exactly, but not too long before he died."

I didn't understand why that would cause Jake such discomfort. "You should have said hello. Kick always liked you."

"It wasn't that," he said, and came to an abrupt stop, as if he'd thought better of sharing the reason he'd decided not to approach my brother.

"You're freaking me out a little bit, Jake. Just tell me."

"The reason I didn't say hello was because your brother was very cozy with this woman—"

"Did she have red hair?"

My interruption startled him. But then I realized Jake wasn't surprised by what I'd said as much as confused.

"No," he said. "It was Rachel. Your brother, he was with Rachel Fischer."

The words hit me like a jackhammer. Kick was cozy—very cozy—with Rachel?

"Are you sure?"

"I shouldn't have said anything," Jake said.

Yes, he was sure. Rachel—my Rachel—was seeing Kick. She was all over him, in fact. My head was spinning with what it all meant, but none of the options I'd landed on were anything other than terrible.

"Is it possible that they were . . . you know, just acting like old friends do?"

"I'm sorry, but no. They were kissing and . . . so, no."

I clung to one other possibility, even though I knew it was too weak a likelihood to hold me for long. "When was this?"

"February of last year, maybe," he said.

"Are you sure it was then? Not earlier?"

Jake shifted uncomfortably, which answered that question. He was sure. Then he told me why.

"I was with Peter and I remember him saying that the place was really romantic and that we should come back for Valentine's Day. So it had to be, at the latest, late January."

That had been my last reed of hope. It snapped with my realization that my wife and my brother were involved at the time of Kick's death.

32.

I pounded on the front door. No answer. So I pounded some more.

It took almost five minutes, but the outside lights finally flickered on. A moment after that, Ben appeared.

His hair was disheveled and his eyes squinty. He was wearing a robe over a T-shirt and, by his naked leg, I assumed boxer shorts.

"Is everything okay at the restaurant?"

"Yeah, it's fine," I said. "I need to speak to Katie."

"She's asleep. It's . . . I don't even know what time it is."

"It's a little before midnight."

"Sean, have you been drinking?"

"No. Not a drop. Now go wake up my sister and tell her to come down."

"Whatever it is, can't it wait until the morning?"

He held his ground, waiting for me to explain why I needed to speak to my sister so urgently. So I told him.

"I know Jenny didn't confess to killing Kick."

Ben flinched. Katie had obviously confided in him about her ruse.

"We can all have a civilized discussion about this tomorrow when emotions aren't running so high," he said. "Why don't you stay the night. We can all talk about it first thing in the morning."

"Ben, listen to me, and listen to me carefully. I'm not leaving without talking to Katie. So, go get her. Right now."

I sat in their living room, in the same chair I'd occupied when Katie first told me about Kick's passing. I recalled the ease with which she'd lied about the reasons I needed to come home. I now felt the fool for having been tricked by her for a second time.

When she joined me, Katie looked as if she'd been asleep, a robe was cinched around her and her bedhead pronounced. I would have preferred to have this conversation with her alone, but didn't want to get sidetracked by banishing Ben, so I didn't object when he sat down beside his wife.

Katie gave me her best Mom-sucking-lemons expression and said, "Ben tells me you haven't been drinking, or so you say, but he also told me that you need to talk to me about Michael and it couldn't wait. So I'm here now. Talk."

"Jenny never confessed to killing Michael, did she?"

Katie's silence was as good as an affirmation. Still, I needed to hear her say it.

"I know that you did what you did because you thought it was best for me," I continued in a measured tone. "But lying to me about Jenny is the farthest thing from what's best for me right now. So, for the love of God, Katie, please tell me the truth."

I stared as hard as I could to convey that I meant every word I'd just said. Katie broke eye contact with me to look to Ben, who nodded almost imperceptibly at his wife. Then my sister turned back to me.

"No. Jenny didn't confess," Katie said, defeated.

I'd known the truth for the better part of an hour by then, since Jake had told me that Kick's mistress was Rachel and not Arielle. For a fleeting moment, I considered whether Kick could have been cheating on Jenny with two women, but it made much more sense that everything I'd believed had been a lie.

"What did Jenny actually say to you?"

Katie looked as if she was still wondering whether honesty would serve her well. She turned to Ben, but this time I saw no signal between them.

She shook her head. There was no way out for her, and she knew it.

"If you really have to know, Jenny said that you were crazy. That we should think about institutionalizing you because you had broken with reality. She called Arielle while I was there and Arielle laughed at the claim that she and Michael were lovers. And when I heard that, I realized that she was right about you. You were clearly obsessed with proving something that just wasn't true. I was angry at myself for allowing you to plant doubt in my mind about Michael. In the name of absolving him of one sin you'd accused him of something much worse."

Katie was only half right. Maybe even less than that, depending on whether Kick's infidelity with his ex-girlfriend was a greater sin than if he'd been cheating with his niece.

"I thought you were beyond reason, Sean. I just didn't know what else to do."

"So you thought lying to me was the answer?"

"I'm sorry. But I didn't see any other way. Hand to God."

Katie was apparently still of the belief that a lie to bring about a greater good was justified. And like the night I came home from New Orleans, being angry about her deception took a back seat to my need to learn the truth.

"What did you tell Jenny?"

Katie paused a moment, as if she was trying to recall what had happened that day. I couldn't imagine that she'd forgotten a single detail, however.

"I told her I was sorry. I apologized for you. I said you were under a lot of pressure."

"I meant did you tell Jenny that you were going to tell me she confessed to killing Kick?"

"Not then, but after, yeah. I didn't say that, exactly. I told her that you believed she'd killed Michael, but I knew she hadn't. That I was very sorry that on top of everything, she had to deal with such a horrible accusation. She said she understood why I had to choose you over her in that way, especially after I'd just lost one brother. Since then, I've kept in touch with her. I reach out to her every month or so, just to remind her that we're still family."

I slumped back, exhausted by what I'd just heard. Like awakening from a particularly realistic dream, I needed time to acclimate to my new reality.

"I'm sorry, Sean," Katie said.

Ben, who had been silent up until that point, added, "We both are."

"How did you know?" Katie asked.

I wasn't ready to reveal that part yet. Maybe I never would.

"I just do," I said.

"Okay. You don't have to tell me right now if you don't want," Katie said. "But please, stay here tonight. It's late. We can talk more about everything in the morning."

"No. I need to get home."

They both tried to persuade me otherwise, but I didn't relent. Another important discussion was still awaiting me that evening.

Soon enough they saw that it was a losing battle to change my mind. They both walked me to the door. Before taking my leave, I said one more thing.

"I know this is going to sound scary, but I need to say it anyway."

"Okay," Katie said, already seeming scared.

"I'm not suicidal. Or accident-prone. If something happens to me, I promise you that I didn't kill myself."

I shook Rachel awake.

"I need to talk to you."

She groggily opened her eyes, and then rubbed them. "What time is it?"

"It's late. But there's something very important I need to discuss with you."

"Okay," she said hesitantly. "Just give me a second, okay?"

She sat up and rubbed her eyes again. Then she checked her phone for the time.

"Did you just get home?"

I'd called Rachel earlier that evening to tell her about my chance encounter with Jake Marshall and that we'd agreed to get a late-night drink. I invited her to join, but she said that one reunion was enough, while promising to come the next time.

I hadn't communicated with her after that, however. So she had no idea what I'd learned in the intervening hours.

"Yeah. I stopped at Katie's house first, though."

"Is Katie okay? The kids?"

"They're all fine. I need to talk to you about you."

"Did I do something wrong?"

I was studying Rachel's face, looking for a sign that might

reveal whether she was going to lie. She offered no such tell, however. At least none that I could discern.

"Jake told me that he saw you and Kick together in the city," I said.

I'm not sure what reaction I'd expected, but what I got was an impassive stare. It wasn't clear to me if Rachel was being careful, or if she truly didn't understand the import of what I was conveying.

Then, as if all of a sudden, she realized that the truth was at hand. She looked away, ashamed. "I thought you'd be upset if you knew."

"I am upset. But I need to know."

She nodded as if she agreed. "Okay."

I waited for Rachel to gather herself. When she still hadn't come out with it, I prodded.

"So tell me."

She sighed, but that was thankfully the last of her stalling. Then she came out with it, at first speaking in a slow, measured pace, but gradually becoming more animated.

"After you left town, Michael reached out to me. He told me about your fight—the one in which you told him about us—and . . . you have to remember, he had no idea where you'd gone, and so he thought that maybe you were still with me. Or that at least I'd know where you were."

The explanation struck me like a baseball bat to the head. It was my fault. If I hadn't told Kick about Rachel and me, he would have never reached out to her. And what ended up happening would never have occurred.

I needed Rachel to come out with it all. To spare me from further interrogation. To just put me out of my misery by telling me the truth.

She didn't, however. She was still, only her eyes moving, as if she were searching for an escape route magically to appear.

My face must have made it crystal clear that wasn't going to happen. The only way this was going to end was with Rachel telling me everything.

"He wasn't having an affair with Arielle. He was having an affair with you, right?"

Rachel didn't deny it. Instead, she stared out into the middle distance, as if she was in a trance.

"That was the whole point of introducing me to Dolev in the first place," I continued. "To prevent me from finding out about you and my brother. *You* were the problem that Kick told me about in our last phone call. The one he had to take responsibility for. That's why he reached out to me. Because he knew that I could help him manage *you*."

I bore down on Rachel. The intensity of my stare caused her to look away. It was enough for me to pull back. To let Rachel know that there was, in fact, a way out for her. For us.

"I love you, Rachel. I hope that you believe that because it's true. Before Jake told me about seeing you with Kick, I was going on and on about how I was the luckiest SOB on planet earth and that was all because of you."

She offered me a shallow nod. It wasn't clear to me whether she meant it to denote that she agreed with what I'd just said or simply that she'd heard it.

I was fairly certain that Rachel was well aware that her undisclosed relationship with Kick wasn't the problem. It was how that relationship ended that mattered.

"Maybe I'm a hopeless romantic," I continued, "but I truly think that one of the things about being in love with somebody means forgiving them, even for their worst sins. And the truth is, I have to believe that, because look at all the people in my life that I needed to forgive me. My daughters. My sister. Kick. Meghan. And you. So now I'm asking—begging, really—for you to show me that you believe I'm capable of that kind of forgiveness too."

"How can I do that, Sean?"

"By telling me about the day Kick died."

For a good ten seconds, Rachel didn't say a word. Maybe longer. The only sound was that she'd started to cry. Not sobbing, not yet, at least. More like when it begins to drizzle but you know it's a prelude to the fierce storm to come.

Then she sighed deeply, revealing that the truth was finally at hand. I waited for her to say what I already knew she would, still unsure how I'd react when it was all finally laid bare.

"I arranged for the hotel. It was my birthday gift to him," Rachel said slowly.

I'd intuited that much already. That was what people who had affairs did on their birthdays. They had sex with their mistresses at fancy hotels and then went home to their wives.

Still, hearing her say it conjured the image in my head of Rachel naked, a red satin bow across her breasts. As if she saw the scene through my eyes too, she turned away.

I waited for her to lift her gaze back to mine. When she did, I posed the question I'd been asking myself since Jake told me about his chance encounter with Kick and Rachel. The only question that mattered anymore.

"Did you kill him?"

She didn't seem shocked by my accusation. If anything, she looked as if she'd been expecting it.

"No," she said defiantly.

But she knew who did. There was someone she was protecting.

"Rachel, you need to tell me what happened at the hotel. Dragging it out isn't doing either of us any good."

I wasn't sure what I expected Rachel to say next. To lie,

probably. To explain that I had it all wrong. To go back to the party line that Kick had killed himself.

But in the softest voice that could be audible, she said, "Dolev. He killed Michael."

33.

After telling me that Dolev had murdered my brother, Rachel filled in their story.

She spoke in a monotone, intermittently stopping to cry. I sat beside her, holding her hand.

Dolev was former Israeli intelligence. Or so he told her. She said there were things about him that never truly added up. He was employed by an IT firm of some kind. He didn't do any work for Rachel's law firm. She'd met him on a dating app.

"I obviously didn't know him the way I thought I did, or I would never have been involved with him," she said, a reference to the fact that she didn't knowingly sleep with murderers.

"How long were you and Dolev together?" I asked.

"Six months, more or less."

In other words, the same amount of time Rachel and I dated the first time. Long enough to fall hopelessly in love and to be shattered when you found out that your love was unrequited.

I had resorted to self-harm: drinking to excess and self-banishment. Dolev had seemingly found another way to deal with the pain.

"So, like I said, after you left town, Michael and I spoke a handful of times. Whenever we did, it was almost entirely about you. And then, that stopped . . . I don't know, maybe after six months. But after the New Year, he called and said that he wanted to see me. We met up at this place near my office and he told me that things were tough for him at work because of the SEC investigation. He said he had no one he could really talk to. He was afraid to tell Jenny because he didn't want to worry her, and . . . well, I'd always kept his secrets, and so he figured he could trust me."

The words hurt. I should have been the person my brother confided in. Not his high school girlfriend slash mistress.

"One thing . . . led to another," she continued, her eyes downcast. "I'm ashamed of it now, but at the time it really seemed like Michael needed me and . . . I don't know, I needed him too, I guess. But after, I realized that, I think, for both of us, it was a kind of self-punishment. I truly believe that he was only seeing me to make himself feel guilty. Practically every single time we were together, he told me it had to be the last time. And I sometimes think maybe that's why I was seeing him too. Just to make myself feel worse about myself. Does that make any sense?"

None of it made any sense. At the same time, I could finally now see how it all fit together. The three sides of this love triangle on a fatal collision course. It would all end with my brother shot dead at close range.

"I begged Michael to see me on his birthday, dangling the hotel room as a special present. Like I said, he wanted us to be over, but I told him that this would be the last time and after I'd go away quietly. I told him that I needed the closure. If I hadn't pressed, I'm certain he wouldn't have seen me. And if Michael hadn't gotten to the hotel first and paid for the room, even though it was my gift to him, the police would have instantly known I'd been with him."

I needed her to get to the point already. To tell me what I already knew was coming.

As if she intuited my distress, Rachel said, "Right after I got there, there was a knock on the door. Michael might have asked who it was, and maybe the answer was *room service* or *front desk* or something, but it's also possible that he answered the door without saying anything. I just don't remember. But what I do remember, what I can see as if it was happening right now, was that right after Michael opened the door, Dolev jammed a gun into his face."

I was frightened for my brother in that moment, even though it had all happened eight months earlier. How Kick was surely in fear for his life. How he'd never get the opportunity to set things right the way he told me just a few minutes earlier that he was determined to do.

"I swear to God, I don't know how Dolev found out about Michael and me. Or how he found us that day. As soon as he entered the room, I started screaming and ran to the phone. Dolev hit me across the face—hard—with the back of his hand, knocking me down. I think I blacked out for a second, because when I looked up, Dolev had the gun pressed up against the middle of Michael's forehead, and Michael was sitting up at the foot of the bed."

According to Rachel's recounting of the last moments of my brother's life, Kick tried to calm Dolev down. He said that they should talk things through, that Dolev just needed to put the gun away.

"Dolev, he was like a wild animal," she said. "He kept screaming that he was going to kill us both. And I was certain that he would. I couldn't imagine how Michael or I was going to get out of there alive."

"But he only killed Kick. And you did get out of there alive."

She mouthed *Yes*, but no sound came out. She followed the silence with a short nod.

"So, keep going," I urged. "Dolev has the gun to Kick's head. You're on the floor. What happened next?"

"For a second I thought Dolev had finally calmed down. He did this shrug, and the hand that was holding the gun kind of fell to his side. But then without saying anything, he put the gun to Michael's temple and fired. Point-blank. I screamed. I've never screamed like that before. I don't know how no one from the hotel heard it. Or the gunshot. It was so loud. Like the worst thunder you can imagine."

I heard the clap in my head and winced. It was enough for Rachel to put her hand on my now bowed head.

In a soft voice that was at odds with the frenzy that must have epitomized that hotel room, Rachel said, "Dolev then pointed the gun right at me and started shouting, *Shut the fuck up. Shut the fuck up or I'm going to fucking kill you.*"

She came to an abrupt stop. I imagined it was a little like what had happened at the hotel too. How she'd followed Dolev's command to keep quiet.

I knew the plan that Dolev hatched in those next few moments. Still, I wanted to hear Rachel say it. More than that, I *needed* her to say it.

Thankfully, she didn't make me wait.

"Dolev said that he could make it look like a suicide. If he did that, it would be like it never happened. I remember saying that made no sense. Of course it had happened. Michael was dead. But Dolev said the choice was simple: throw our lives away or protect ourselves. He said it as if there wasn't even a possibility that we weren't in this together. I called him on that, saying something like, *I didn't kill him, you did.* But he said no one would ever believe me. This I remember almost word-for-word: *The story is going to be that your married boyfriend dumped you and you killed him in a jealous rage.* Then Dolev pointed the gun right at me and he said, *Or I could stage a murder-suicide. It's your choice.*"

Rachel was crying hard now, her face buried in her hands. Through the tears she told me how Dolev wiped the gun clean of his fingerprints and then wrapped Kick's dead hand around the trigger, causing the second shot to fire into the ceiling to ensure that gunpowder residue would be found on Kick's hand. Then he placed the gun on the floor where it would have fallen if Kick had shot himself.

"What about cameras in the hotel?" I asked.

Rachel shrugged. "I must be on them. Dolev too. But I didn't arrive with Michael, and it was a busy hotel. I think there was some party going on there that night or something."

I had thought that the police would have questioned every person who showed up on the video footage, but of course they didn't. That would have been hundreds of people and they didn't believe they were investigating a murder because the room key had only been used once.

"I just walked out of the hotel and got into my car," Rachel continued. "Dolev had taken my phone, but nothing stopped me from pulling into a gas station and getting someone to call the cops. But I didn't. I drove home. Dolev followed me there. Once we were inside, he told me to give him all of the clothing I was wearing. After I did, he gave me my phone back, and left."

Like learning a magician's trick, it was all so stupidly obvious. Dolev not being a private investigator, as Rachel had claimed. Kick not having an affair with his twentysomething niece, as Dolev had claimed. Jenny not actually confessing, as Katie had claimed.

Two questions remained. Neither had to do with Kick, however. They both were about me. Or more specifically, about Rachel and me.

"So, you and me, that was just to keep tabs on what was going on in my family?"

Even as I said it, I realized that it made little sense. Rachel could have ended things with me when I'd accused Jenny of murder and considered the case closed. Instead, she'd married me.

"I swear to God, Sean, no. Not even for a second. I know this sounds like I'm some type of sociopath, but I just told myself that I couldn't think about what happened to Michael. That I needed to pretend I was like everyone else, shocked at his suicide. And when I saw you, I thought—"

"What? What did you think when you saw me?"

"I thought that maybe it would make Michael happy if we were together. If I could help you, maybe I could be forgiven for what I'd done to him. So, I guess, you and me wasn't totally *not* about Michael. But it definitely wasn't an act. I love you. Right up until about an hour ago, I thought we would actually be that rare couple that got to live happily ever after."

I wasn't ready to talk about the future, however. I was still very firmly in the past.

"And so you decided that the way to get there was to have Dolev pretend he was a private investigator to convince me that Kick was having sex with his niece? That's just too fucked-up, Rachel."

"You were pushing too hard. You were going to find out about Michael and me. What other choice did I have?"

I could have told her all the other ways she could have gone besides the one she selected, but there was little point. I understood everything now.

"I love you so much, Sean," she said, as if that erased everything that preceded it, and then she wiped a tear from under her eye to further punctuate the point that it could all somehow be put behind us.

I allowed that thought to envelop me. There was a certain symmetry that both Rachel and I had failed Kick, and later found redemption for our sins in each other's love.

But I knew that simply wishing it to be was not the answer. I'd done enough pretending in my life.

"Here's what I'm going to need you to do if we're going to have any chance of a future, Rachel. You have to call Dolev and tell him that we need to meet."

"Why?"

"So I can look him in the eye and tell him that I know."

It was the same rationale I'd presented to Katie once upon a time about Jenny. Only now I'd be confronting my brother's actual murderer.

As terrified as Rachel was while telling me what had transpired at the hotel, she suddenly looked even more frightened. "He's not going to agree to meet with you."

"With us," I corrected. "You and me. And the reason he will is because you're going to tell him that he either meets with us or he meets with the police. You'll explain that I figured out what happened and I confronted you about it. That you said that you weren't involved, and that if I went to the police, Dolev would make sure you'd take the fall. The same thing you said he told you. The only difference is that now you'll be telling him that the only hope you both have of avoiding prison is if he meets with me. If he does, then I won't call the police because I don't want anything bad to happen to you."

She looked far from convinced by my logic. The opposite, actually. Her expression told me she thought my plan was insane.

"You don't understand what Dolev is capable of. He's more likely to murder you than to tell you anything."

"He won't be able to do that."

I said it with confidence, as if I had it all figured out. Nothing could have been further from the truth.

"You'll tell him that we've left a video with Katie of you saying that Dolev killed Kick and that I was going to confront him. If anything were to happen to either of us, that video goes straight to the cops."

It was obvious that Rachel still thought my plan was a suicide mission. Unfortunately, not going along with it was even more fraught for her.

I had one more card to play. "You know that I'm not going to hurt you in all of this, Rachel, because, well, because I love you. We're still newlyweds for Chrissakes. But even if that isn't enough assurance, you can take comfort in the fact that when I thought Jenny had killed Kick, I let it end there. I didn't turn her in. And I wasn't in love with Jenny and she wasn't my new bride. But like with her, I need to know the truth."

That apparently was enough to convince her. Rachel reached for her phone. A second later she said, "Dolev, it's me . . . Rachel."

34.

Two days had passed. Two very long days.

Katie called me the first of those two days, worried sick. I apologized for my melodramatics from the night before, and told her that everything was fine.

"I don't believe you," she said.

"Well, I don't know what to tell you, then," I replied.

"You could tell me the truth."

"Why should we start with that now?"

"Okay, I deserve that. But just tell me that you're going to be okay."

"I'm going to be fine," I said, wondering if that was just another lie.

Rachel had taken every opportunity in the last forty-eight hours to convince me to abort the plan. Even after we'd arrived at the Dunkin', she tried one last time.

"We don't have to do this, Sean. We could leave right now."

But I had to do it. There was simply no way that my life could otherwise go on.

Once inside, I went to the counter and ordered coffees for Rachel and me. Then we sat side by side at the table in the middle of the place and waited.

I felt some relief we weren't alone. Two men in sports jackets and ties were beside us at the table nearest the door and two women in their thirties occupied the one in front of the counter.

Dolev arrived a few minutes later. He looked at our coffees and laughed.

"Nothing for me, I see. That's okay. I had some on my way over."

Without saying anything else, Dolev swiped his hand under the table and all four chairs. Obviously, he thought I'd planted listening devices.

I hadn't, which he realized soon enough. But that apparently was still insufficient to satisfy him that this wasn't a setup.

"Before anyone says anything, I'm going to need you both to accompany me to the men's room, please."

In all our prior meetings, Dolev had pretended we were allies, but now I saw him clearly for the sociopath he'd always been. "No fucking way are we going anywhere with you," I said.

He looked behind him at the table of businessmen and then past my shoulder to the women on our other side. None of them had stirred as a result of my profanity.

"No harm is going to come to you," Dolev said with a smile discordant to that sentiment. "This place has a million cameras everywhere. I'm on tape as clear as day entering and now sitting at your table. Not to mention that there's this video—the one you say is with your sister—you're blackmailing me with. So, trust me on this, Sean, you and Rachel are going to make it out of here alive. But, I don't trust you. You've made some pretty serious allegations—none of which are true—and if we're going to have a discussion about those lies, I need to know it's for our ears only. Or you can leave. Be my guest. There's the door. Fine with me if we part ways right now. But if you want to hear what I have to say, you'll follow me."

Rachel's expression made clear that she was equally concerned as I was about being behind a closed door with Dolev. But I was already coming to my feet, which caused her to reluctantly follow my lead.

The bathroom was single occupancy but outfitted to comply with ADA requirements, so the three of us fit comfortably inside. I stood closest to the toilet, with Rachel beside me. Dolev was leaning up against the sink.

"Strip down to your bare ass," he said.

I knew this request was coming, but it still shocked me. Nonetheless, I didn't protest; instead, I quickly pulled off all of my clothing.

I was unaccustomed to men staring at my naked body, and it was doubly disturbing with Rachel bearing witness. If Dolev was uncomfortable, he didn't show it. Without so much as a blink, he held his index finger up and spun it around.

When my pirouette was complete, Dolev said, "Toss over your clothes."

First he went through the pockets of my jeans, turning them inside out until he was satisfied they were empty, at which time he threw them back to me. My underwear required less inspection. As I was reapplying the bottom half of my clothing, he returned my shirt. My socks went back to me quickly, but Dolev spent time massaging my shoes to the point I half expected him to break off the heel to check whether I'd hidden a bug inside.

The last garment he inspected was my coat. Dolev turned out the pockets, taking my phone and putting it in his own coat pocket. After that, he paid special attention to the collar, massaging it between his fingers.

"Okay, you're smarter than I gave you credit for," he said.

"Thanks. I can't tell you how much I appreciate that. Especially coming from you."

He laughed a mocking cackle. "Now you," Dolev said.

"You're kidding," Rachel said.

"Nothing I haven't seen before, sweetheart."

Rachel sighed audibly, but didn't put up much more of a fight than that. Once she was laid bare, Dolev went through the same ritual as he had with me before returning her clothing. After she was dressed, without saying a word, Dolev opened the bathroom door, and motioned for us to lead him back to the table.

Back in our seats, Dolev said, "Okay, so now that we know we're just among friends, why don't you tell me why we're all here, Sean."

"Because you fucking killed my brother, that's why."

Like when I'd cursed at him before, Dolev looked over his shoulder, and once again the men at the table behind us were oblivious. Next Dolev turned toward the women, and as I followed his sight line I saw that they were equally engrossed in their own discussion.

"I read somewhere that people crave apologies when they've been wronged," Dolev said, as if we were friends and he was recounting some anecdote he thought might have interest to me. "It triggers some brain neuron or something. Doesn't make much sense to me, though. What's done is done. Saying you're sorry. Or even actually being sorry, doesn't matter."

"It does to me," I said.

"I gather, which is why we're all here."

I had assumed Dolev wouldn't have agreed to come if he wasn't prepared to uphold his part of the bargain. But in that moment, I wondered if he was going to resist taking that final step.

"Maybe confession will be good for you too," I said. "For your soul, I mean."

He laughed. "I doubt that very much. My soul is what it is, for better or worse, I suppose. I will tell you that I wish I could take it back. That's the honest truth. I think about that day a lot. I know your brother had a family. It's just a tragedy that it turned out the way it did. I . . . wasn't in my right mind. That's all I can say. I don't even remember what I was thinking when I pulled the trigger."

I looked at Rachel. She averted her eyes.

"So, here's how this ends," Dolev said, returning to a menacing tone. "We never see or speak to each other ever again. Because if we do, then you're giving me no choice but to kill you. And when I walk out of here, you should thank Rachel from the bottom of your heart because the only reason you're still alive is she said she'd turn me in if you weren't. Call me sentimental, but I didn't want to have to kill you both."

He smiled as if he was actually amused. "Don't get me wrong. I will if I have to. But Rachel assures me that won't be necessary because you love her and won't do anything stupid that'll make you both dead. For both your sakes, she better be right. And believe me, you're not going to be doing her any favors if you go to the cops. I'll turn on her in a heartbeat. It was all her idea. I'm just the hired gun. She seduced me to kill him. I'm the real victim."

He flashed another grin, this one had cruelty as its defining feature. His monologue of fear concluded, I turned to Rachel. She put her hand on mine.

"Good," Dolev said.

He stood and walked toward the exit. Rachel and I watched him push the door open, just as another man approached it.

Dolev wasn't the kind to give the right-of-way. I'm certain that in any other situation, he would have made the man wait for him to leave before allowing him entry.

Dolev yielded, however. It wasn't out of politeness, though. The other man had a gun pointed right at him.

35.

Theodore C. Quinn Field had changed since my last visit. A bleacher had been erected on the far side. The signage was different too. Back in my day, the scoreboard said *East Carlisle* and *Guest*, but it was computerized now, displaying the name of the visiting team too. It wasn't turned on, rendering the spaces dark.

I entered the field from the back, which allowed me time to watch the action in front of me. The sprinters practicing their starts. The pole-vaulters planting but not elevating. The hurdlers doing two-foot jumps, the exercise that they always hated. And, of course, a pack of runners, whom I guessed were 1600-meter kids by their pace, rounding the first turn.

I waited along the straightaway for them to pass me, hearing the familiar rhythm of the galloping footsteps. It brought me back faster than any time machine ever could.

―――

Dolev had been armed in the Dunkin'. I wonder if he would have considered reaching for his gun if it hadn't been for the fact that when he turned to plot an escape through the back, he saw that the other patrons—the men wearing the sports jackets and the women in their thirties—were pointing their service revolvers at him.

The recording devices had been on them. Every word Dolev said was preserved for use at trial.

It hadn't been easy to get the cops to go along with my plan. Even after I explained that Rachel had confessed that Dolev had murdered Kick in her presence, Detective Montedesco reminded me, rather forcefully, that the case was closed and the cause of my brother's death was a suicide. She said she wasn't going to deploy six officers to humor a bereaved family member conducting his own sting.

I hadn't referenced my running to anyone in almost twenty years, but at last my past success on the track had a purpose. It was a way to get the police to do my bidding.

"You may not know this about me, Detective, but I'm a former United States champion and NCAA champion in the 1500 meters."

"Okay. Congratulations on that, I guess."

"Yeah. Thanks. The reason I mention it is that it's going to make a great lead-in for someone's true crime podcast, don't you think? Former All-American unwilling to accept the police's conclusion that his brother committed suicide and conducts his own investigation. And the way I see it, the story ends one of two ways. All goes well, and I get Dolev on tape myself, and I'm the hero of the piece. Don't worry, Detective, I'm sure they'll want to get your side of things too. Why you refused to believe me most especially, given that I solved the case that you had erroneously closed to allow a murderer to go free. But you can always hope for the other outcome. In that one, Dolev finds the recording device and kills me and Rachel. I suspect you'll come off even worse if it goes that way, though. That's because my sister has a video of me telling her that I begged you to help and you refused."

I let that sink in for a second. "But maybe there's a third ending. The one where the police save the day. How they're the heroes, capturing the confession on tape and securing a conviction. I bet someone like Kate Winslet even gets cast to play you in the movie version."

"And what if it's all a big waste of time?" she countered. "If Dolev doesn't show? Or if he says you're crazy when he does?"

"I'll spring for the donuts, then," I said. "Win-win, right?"

A short while after everything went down with Rachel and Dolev, I visited East Carlisle High School a half hour before school let out.

"I used to go here," I said to the young woman working the front desk.

She gave me an *I hear that a lot* smile. "What can I do for you?"

"I'm here to see Andrew Leeman, the coach of the track team."

"Is Mr. Leeman expecting you?"

"No. But he knows who I am. Our former coach, Mr. Palomino, suggested I contact him."

"Okay, let me check where Mr. Leeman is right now."

A few pecks at her computer later, she told me he was in the gym. I would have guessed.

"I'll take you to him," she said. "We're not supposed to have unaccompanied visitors on campus during school hours."

We walked out into the hallway, right in front of the Wall of Fame. I stopped for a second and then pointed into the case.

"That's my father," I said. "State champions of 1979. The black-and-white photo in the back."

"That's nice," my escort said, without studying the picture. It must not have registered with her that the larger photograph in front was a much younger version of the man beside her.

When we reached the gym, she pointed to the only adult in the room, a tall, thin man, a few years younger than me, wearing green gym shorts and a white polo shirt. A whistle hung around his neck. He was officiating a volleyball game.

"I need to get back to the office," she said. "Mr. Leeman can walk you out when you're finished."

I thanked her for accompanying me but didn't make my way any closer to the man I'd come to see. Instead, I watched half a dozen points. Few of the kids could jump high enough to get their hands over the net, but that didn't stop some of them from trying to spike, although I didn't see anyone succeed.

At five minutes to three, Coach Leeman blew a long whistle. Then he clapped his hands.

"That's it, everybody. Good job today. See you all tomorrow."

He was already walking toward the locker room when I called out his name. "Coach Leeman?"

"Can I help you?" he asked.

"I hope so. I'm Sean Kenney."

I was about to explain that Coach Pal had suggested I pay this visit, but his smile confirmed that he already knew who I was and why I was there. "Coach Pal told me that he'd asked you to contact me, but . . . well, that was last year, so I didn't think it was going to happen. I don't want to fanboy too much, as the kids say, but it's truly an honor to meet you, Sean. Coach talked about you so often, when I was his student, and then when we were both colleagues and I was his assistant, that I feel like I know you."

"That's kind of you to say."

"It's the truth. Coach sometimes made me feel . . . you know, one of those *Dad likes you best* kind of feelings. I worshipped that man, but there was no denying that you were always his favorite. I should add, you and your brother. The brothers Kenney, as he called you."

Coach Leeman and I sat on the bleachers and talked for about an hour. About running mostly, but a little about our old coach, and some about me. It didn't seem like a job interview, but I guess it was.

When we were done, he told me to come back in two days. At that time, he said, he'd introduce me to the team.

After arresting Dolev and Rachel, the cops told me that I was free to go. I didn't feel free, though. There was still an important matter weighing heavily on my mind.

I drove straight from the Dunkin' to Jenny's house. I should have told her I was coming because in response to my knock she threatened to call the police if I didn't leave immediately.

"I'm here to apologize, Jenny. I know you didn't kill Kick. If you let me come in, I'll explain."

She opened the door halfway, looking at me like I was a wild animal she didn't want getting too close. Then she told me that, rather forcefully.

"Step the hell back, Sean. I don't want you anywhere near me."

I did as requested and once again assured her that I came in peace. "If it will make you more comfortable, call Katie. She can be on the phone while we talk."

My suggestion seemed to relax Jenny, but not enough that

she didn't see the wisdom of involving my sister. She pulled her phone from her pocket and pressed a button.

"Hi Jenny," my sister said on speakerphone.

"Your brother is here."

"Sean is there?"

"Hi Katie," I shouted.

"Sean, what the hell are you doing there?"

I'd expected to have this conversation indoors, imagining it in the same place I'd first discussed Kick's death with Jenny and the same spot in which I'd later accused her of murdering him. But it made sense that I was outside in the cold. That had its own symbolism.

"I know what happened," I said. "Finally, I know. And I'm sorry for so many things, Jenny. Of course for falsely accusing you. But also for what I'm going to say now, which I know is also going to hurt you."

I saw Jenny recoil, as if she thought that perhaps I was going to pull out a gun and fire. I was mindful to keep my hands where she could see them.

"Kick was having an affair," I shouted, loud enough for Katie to hear too. "Not with Arielle, though. But with Rachel."

Having falsely accused my brother of infidelity before, there was no reason for Jenny to accept my claim at face value. Her stern expression told me that she didn't.

"Rachel admitted it to me," I said. "She said that it didn't last very long. It started shortly after the New Year. She said that almost as soon as it started, he told her that he wanted to end things, and she thought that his birthday was going to be their last time together."

"Rachel was with Michael when he died?" she asked, sounding as if it couldn't have possibly been true.

She apparently still didn't believe that Kick had been

murdered. I knew that this was a lot of information coming at her fast and without warning, but having waited a long time to hear it myself, I also knew it was best not to dribble it out.

"Yes. I'm sorry, Jenny, but yes. Rachel had been seeing this guy named Dolev Attias. He was the one who killed Kick. Somehow Dolev found out about Rachel and Kick and followed them to the hotel that day. Rachel swore to me that she wasn't involved. She claimed she'd kept quiet all this time because Dolev threatened to kill her if she said anything."

Jenny looked lost, her expression not dissimilar to the one my father wore in the last months of his life. I couldn't imagine what was going through her mind, even though I'd been confronted with these same facts only two days earlier—my spouse's affair leading to my brother's murder.

Katie's voice came through the phone. "That's convenient of Rachel to put all the blame on her boyfriend."

"I'm not going to tell you that I believe her," I said, "because I don't expect that to hold much water. The police have arrested both of them. Dolev is on tape admitting to everything."

Jenny dropped to the ground. With me still standing twenty feet away and my sister on speakerphone, she began to sob.

I knew the tsunami of emotions swirling through her at that moment because I'd experienced them too. The realization that my brother—her husband—had not willingly left his loved ones, and yet he was still not without blame for the choices he'd made and the consequences that resulted. And, of course, regardless of the reason, he was still gone.

———

With the recordings from the Dunkin' meet, Detective Montedesco said that they had Dolev dead to rights. As he promised he would, Dolev was trying to shave time off his sentence by claiming Rachel had masterminded Kick's murder, and he'd done her bidding because he was under her spell.

Rachel was sticking to her story that she had no idea Dolev was going to kill Kick. Either the police believed her or they were still gathering evidence because she hadn't been charged with any crime.

Detective Montedesco told me that because Rachel hadn't disturbed the crime scene, she couldn't be charged with obstruction of justice. She likewise hadn't assisted Dolev with anything before or after the murder, so she wasn't guilty of aiding or abetting either.

I believed Rachel was innocent. I just couldn't imagine what was in it for her to kill my brother. But I know that jealousy can make you do crazy things. Which means that I couldn't completely rule out the possibility that Dolev was the truth-teller, and the woman I was prepared to love until death did we part, the liar.

I've tried to come to terms with the fact that my brother and I had both loved, and ultimately were betrayed by, the same woman. I don't know what it says about either of us, but I find an odd comfort that it's yet another thing that bonds us.

Like when I wear his suit. Like when I run.

Or just every single day when I think about him.

———

A few weeks after she was arrested, Rachel appeared at the restaurant. She hadn't reached out to me since I'd left her at the Dunkin'. I hadn't expected her to, of course. I was reasonably sure that she was under strict legal advice not to go anywhere near me. Not to mention that I suspected she hated my guts for not telling her that the Dunkin' meet was a setup.

"I only want a few minutes, Sean," she said. "And then you won't ever hear from me again."

I looked behind me into the crowded restaurant, as if to suggest I was too busy to grant her wish. But when I turned back to Rachel, I nodded, and followed her out into the street.

Even now, after everything, I still couldn't resist her.

It was a warm night, but with a wind that gusted from time to time, which seemed to be a special effect for Rachel's hair to billow. I half expected her to ask me to hand over my iPhone before we began talking, but either she trusted me not to be recording her, or had kept a careful enough eye on me since she entered the restaurant to know that I hadn't reached into my pocket.

We walked away from the front door, stopping under a streetlight on the next corner. She looked up at me, almost as if she was thinking about whether we should kiss.

"You look good, Sean."

She did too. As beautiful as I ever recall her being, in fact. But I resisted telling her that.

She got the message that she was on the clock. "When I think about my life, I realize that I've only loved two men," she said. "And in one of God's little pranks, they happened to be brothers. Michael betrayed me and I betrayed you. I hated Michael for a very long time after, and I can only assume you hate me right now. But I also never stopped loving him, and in time I came to forgive him. I know that's too much for me to ask of you now, but I want you to always remember that I'm asking for your forgiveness, even though I know I don't deserve it."

There was that word again—*forgiveness*. It seemed to be the sun around which my life orbited. I remembered Meghan's thoughts on the matter, shared with me that day on her front lawn. About how in time we become different people, such that our prior sins almost belong to someone else.

"I think we're all worthy of forgiveness, Rachel. It just takes time, is all."

She was crying, the tears illuminated by the faint glow of the streetlight. "Thank you for saying that. It means . . . everything to me. Truly."

My decision to involve the police had nothing to do with my not loving Rachel. I'd swear that I loved her as much as I'd ever loved anyone. Meghan included.

Rachel had brought me back from the edge of the abyss, and I once believed that we could live happily ever after. But that life could not be built on a lie, which meant that it couldn't be had at all once I knew the truth.

"I hope that, in time, you'll find it in your heart to forgive me too," I said.

"I don't need time," she replied quickly. "You're more than forgiven. I'm grateful that we had the time together that we did, even if it is going to make me a two-time divorcée before I'm forty." She tried to eke out a smile. "I know the path for me now. I sometimes doubt that I'm a . . . good enough person, I guess, to make it down that road, but before I met you, I didn't even know what direction to go."

"Maybe we'll see each other at the end of that journey," I said.

"I'd really like that."

She reached over to take my hand, and I held hers for a few seconds. She was the one who broke our contact.

"You have been more generous than I had any right to expect," she said, "and so I'm not going to take up any more of your time. I'm sorry to have ambushed you, but I felt that I needed to say what I did."

I understood the compulsion for closure. More than most people.

"I want you to have a happy and meaningful life, Rachel.

I truly do. The one thing that I'm absolutely certain about is that everyone is entitled to a second chance to make amends for their mistakes."

She smiled in a way that suggested she was actually pleased by what I'd said. Then Rachel kissed me on the lips in a soft, but lingering way. I can't deny that it reminded me of our first kiss at the Orchard all those years ago, right down to the way her eyes were glistening when I opened mine.

The streetlight was broken on the next block. I watched Rachel walk underneath it and into the darkness.

Coach Leeman blew his whistle three times in rapid succession.

Then he yelled at the top of his lungs. "Everybody, gather up. Gather up, everybody."

About thirty boys and girls jogged onto the infield. My youngest was among them. I'd discussed this next step with Harper at some length, telling her more than once that I would be happy to refrain until she graduated. She never hesitated. Her only request was that I not show her any favoritism.

Coach Leeman was wearing a green ECHS hoodie, matching sweatpants, and running shoes. Nearly every member of the team was similarly attired. I, on the other hand, was dressed in slacks and a button-down shirt, over which I wore a sports jacket and leather-soled shoes. The outfit of a man who managed a very successful restaurant.

"Quiet down. Quiet down." Coach Leeman said even though no one was talking. "I've got a real treat for you all today—and for the rest of our season."

The kids looked bored. I remembered that feeling from my days too. I just wanted to run. I didn't want to meet old men.

"Ryan, who holds the ECHS record for the 1600 meters?"

One of the few members of the team with a runner's physique answered without hesitation. "Sean Kenney. 3:43:52."

Coach Leeman smiled at me but didn't say anything. I wondered if that was my cue to introduce myself to the kids, but then he said, "Ladies and gentlemen, the legend himself stands before you. Give it up for Harper Kenney's father and the former two-time NCAA and US champion, Sean Kenney."

They all clapped. Not too enthusiastically, but not like they were doing so under pain of punishment either.

I put my hand up to quell the team's applause.

"It's funny, but that's the first ovation I've had on this field since well before any of you were born. A very long time ago, I ran track and field for this team. And, like your coach said, or actually, it was you, Ryan, who said it, I ran the 1600 meters faster than anyone had done before or since. But like I just said, I did that before any of you were born. So what does it matter now, am I right?"

If nothing else, I had their attention. I suspect that none of them, Coach Leeman included, expected me to wax philosophical.

"The answer is: it doesn't. Not to any of your lives. Not even to my own, if I'm telling the truth."

There it was. The reality that for a very long time I had difficulty accepting. I had been a great runner. And then I wasn't a runner at all.

For years I told myself that it was only while I was running, and not when I was being a husband or a father, or any of the other things I tried to be through the years, that I was the version of myself that I wanted to be. That I could be happy. That everything would be okay.

But that wasn't true. It never had been.

It had taken me a very long time to understand, but I was grateful I finally had. Even though I'd done so too late to salvage my relationship with Kick, there was still time for me to be the man my brother always knew I could be.

After all these years, time had once again become my ally.

"Here's what I want to teach all of you while helping Coach Leeman this season," I continued. "It's not what you do on the track, but the person you are off the track, that matters. I had a coach once who used to scream at us, *You gotta leave it all on the track every single time*." I chuckled and turned to Coach Leeman. "God, I hope you don't say that, Coach."

He shook his head. "No. I don't."

"Good. Because I believe exactly the opposite. Don't leave it on the track. Instead, take what the track has to offer with you. That's what running is all about. Pushing yourself to be better than you ever thought possible. That's what life is about."

During my glory days, I would have unequivocally said that my time on the track was a blessing. Then when it all ended, I would have just as vehemently claimed it was a curse. Now I knew it was never actually either. It was just a part, but not all, of me.

"So, I've got two pieces of very good news to share with all of you," Coach Leeman continued. "The first is that Mr. Kenney, who shall be hereafter referred to as Coach Kenney, has agreed to help me out this season, for which I am very grateful. And you should be too. It's not every high school athlete who can say that they were coached by a former US champion. And second, that Mr., excuse me, Coach Kenney has established a college scholarship to be awarded to the most deserving athlete of the East Carlisle High School track and field team. Coach, why don't you tell them a little bit about what you're looking for in that regard."

Since my unannounced visit to Jenny's house on the day of

the arrests, I've reached out to her a few times. Most recently, to tell her that I wanted to honor my brother's memory through a scholarship. Jenny offered to fund it, but I said that I wanted to put up the money. It was the least I could do, I told her.

"You did a lot for Michael by loving him," she said. "He never doubted that. Up until the last moment of his life, you were the person he turned to when he needed help."

I hoped that was true. But even so, I still needed to do more in the future to make myself worthy of my brother's belief in me. One way to do that was to make amends with Jenny. Another, maybe more important way, was to be there for Jack and Molly. To do my best to make sure that they remember him the way I do. When I asked Jenny for permission to do that, she didn't hesitate to grant it.

"The scholarship is called the Michael Patrick Kenney Award for Excellence," I told the boys and girls arrayed before me. "It's named after my brother, who, before me, held the school record for the 1600 meters. But far more important than anything my brother did on the track, is that he had the biggest heart of anyone I'd ever met. Which is why, to be worthy of an award bearing his name, I'll be looking for the athlete—boy or girl—who exemplifies my brother's heart. That's the best way I can say it. I'm not looking for the best runner or shot-putter or pole-vaulter. I'm looking for someone who's working as hard as he or she can every day to be the best version of themselves possible."

I looked back at Coach Leeman. He clapped his hands.

"Okay then, you're going to be seeing a lot of Coach Kenney this season, so we can end it there for right now. Remember, we have our next meet on Thursday against South River, at home. Good job today everyone."

"Coach," I said, "can I bring something of a closing ritual to this practice?"

"By all means, Coach."

"When I ran here, my coach, who was Coach Leeman's coach too, always made me say these few words to myself before the start of every race. I used to call it Coach Pal's Prayer, because I'd recite it like it was a prayer. It goes like this: Legs fast; mind faster; heart unstoppable."

Coach Leeman smiled. "I can hear Coach Pal's voice saying those words." Then turning back to his team, "Let's all say it. First Coach Kenney, and then everybody else."

I recited the lines again. After which the team repeated them back to me.

ACKNOWLEDGMENTS

Although we will likely never meet, I firmly believe in the bond between author and reader, and so allow me this opportunity to thank you for reading *The Brothers Kenney*. I hope you loved it.

If you have the time, please email me your thoughts about the book at adam@adammitzner.com. I'll reply. Promise.

Now for all the rest of my thank yous.

The fine people at Blackstone Publishing went above and beyond to make this book as good as it could possibly be. Michael Signorelli and Celia Johnson provided absolutely killer suggestions to move the story along, and then Cole Barnes made sure that the words and grammar were right. Josie Woodbridge, Becca Malzahn, Rick Bleiweiss, and others whom I never met, helped guide the book and me along the way.

My agent, Scott Miller, has been with me my entire career, and I could never thank him enough for everything he's done over the years to make me a writer. Thanks again to his colleague, Kristen Bertoloni, for all her help and attention.

While writing, I continue to practice law at Pavia & Harcourt in New York City. My firm is very supportive of my extracurricular activity, and special thanks are owed to my colleagues at Pavia, George Garcia and Donatella Santillo.

I rely heavily on early feedback from readers, most of whom have no choice but to read the manuscript because we've been friends for years or they're related to me. Still, I appreciate that they do so cheerfully. Thank you to Jessica and Kevin Shacter, Jane and Gregg Goldman, Matt and Deborah Brooks, Margaret Martin, Lisa Sheffield, Jodi (Shmo) Siskind, Carie Sax, Bruce and Marilyn Steinthal, Debbie Peikes, Bonnie Rubin, Clint Broden, Ellice Schwab, and Lilly Icikson.

Most of all, none of my writing, or anything I do, could be accomplished without the support of my family. My wife, Susan, is my first and best critic (and also my second and third critic too), in addition to being a world-class finisher of 5000-piece jigsaw puzzles. My daughters, Rebecca and Emily, are always at the forefront of my thoughts when I write, and I hope someday they'll read my books and be proud of their father.

Finally, *The Brothers Kenney* is a book about brothers, and therefore I've dedicated it to my favorite brothers, Michael and Benjamin. Being able to be a part of their lives has been one of the most enriching parts of mine.